DEDICATION

To the horses, for they make life worth living.

Other Books by Lisa Wysocky

Nonfiction

The Power of Horses
Success Within
Front of the Class (with Brad Cohen)
My Horse, My Partner
Horse Country
Success Talks
Two Foot Fred (with Fred Gill)
Horseback
Walking on Eggshells (with Lyssa Chapman)
Hidden Girl (with Shyima Hall, 2014)

Fiction

The Opium Equation

CAST OF MAIN CHARACTERS

Cat Enright: A horse trainer who lives near Nashville, Tennessee. She is twenty-nine, single (but in a relationship—she thinks), impulsive, vulnerable, and the owner of a small stable.

Jon Gardner: Cat's stable manager and right hand. No one, Cat included, knows much about him, which is the way he likes it.

Darcy Whitcomb: Seventeen-year-old teenager with a trust fund. She's spoiled, but Cat loves her like family.

Agnes Temple: Eccentric woman of a certain age with short, spiky, electric-blue hair. She owns two horses in Cat's barn.

Amanda Prentiss: Eleven-year-old youth kid who trains with Cat. Amanda suffered a prenatal stroke and has some weakness on the left side of her body.

Annie Zinner: A horse trainer from Oklahoma and a mother figure to Cat. Annie has experienced a lot of hard times in her life.

Tony Zinner: Annie's husband and training partner. He worked a factory job for decades to keep their training business going.

Noah Gregory: Horse show manager and long time friend of Cat's. His reputation is on the line when things go very wrong at a prestigious all-breed horse show.

Bubba Henley: Budding juvenile delinquent and ten-year-old son of a neighboring Tennessee trainer. He and Cat became close after Bubba was kidnapped earlier in the year.

Hill Henley: Bubba's father and fourth generation Tennessee Walking Horse trainer. He may know more than he's telling.

Keith Carson: A neighbor and country music superstar. Cat has a secret crush on Keith and is thrilled that he is performing at the horse show exhibitor party.

Brent Giles: A small animal veterinarian from Clarksville who is dating Cat. Cat likes him, but isn't sure she wants to take it to the next level.

Martin Giles: Local deputy from Cat's home in Ashland City—and Brent's brother.

Mike Lansing: Texas horse trainer. Youth rider Melanie Johnston shows out of his barn.

Judy Lansing: Mike's wife and youth coach.

Cameron Clark: A trainer, and Cat's former boyfriend. He is tall, dark, and handsome—and knows it.

Debra Dudley: Owner of the beautiful Arabian colt, Temptation.

Zach Avery: Debra's trainer.

Reed Northbrook: Olympic caliber competitor.

Hunter Northbrook: Reed's son.

Melanie Johnston: Youth exhibitor who has a love/hate relationship with Darcy.

Ambrose: Show security guard hired by Cat.

Lars: Agnes's oddly named driver.

Linda Carruthers: The show's equine veterinarian.

Hank: Cat's incorrigible Beagle-mix puppy.

Mickey: The Zinners' Jack Russell terrier and a friend of Hank's.

Sally Blue: A (possibly) psychic, red roan Appaloosa mare owned by Agnes Temple. Sally is very loyal to Cat.

Redgirl's Moon: A tall and elegant chestnut mare owned by Agnes. Reddi is a go-getter who excels in English events.

Peter's Pride: A tall, older black gelding owned by Darcy Whitcomb. "Petey" is a calming influence on Darcy, but he also likes to play.

Hillbilly Bob: Bay, aged gelding owned by a local orthopedic surgeon. Cat swaps training fees for treatment of broken bones and other injuries, and has won several championships on Bob.

Glamour Girl: Gorgeous, excitable, yearling filly. Gigi is owned by Mason Whitcomb, Darcy's dad.

Wheeler: A short, stocky palomino gelding owned by Amanda Prentiss. He is not all that athletic, but is very confident about what he can do.

Middle Tennessee State University (MTSU) Equestrian Facility

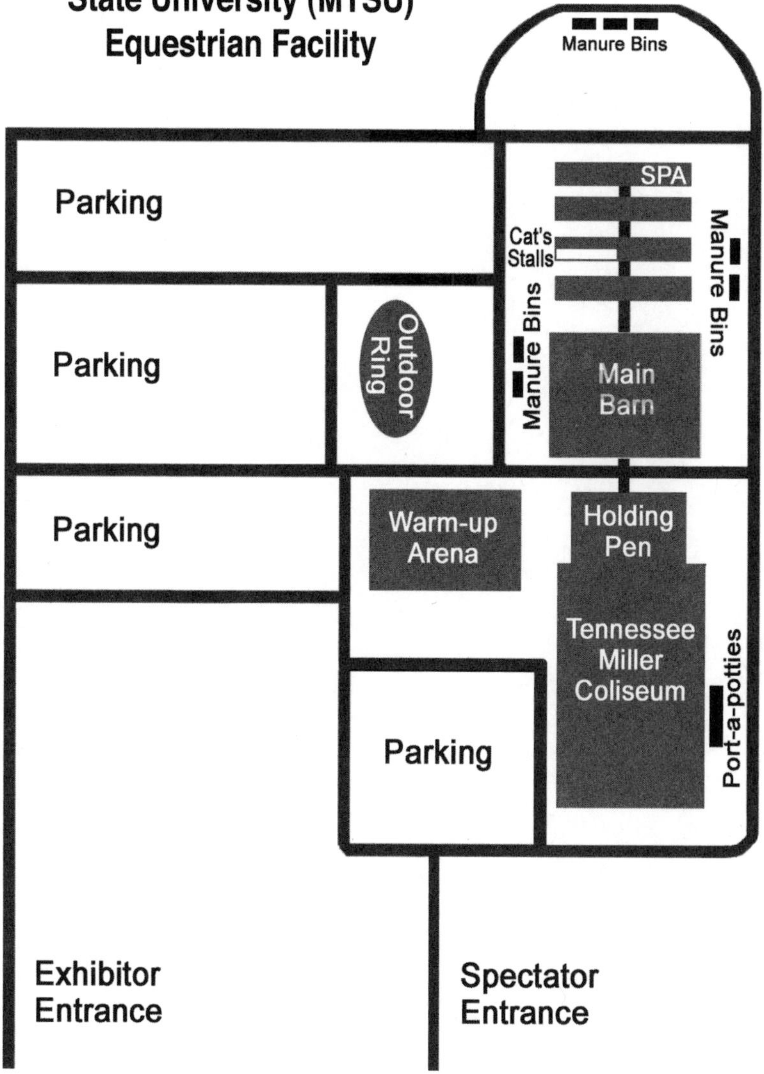

1

THERE WAS NO MISTAKING IT. The colt looked quite dead.

There is something unsettling about a dead horse. The enormous size, maybe. Or, the absolute stillness. This yearling lay diagonally across the stall floor, his brown and white speckled body pillowed deep into wood shavings. Flies buzzed around his face and his tongue protruded slightly. His nose showed the hint of a wrinkle, as if he found his predicament distasteful.

The veterinarian, a slim, grim-faced woman I didn't know, was putting her gear away. I caught her eye and she said a single word: "Colic."

My heart sank. Colic was a dangerous, unpredictable gastrointestinal ailment and horse owners took great care not to stress a horse's system, as stress was a main cause. Simply put, colic was a big tummy ache and because horses cannot vomit, it often became deadly. Horse people knew that many things besides stress could cause colic: heat, overwork, bad food, too much food, not enough food . . . the list goes on. Here, at this prestigious all-breed show, any number of things could have caused this champion colt to become ill.

I felt dizzy all of a sudden and sank to the stall floor. Then I made a pretense of examining bits of shavings in hopes the others wouldn't think me faint hearted.

"You all right?" a voice asked from somewhere behind my left shoulder.

"It's so unfair," I replied, dusting off the shavings in my hand. A few pieces landed on the colt's right foreleg and I quickly brushed them off. Leaving them there felt disrespectful. "You and Annie worked so hard, Tony. To do so well and to bring Starmaker this far . . . I feel bad for you and I don't know anything I can do to make things better."

"Nothing you can do, except keep on being a friend. You're here when we need you and that helps," said Tony's wife, Annie, who joined us at the open stall door. I blinked back tears as Annie pulled me up out of the shavings and gave me a tight hug.

"It's me who should be crying, not you," she said with a wry smile.

She was right. Annie Zinner had a lot to cry about.

Tony and Annie were childhood sweethearts who married a week after their high school graduation. Both sets of parents were against the couple marrying so young and offered no help whatsoever. But Tony worked at a local factory and Annie waited tables, and they were able to make ends meet. Not only that, they were also able to put a little money aside to get Tony started part-time as a conditioner and handler of halter horses, horses that were judged on their build.

There had been medical issues for both, too. Annie's high blood pressure, and Tony's diabetes and asthma, kept both on their toes with regard to diet and exercise. Despite rigorous attention to their health, as the couple had gotten older the conditions had worsened. Nothing critical yet, but it was possible that not too many years down the road that any of their medical concerns could turn serious.

A few years ago the couple, both pushing fifty, risked everything they had to buy a world champion mare. Some successful halter horses do not produce champion offspring, but this mare had produced several. The Zinners bought her and bred her to the current world champion aged stallion. Starmaker had been the result. As luck would have it, the mare died shortly after the colt was born, the victim of a misguided bolt of lightning. The insurance company, a firm of callous, capitalistic tycoons (in my opinion) explained the Act of God clause in the Zinners' policy and refused to pay out the fifty grand I and everyone else I knew felt the couple was due.

A year ago Tony and Annie had one of the top Appaloosa mare and colt combinations in the country, the Appaloosa being a versatile, spotted breed. An hour ago Tony and Annie had what was very possibly the nation's top yearling colt. Now it looked as if the demise of the Zinners' life-long savings, and very possibly their livelihood, was near.

"If I were you, Annie, I'd throw myself down right in the middle of the aisle and scream and kick until I didn't have an ounce of energy left," I said.

"Fat lot of good that would do," she replied. "Tony and I have been through a lot in the last thirty years, and I'm sure the good Lord will put us through a lot more. It's hard, but we'll manage. Especially with friends like you. Please don't worry about us. You've got a lot of your own worries right now, namely six horses and a stray kid waiting for you at your stalls and each needs your help in winning a championship at this show."

As usual, Annie was right. It was sad that she and Tony never had kids because Annie was the kind of woman who could have handled a dozen of them with one hand tied behind her back. No matter what happened, she coped.

I had just turned to head to our stalls, two aisles over, when the colt's right foreleg, the one I had just brushed the shavings from, twitched. Then a few small pieces of shavings in front of his nose fluttered and his dull eye blinked.

Even before I could give a cry of surprise the veterinarian rushed in with her stethoscope. Then she gave staccato orders to her assistant, and after a few shots an IV drip was set up. I was so focused on the colt, who was now breathing lightly, but steadily, that I didn't see Tony and Annie wrapped in each other's arms, unbridled hope on their faces.

The veterinarian consulted with the Zinners, and Annie pulled me into the conversation. "I'm not sure what to think," said the veterinarian, whose bright blue polo shirt read LINDA CARRUTHERS, DVM, in white stitched letters. "There was no heartbeat, no pulse. I was sure we had lost him.

"We need to move him to an equine hospital," she continued, "but I don't want to load him into a trailer until he's stable. You can go to the University of Tennessee in Knoxville, but Tennessee Equine Hospital in Thompson's Station is two hours closer. They are very good there. Wherever he goes, we have a horse ambulance here on site and I'll ride with him. We have a vet on call who can cover for me here."

Tony and Annie looked at me, and I nodded. An equine hospital was expensive, but it needed to happen. If Starmaker survived, he was well-bred enough that he could command sizable stud fees. Plus, it was always possible that he could compete again in the future and earn other championships. The possibilities were endless.

If he survived.

2

It was with a heavy heart and a nervous stomach that I headed to my temporary headquarters two aisles away, the seven roomy box stalls assigned to Cat Enright Stables.

I arrived to find Jon Gardner and Darcy Whitcomb, my stable manager and outrageous youth kid respectively, making good headway in getting the horses settled. Hank, my incorrigible Beagle mix puppy was helping, too. He'd found a short, but potentially dangerous stick somewhere and carried it around in his mouth as he wagged his tail at everyone who walked by. We arrived less than an hour ago at this very special national all-breed horse show in Murfreesboro, Tennessee, an hour southeast of Nashville. The show was a ten-day extravaganza and was being held at the Tennessee Miller Coliseum on the campus of Middle Tennessee State University (MTSU).

The event was special because it was an "invitational challenge." This meant trainers had to be invited to attend. There were a lot of rules, but basically, show organizers invited six trainers from each of the major breeds or disciplines. The difference between a "breed" trainer and a "discipline" trainer was that a breed trainer, like myself, only competed with horses of a specific breed. My breed was the Appaloosa. A discipline trainer competed with horses in a specific type of class such as jumping or Dressage (the English discipline of precise movements that can make a horse look like it is dancing). Discipline trainers competed with horses of many different breeds.

Each trainer could bring six horses to the competition and it was going to be breed against breed, trainer against trainer, for the duration. Represented were the Quarter Horse, Appaloosa, Paint, Pinto, Arabian, Thoroughbred, Morgan, Tennessee Walking Horse, Saddlebred, Haflinger, Peruvian Paso, Paso Fino, Spotted Saddle Horse, and various Warmbloods and sport horse crosses along with some pony and exotic breeds. More than four hundred horses were competing and with stalls filled with horses, equipment, and feed, all of the barns on the grounds were full. This was the first time this event had ever been held and there was a lot of buzz about it in the horse world. All of the major equine magazine, blogger, television, and radio people were here and it was going to be great exposure—for those trainers who won.

I, by the way, am Cat Enright, horse trainer. I'm single, twenty-nine, with a long mane of wiry hair that, if you were flattering me, could be called mouse brown. A genetically slim build, and a quick temper to match my Irish Catholic heritage complete the package. I've been horse crazy as long as I can remember, and opened my own stable seven years ago with a legacy from the untimely death of my grandmother. My mother's been dead for years. Dad is still around somewhere. He pops in every now and then to say hi and to borrow a few bucks, which he never repays. I'm usually glad to see him go.

Word travels fast on horse show grounds and the incident with Starmaker was no exception. Jon and Darcy had heard the gory story of Starmaker's death several times by the time I got back to the stalls.

"Can you believe it?" gushed Darcy, pushing yet another wad of bright purple bubble gum around in her mouth. "I mean, it's so unreal, but it isn't, you know? Like I'm not going to the hotel at all. I'm going to stay here the whole time and make sure nothing happens to Petey."

Petey was Darcy's tall black gelding. He had dime sized white spots evenly spaced across his body and if he had been a second grader, would have been considered the class clown.

"Spare us the dramatics Darce," I sighed. "We've a lot of work to do to get the horses settled in."

"But Cat," pleaded Darcy, her round blue eyes forming big drops of tears, "we can't take a chance that Petey—"

"Or any of the horses, or you," I finished. "We won't take any chances. I promise. But right now we've got horses to walk, a tack room to organize, a trailer to unload, and a hotel to check into. Besides," I paused dramatically. "Starmaker isn't dead."

After I relayed the developments to my astounded crew, Jon, Darcy, and I put down bedding, settled one placid and four grumpy horses, and one that was just too darn dingy to know the meaning of the word.

Competing on a national show circuit much of the year as we do, trainers often become close friends with some of their stiffest competitors. The collective rigors of traveling with horses worth tens of thousands of dollars apiece (or more), lengthy stays away from home, shared camaraderie at the local Laundromat, and hotel high jinx developed lasting friendships in a short amount of time.

My relationship with the Zinners began like that. I hadn't known them at all until we'd been stalled next to each other at the National Appaloosa Horse Show five years ago, and then by coincidence, the world championships later that year. We'd gotten along well and the association had deepened until I now thought of them as a favored aunt and uncle, and truly looked forward to seeing them at the larger shows.

The Zinners' misfortune had me on edge and I decided to calm my nervous stomach by taking Hank and our young mare, Sally Blue, out for a much-needed walk around the grounds. Sally was only a three-year-old, but was wise beyond her years. Not flighty like many young mares, Sally was steady as a rock. She always listened calmly to my problems, and responded at the right moment with an understanding flick of her ear or an affectionate bump of her nose.

Sally was a heavy, bulky roan, about 15.2 hands, and I'd never understood why her owner, a wonderfully batty woman named Agnes Temple, named the mare Sally Blue when, in reality, she was red in color. But then again I never understood anything Agnes did. Besides, Sally's name was the least of my problems.

The three of us walked companionably around the show grounds for a time, greeting other exhibitors and spreading news of Starmaker's miraculous recovery. Technically, Hank was supposed to be on a leash and I had one wrapped around my waist in case anyone complained. Hank did so much better on his own, though, that I always tried to leave him free to roam.

Eventually we headed for peace and quiet in the form of the outer road around the grounds and found a suitable area on the paved track that ran parallel to the back of the huge coliseum. It was there I finally let my tears fall and buried my face in Sally's sleek neck. I didn't cry long. I never do. This time I wasn't even sure why I was crying other than the fact I was dog tired and overly upset by the Zinners' tragedy. I knew how I would have felt, had the horse been in my care.

Feeling somewhat restored I turned my shoulder to Sally's ear, which was a signal for her to walk with me, and headed toward the barns. Walking next to it, it was hard not to notice that the coliseum, for all the wondrous glory that would happen inside during the coming week, was covered with a greenish-beige vinyl over a cement block base. Within seconds I was happily discussing with Sally other, more suitable colors, for the coliseum. That's the thing about horses. They're very knowledgeable. With a blink of her beautiful eye, Sally let me know that she preferred sky blue while I leaned toward charcoal gray.

We had just compromised with a nice blue-gray, which we both thought would look quite nice with the building's green awnings and trim, when Sally stopped, turned at a right angle to face the coliseum and snorted. Sally often acted oddly and it was sometimes difficult for me to determine when she was just being a young mare, or when she was, as her owner would phrase it, "being psychic."

Several times in the past, Sally had bumped blue things with her nose before she won a championship. She had also blown bubbles in her water bucket and pawed holes in her stall. Some people said those "clues" could maybe have been put together to solve a murder and a kidnapping—if one believed that sort of thing.

Now Sally refused to move forward when I asked her to walk on, and instead angled her body to block me from moving. I had learned from experience that when Sally acted like this we'd get past it a lot quicker if I lowered my body energy, focused entirely on her and acknowledged her with my voice.

"Okay, Sally. Smart girl. I'll think about it but now we have to get back to your stall." And with that, Sally deigned to walk toward the barn. I was so glad that none of the other exhibitors had seen Sally's "episode." Despite the friendships, showing horses was still a business and here on the show circuit rumors spread quicker than a hen on a June bug. No need for anyone to think Sally was obstinate.

Just before we reached the end of the coliseum, Noah pulled up on one of the show's faster transports, a golf cart.

"Man, Cat, you pull the disappearing act on me before I even know you're on the grounds. I've been looking for you everywhere."

"Just like you, Noah. Start complaining right away. Don't even give me a chance to say hi or anything," I said, as Sally and I continued our walk. My words were sharp, but my voice was as good-natured as my smile.

If such things exist, Noah Gregory and I were platonic soul mates. I wouldn't be the least bit surprised to find we had been twins in another life. As show manager, he was fully responsible for everything from securing the facility, to the tiny day-to-day details of running the show. Needless to say, his job was filled with a great amount of pressure. A decade earlier Noah and I had gone to school together here at MTSU, and both of us had come away with degrees in equine science. Over the ensuing years we had developed a special relationship and as soon as I'd seen Starmaker lying in his stall, I knew Noah would seek me out as soon as he could. I also knew, without even talking to him, that Noah felt responsible. The health of all the horses on the show grounds was one of his areas of responsibility. A responsibility, he was sure to feel, he had failed.

"I guess you heard," he said, rolling his cart along slowly next to us as Hank jumped in to lick his face. "It's got all the exhibitors upset. Colic can happen to any horse at any time for just about any reason, but still. Every trainer here is thinking he could be in Tony's shoes and no one needs to pull a horse out of the competition. The stakes are too high, especially as the trainer with the most points and the owner of the horse who scores the highest in all the classes each get a twenty thousand dollar bonus."

I realized Noah was talking to himself as much as he was to me and I let him ramble. Hank, Sally, and I responded noncommittally at the appropriate places.

As we reached the first of the horse barns, Noah's cell phone rang at the same time his walkie-talkie squawked. Hank jumped out of the cart and took up a spot on the other side of Sally. Sally didn't bat an eye at the sudden noise—or at Hank—but I jumped a foot, proving the walk had done Sally a lot more good than it had me. Noah listened to the scratchy words coming through the walkie-talkie, his finely chiseled face a mask of tightly controlled emotion.

"I've got to go," he said. "Security found a gun. And hey," he added, "put that dog on a leash."

3

AS MUCH AS I WANTED to follow Noah, I knew I couldn't. There was just too much to do. So as Noah sped away, the three of us turned to head in the direction of our stalls. We hadn't gone ten steps when I heard a familiar, and dreaded, voice.

"Hey Cat, wait up."

I ignored the request and instead encouraged Sally to break into a jog trot.

"Cat, come on. You're not still mad at me, are you?"

I increased my pace, resolutely keeping both my head and my shoulders facing forward.

"Cat, please."

As the voice was now directly beside me, I could no longer avoid it or the person to whom it belonged.

"I have nothing to say to you, Cam," I replied.

"Aw, Cat, come on," he pleaded. "I said I was sorry. And I am. I really am."

I looked up into Cameron Clark's exquisitely handsome face, but could read nothing in his deep-set gray eyes. They were as blank as I'd found his soul.

"Sorry? Yeah, right," I said, surprising myself with the strength of my feelings. "You don't even know the meaning of the word."

Cam and I had over the course of several years been what my grandmother would have called "an item." Superficially, he was everything I had thought I wanted in a man: tall, strong, dark, handsome, and nicely packaged with a small trust fund, courtesy of his late mother. However, over time, I found that Cam was also vain, egotistical, conceited, and self-absorbed. Time after time he put himself before others and it was a source of amazement to him that others didn't do the same.

The final straw, for me, was last fall at the world championships when the owner of an up-and-coming stallion missed his wife during the exhibitor party. He went back to their room to look for her and found her gaily romping in bed with none other than the amazing Cam. Cam couldn't seem to figure out why the husband, the wife, and I were all upset. I hadn't bothered to talk to him since. Besides, I'd recently started dating a veterinarian who lived near me just west of Nashville and I, at least, only dated one person at a time.

"Cat, you never gave me a chance to explain—"

"Explain! There's nothing to explain. You don't get it and you never will."

"At least let me buy you a drink and we can work it out."

By this time we had arrived at our stalls, and Jon and Darcy were staring at us, open mouthed at the heated exchange. I handed Sally to Jon, who busied himself settling Sally back into her stall. But, I could tell Jon's ears were still turned in my direction.

"Cam, look. It's over. We're through. We were headed in that direction before the 'worlds.' That just finished things for us, that's all."

"Okay. So we won't get personal. I can see you're not ready for that. So we'll talk. About horses, about the show! My yearling colt is really coming on—"

"You, you, *you*!" I screamed. "That's all you think about. You. What about Tony and Annie? What about the colt they had that was not only coming on, he was already there? And now he's out of the competition. He may not even survive. Go away, Cam. Stay out of my life. Just. Go. Away."

In tears for the third time in the last thirty minutes, I ducked into the tack room and plopped myself down on a stack of bridle bags. Whew! I felt like I was on an emotional roller coaster. Luckily, both Jon and Darcy were used to my passionate Irish outbursts and gave me a few minutes to compose myself. I hate it when I get overly emotional and Cam knew just what buttons to push to achieve that effect.

"Ah . . . you'll squash those bridles permanently if you sit on them much longer," said Jon. I looked up at him and smiled. Jon was the epitome of tact. Whatever his true thoughts, he never verbalized them, and instead chose to get on with the task at hand. He was a wonderful assistant and definitely worth his weight in bridles.

We'd only recently gone back to that close camaraderie. Last spring I'd gotten a little too involved in the brutal murder of my next-door neighbor. In the process, the daily workings of the barn fell solely on Jon's shoulders and he resented it more than

I knew. Conversation at the barn was pretty slim until we went on the road last April. But time had done its job and now things were back to normal. Well, as normal as things ever got around my barn.

"Sorry." I stood up and brushed invisible specks of dust off the seat of my Wrangler Jeans. "Well, so much for that. Shall we finish here and get something to eat?"

Later that evening Tony, Annie, Darcy, and I dawdled over the remains of apple steak and roast potatoes at The Apple Tree. It was a restaurant favored by show goers as much for its proximity to the coliseum as for its apple flavored menu and the large tree that grew in the center of the dining area and up through the roof. I never could figure out how they built the roof around the tree and why they never had any leaks. Shows you the type of life I lead if that's all I usually have to worry about.

When we were at shows Jon spent the night in the tack room, unless we hired a security firm to watch the horses, which we often did. Even then, he still preferred to bunk with the horses. He knew that our client's horses were too valuable, and we had spent too much time with them, for anything to happen.

Besides the fact that I felt each of those horses were part of my family, horses are actually quite delicate and can get hurt on seemingly invisible dangers. Put a horse in a padded room, I often joke, and she'll find a way to hurt herself. Tonight I would bring dinner back to Jon in a "to go" box.

"It's interesting," I said to Annie, "to see which of the exhibitors eating here tonight have stopped by to ask about Star, and which of them have ignored your existence."

"Oh now, Cat, don't be down on everyone who hasn't come over," said Annie. "Some people just have a problem knowing what to say, so they don't say anything."

"Bunch of ingrates if you ask me," I said, picking the remains of a biscuit from Darcy's plate, slathering it in apple butter, and popping it into my mouth. "Can't say a word to you now, but just wait until the next show when they need to borrow a lead line, or a cinch. They'll come running then, because they know you'll both do whatever you can to help."

Annie and Tony were probably the nicest people in the "show business." Plus, Tony had a knack for spotting top horses and earned a good local reputation as a horse trader when he was still a kid. Annie often said it was a mixed blessing that the children they so longed for never came as it allowed more time, and finances, for the horses.

After they were married, Annie spent ten years waiting tables before she put down her order pad for good and began to help in the barn during the day while Tony was at the factory. She also began training horses for pleasure classes, horses that were judged at the walk, trot, and canter (or lope if the horse was ridden in western gear). Another ten years and Tony took an early retirement to finally follow his dream of breeding and handling top halter horses full time. Conscientious and hardworking, the Zinners had spent the last decade doing reasonably well with their own—and with their clients' horses. They lived on a modest twenty-acre tract just south and a little west of Oklahoma City, housing their horses in a vintage hay barn that Tony had skillfully remodeled for their prime show string.

Maybe it was the lack of a fancy rig or want of state-of-the art facilities, but the Zinners had never quite been to the top. Their many clients sent them good, but not great, horses to work with and I'd always felt it was a testament to Tony and Annie's skill and dedication that they'd done as well as they had. Their horses were consistently tough competition at local and regional levels, but the Zinners had gotten very used to taking home third, fourth, and fifth place ribbons at the big national shows, the shows that really counted.

They had been invited to this show only because they were so consistently close to the top with every horse they had, and because everyone loved them.

That's why the colic of their spectacular yearling colt, Starmaker, was so devastating and why the snobbish owners of past national and world champions made little effort to stop by the Zinners' table.

"Ooohh," squealed Darcy as she looked at the doorway. "There's that awful Melanie Johnston coming in. Just watch. She's one who'll see us over here right off, but she'll turn up her nose and walk right by us. She hasn't spoken to me at all since I beat her in our equitation class in Lexington last month. Then on the way out the gate she tried to pin Petey and me against the wall with that big old ugly cow she rides. Ooohh, how I hate her."

I sighed. Darcy was the very privileged and only child of publishing mogul Mason Whitcomb and tended to be spoiled, which was reflected in her views on life. Or maybe it was because she was seventeen. I tried to remember what it was like to be that age, but only recalled a monk-like dedication to horses.

I'd taught Darcy for about four years. Her jet-setting parents were divorced, and consequently, Darcy ended up more and more in my care until last month when she announced to the world that she was moving in with me. I thought it would have been nice if she had consulted me first, but looking at it as a whole, it really was the best decision. She could ride and train with me every day, and was with people who not only cared about her, but let her know it.

Although Darcy felt a fierce devotion to her tall, black gelding Peter's Pride (Petey), over the years she had lost the giddy exultation about horses common to most horse-crazy girls. But she was a tough competitor and, I think, saw horse shows as a way of excelling in her own world, rather than her mom's glamour world of beauty or her dad's world of business and finance.

Unfortunately for Darcy, Mason's only reaction to her new place of residence was concern about the tuition he had already paid for her senior year at the very upscale, very private Nashville school he sent her to. Darcy's mother had lived on "the continent" with a series of aging boyfriends for the past several years. But I convinced Mason that Darcy could finish out her senior year from my place. She drove her vintage Corvette to school anyway. Now she'd just drive a little farther.

Our after-dinner conversation drifted around to the show, and, of course, to Starmaker.

"Fill us in," I asked Tony and Annie. "We arrived in the middle of everything, so I really don't know all that happened."

"Oh Cat, like I heard—"

"Darcy," I replied evenly, "Tony and Annie were there. I'm sure they can tell it at least as well as you can."

Darcy flushed under my rebuke, but stopped short of going into an active sulk. She, too, was interested in what the Zinners had to say.

"Well," began Annie, who was for once tentative, "Tony and I got here Tuesday, two days ago. You know that much. In fact," she said turning to Tony for confirmation, "I think most of the exhibitors pulled in then, didn't they?"

Tony nodded his round gray head, and continued. "All was well. Today we visited with folks and got the horses exercised, same as we always do before a show starts. We finally got where we had just the one filly left to work and then we were going to get something to eat."

"It was about one o'clock. Tony was in the arena with the filly, that nice two-year-old who was third at the Appaloosa nationals last month, and I took a moment to go to the ladies room, hadn't gone all day, you know," said Annie, picking up the story again. I smiled inwardly as I realized that although they were in shock, Tony and Annie were still in tune enough to finish each other's thoughts, just as they always had.

"When I came back, Mickey, our little terrier, was whining and acting very strange. I took him over to the grass to do his business, but he ran right back to the stalls. So I checked the horses and they were all as they should be. All except Starmaker. He was sweaty, groaning, and standing all stretched out with his head hanging. The next thing I remember, I was inside the stall hugging Star's neck and screaming for Tony."

Tony, who was just returning with the filly, heard Annie's screams and came running. "Mike Lansing's crew got there about the same time as I did. He and Judy are stalled just behind us," explained Tony, indicating another Appaloosa trainer and his wife, "and a few of the kids that train with them came over. Noah, of course, came, too."

Tony rubbed a weathered hand over his face and sighed.

"Do you know why Star colicked?" I asked.

"No," said Tony. "He traveled well. The trip took us about eleven hours. He ate and drank well during, and after he got here. Today he seemed fine, then he colicked, lay down, stopped breathing, and we all thought he was dead."

"Dr. Carruthers rode with him to Tennessee Equine Hospital this evening. After they got there one of the veterinarians called us. Star has an intestinal blockage so they are going to do surgery. Probably doing it right now," said Annie. "Dr. Carruthers thought it might be too upsetting for us to be there, so Tony is going to go in the morning. She also said Star would do better if we weren't there. We're so anxious, and Star would pick up on that." She took Tony's hand. "I don't . . . I don't know what we'll do if Star doesn't make it."

Tony suddenly looked old and unsure, and together, the couple turned to me with questions on their faces. I studied them, my dear friends, as I wondered what the colt's death would mean for their future. Physically, Tony was a man overwhelmed by gray and roundness; round head and belly, bowlegs, short to average height. He carried the weight of middle age comfortably. A slow, quiet man, Tony had a comfortable, seasoned look. He'd lost most of his hair ages ago and what remained was short and gray. A pair of round horn-rimmed glasses, as always, perched on his good-natured face. The glasses normally enhanced the twinkle in his eye, but now served just as well to diminish it.

I turned my attention to Annie, who was different from Tony in every aspect. Taller than her husband by several inches, Annie was outspoken and wore her bleached blond hair teased into in an outdated, shoulder-length flip. Cam had once unkindly said that Annie's hair looked like a cat had sucked on it. His words should have been a red flag for me, but at the time I was still too much in love.

Annie's lipsticked mouth was wrinkled at the corners from years of smoking cigarettes, a habit she finally gave up last year as much for the safety of the horses and the hay in their barn as for her health. Although edging fifty, her figure was holding up nicely, a fact her skin-tight jeans displayed to full advantage. A lot of the froufrou show people didn't like Annie because she still looked like the truck stop mama she used to be, but for my money, you'd be hard pressed to find a better person or a better friend.

I shook my head. "It must have been some sort of internal stress, but until we know the cause of the colic we all have to be on alert. Maybe the shavings had a toxic chemical in them and he ate some. Maybe his feed soured, or there was something that didn't agree with him in his hay."

Tony and Annie gave me looks of no, no, and no. They had checked all of that. They were still feeding the hay they had brought from home. And Noah wouldn't allow less than top quality shavings anywhere near a show that he managed.

Darcy, between blowing face-sized bubbles with her now bright pink gum, mentioned that she wanted to organize the youth exhibitors into a "Youth Watch," "to keep their eyes open for, you know, stuff. Just in case."

The Zinners and I both thought it was a great idea, and, considering the source, very thoughtful. With minimal discussion we gave her our approval, as long as Noah also agreed.

"Oh, Cat!" cried Darcy, leaning to her left to envelop me in an enthusiastic hug. "I just knew you'd let me save my Petey."

When I replied that I was under the impression that we wanted to do everything we could to prevent the tragedy from repeating itself, no matter which horse it was, Darcy just shrugged her shoulders and argued that she was sure she would be, you know, saving Petey from certain doom.

In hindsight, Darcy's Youth Watch may have saved many horses—and people.

4

JON WAS POUNDING NAILS SAVAGELY into the tack room wall. Nail after nail after nail. Then I saw that it wasn't nails he hammered so fiercely, but huge silver spikes, like those used in horseshoes, only a hundred times larger. I begged Jon to stop, but he refused to acknowledge that I was there so I pulled on his sleeve and pleaded with him. When he finally turned around I saw that it wasn't Jon after all, but a horrible, faceless being.

I awoke to what I finally realized was very persistent knocking, and I still wasn't sure if the knocking was in my head or at the door to my room. The knocking got louder and a short minute later I came to the conclusion that the sound was a combination of banging on my door and Hank howling.

"Who is it?" I called. I hadn't yet figured out the time. Not that I couldn't find or see the clock. It was right in front of my face, its big fat numerals glowing a luminous red. I just wasn't awake enough to decide what the numbers meant. Did I mention I'm a heavy sleeper?

"It's Noah. Open up."

I shushed Hank and stumbled to the door without bothering to throw a robe over my faded nightshirt. Once done in bright, neon colors, the knee-length shirt was now a faded version of its former self. Noah had given the shirt to me ten years ago, a year during which we thought we were in love. We'd been such good college friends we thought we needed to take the relationship a step farther. We worked at it pretty hard for half a semester. But, there were never any sparks for either of us and we'd parted. Strangely enough we ended up even better friends than before and had remained close.

"What time is it?" I asked as I let him in.

"Three-fifteen. Another colt has colicked."

The news woke me up pretty fast.

The victim was Temptation, a refined Arabian colt owned by Debra Dudley. I didn't know Debra, but had heard that she was the wife of a former child model who was now a never-present Kansas wheat farmer. She was known mainly for the way she spent money like it was water. No one really thought all the money came from wheat, although, to be fair, few cared.

My personal take on most wheat farmers was not in line with the multi-stone diamond necklace I'd seen Debra wearing when we bumped into each other at the show office. For all I knew she'd won the lottery, or maybe she'd robbed a bank, even though she didn't look the type.

Short and chubby with long brown hair and an olive complexion, I'd also heard that she and her resident trainer, Zach Avery, had a penchant for parties. Privately referred to as the "dynamic duo," Debra and Zach were quite popular, both socially and professionally. It was, in fact, after a bit of midnight revelry with the owners of several other horses that Debra and Zach went to check on their own herd before turning into their respective hotel rooms. That was when they found Temptation stretched out in his stall in much the same predicament that Starmaker had been in his.

Symptoms of colic are many, and not all horses show every symptom, but typically a colicking horse stands with his head hanging. Or he might paw the ground, bite at his sides, or try to roll. If he lies down, most lie with their feet tucked under them, much as a cat might lie on the sill of a window and observe the world.

Noah's hands fell between his legs and he shook his head at the floor. One case of colic was not abnormal; two in less than twelve hours was disturbing. It was imperative that Noah find the source of the colic—if there was one. His reputation as show manager was on the line and trainers and owners would quickly pull out of this exciting and potentially lucrative new competition if they thought their horses were at risk.

Finding the cause was important for another reason: insurance. Many owners had hefty insurance policies on their horses and would reap tens or even hundreds of thousands of dollars if their horse died. Others had insurance that covered major surgery, such as the kind that Starmaker had. The Zinners, however, could not afford that kind of policy.

"What about security?" I puzzled to Noah. "Did anyone there see or hear anything?"

"Nothing. But you know, our security force here is mostly college kids. The show grounds are part of a university campus and that's what the venue provides. The kids make their rounds once an hour and then go back to their office and watch TV or play video games until it's time to walk around again.

"But you know what the worst part is? The show has spent a lot of money to cordon off the barn area from spectators. As you know, everyone has to have a pass to get back there. In addition to security, the show office had two people on site all evening, because horses are still coming in. We're sure that no one without a pass was in the barn."

"That means either something at the show facility is tainted, or if someone is intentionally causing this, it is . . . one of us."

Noah nodded, exhaustion showing in every ounce of his being. "Tomorrow, of course, we'll advise everyone to hire their own security, and the show's entire management team is coming in early to deal with exhibitors, who are sure to be panicked. But other than that, I'm not sure what else we can do. I'm not even sure what we're dealing with."

"What about the gun that security found?" I asked, remembering how Noah had sped off on his golf cart.

"It was in a mostly-empty dumpster, one of the big tan ones to the left of the barns. We turned the gun over to the campus police and they were especially interested because, other than licensed security, Tennessee has a "no gun" rule on state property. That means no one involved with our show should be armed—even if they have a license to carry—unless the gun is in their vehicle and stays there. If any of our exhibitors has a gun that isn't locked in their truck, I want to talk to them."

Noah glanced at his watch. "Oh, man," he groaned. "It's almost four o'clock. I've got to get back to the grounds."

But instead of rising out of the chair, Noah's eyes closed and he began to snore. I grinned and pulled the spread off my bed and covered him.

Too upset to sleep myself, I tried to figure out how best to protect the horses entrusted to my care. It was bad enough when one of your own horses had the misfortune to colic, but it would be a thousand times worse when a horse owned by someone who trusted you with their care, and paid dearly for the service, wound up deathly ill, or even dead.

Of all the theories that had flitted through my mind in the past twelve hours, I first dismissed the idea that the Zinners engineered the destruction of their own colt. It was an idea that disgusted me, and although it happened rarely in the horse world, unfortunately it did sometimes happen.

Tony and Annie, however, had worked too hard for too many years and could only afford minimal insurance. For them, there was too much at stake and not enough motive. Besides, if this idea was to be given any consideration, then why did Temptation also colic? I also dismissed the idea that the colic was the result of the two colts eating any hay, grain, or bedding that caused their intestines to knot. One colt? Maybe. The odds of two? Unlikely. Temptation was probably fed an entirely different brand of grain and definitely had a different supply of hay.

I was concerned that both victims were yearling colts. Coincidence? Maybe. Then again, maybe not. Anyone not connected with the show would have a hard time knowing that those two particular horses were going to compete against each other. Especially because, beyond their ages, the two colts were vastly different.

Starmaker was partially named for the unusual spot in the center of his forehead. Most spots like this, which were ironically called a star no matter what the shape, were shaped like a diamond. Starmaker's, however, was in the shape of a five-point star. Star was an Appaloosa who sported a "leopard" coat pattern: a white body covered with quarter-sized brown spots. Most of the spots were clustered on his head, neck, and shoulders, with the spots on the rump area being slightly larger and spaced farther apart. The five-point star on his forehead looked as if the colt couldn't decide whether that area of his face should be white or brown, and compromised. Star was huge, and muscular in build, drawing much from the Quarter Horse blood carried by his mother.

Temptation, on the other hand, was smaller with a delicate build, typical of Arabians at that age. I'd seen him being led down the aisle the previous afternoon and his coat pattern was a bright, rich bay: black legs, mane, and tail, with a mahogany colored body. By the great stallion The Tempest and out of an own daughter of Jubair, the breeding of the two colts couldn't have been more different. Two very unique horses, each exquisite in their own individual way. Both near death due to colic.

Although I didn't dismiss the possibility completely, I put low on my list the likelihood that the colics were a personal vendetta against either the Zinners or the dynamic duo. All were known to be likeable, honest people who prided themselves on representing quality horses.

But maybe, I thought, the glimmer of an idea taking hold, one, or even both of the colics, was a mistake. What if Temptation was the real target, and Starmaker was given something to make him colic by mistake? It was not inconceivable. If the stall numbers were close, maybe Starmaker happened to be in a stall that was mistaken for that of Temptation's. I made a mental note to ask Noah where the Dudley horses were stabled. But then again, I sighed, given the vast differences in the physical characteristics someone would have to be totally unfamiliar with horses to mistake the two. Then again, there would have to be a reason for wanting Temptation out of the way.

It was unfortunate that the two colts were born in the same year. In virtually any other year, each could easily have won the competition here. Last fall Temptation had won the Arabian national championship for weanling colts and Starmaker had won the Appaloosa nationals last month. Plus, Mike and Judy Lansing's yearling quarter horse colt, Master Attack, had been second in his weanling class at the Quarter Horse Congress last year. While the Lansings were mainly in the Appaloosa business, they also had some Quarter Horses.

Then there was the Canadian Thoroughbred colt, Moon Striker, a yearling winner at the big Canadian sport horse show just a few weeks ago. As much as I hated to admit it, Cam Clark also had a really nice colt, as did several other breeders and trainers. Depending on how you looked at it, it was either fortunate or unfortunate that last year's colt crop was exceptionally tough.

I didn't know enough about the background of the MTSU horse facility to know if someone was playing their own game of revenge with the venue, or with the show. Maybe someone tried to schedule a show here and couldn't because this special all-breed event was coming in. Maybe a trainer wasn't invited to the show and got so ticked off that he (or she) was systematically destroying the horses who *were* competing.

With that thought, my neighbor, Hill Henley, came to mind. He was a marginally successful Tennessee Walking Horse trainer who used harsh methods that I didn't approve of. It was his ten-year-old son, Bubba, who had disappeared earlier this year during the murder investigation of a mutual neighbor of ours. On one hand, I wouldn't put it past Hill to do something vengeful, as he had not been one of the trainers invited to compete. But why then wouldn't Tennessee Walking Horses have been targeted, if in fact there was any targeting going on at all. Holy hot cakes. It was all so confusing, and there were too many unknowns for any of it to make sense to me.

I got up and walked aimlessly around the little room. All this speculation did not make my horses any safer and I knew I wouldn't feel comfortable until the problem was resolved. A look at the clock told me it was five-fifteen, almost time to rise and shine. Noah hadn't stirred since he nodded off over an hour ago and a study of his face confirmed that he still looked at least as tired as I felt.

Noah was a study in contradictions. His neat, dark blond hair, perpetual tan, and turquoise eyes hinted of Southern California and plenty of surf, but his accent was pure East Coast Ivy League. Just thirty, he looked years younger. Noah's interest in horses stemmed from his early childhood, and he had since parlayed his equine interest and an MBA into one of the top horse show management firms in the country. He was energetic, enthusiastic, and possessed an innate ability to solve difficult problems, making everyone feel like the winner. He was a good friend and I loved him like a brother.

My alarm finally buzzed, officially starting a new, and hopefully better, day. I yawned as Noah jumped up and acted as refreshed as if he'd enjoyed a full night's sleep.

"Don't worry, Cat," he said giving me a confident hug, "we'll get 'em."

I prayed that he was right.

5

JON WAS POUNDING NAILS SAVAGELY into the tack room wall. Nail after nail after nail. Then I saw it wasn't nails he was hammering so fiercely into the wall, but our bridle and saddle racks.

"Gigi got a bit rambunctious during the night," he explained as I made my way into the almost organized room. "Kicked the wall a few times and knocked everything down on top of me. After the second time I just left everything on the floor. With all that was going on I was a nervous wreck anyway, and the last thing I needed was to be knocked out of a sound sleep by a bunch of metal bits."

I looked around the dividing wall that separated the stalls. Our problem child, Glamour Girl, whom we affectionately called Gigi, was standing at the back of the ten-by-ten box stall, her head and nose raised, fully engrossed in smelling something on the wall. She caught me out of the corner of her eye, frog-leaped her way to the front of the stall and gave me a welcoming splay-legged snort. Gigi was a beautiful copper-colored yearling filly but operated totally without any semblance of an attention span. Gigi didn't care where she was or what she did, she was just happy to be there. Her biggest problem was that she couldn't figure out why everyone else wasn't having as much fun as she was.

I found my main goal as her trainer was not to keep her fit, she did that on her own, but to keep her from injuring herself. Now I did a quick visual check of her legs. All looked good, with no signs of puffiness.

"About one-thirty I took her up to the warm-up ring and longed her for twenty minutes or so. Boy, was she a pistol," Jon laughed and then quickly sobered. "I, uh, suppose you heard."

"About the gun, *and* about Temptation," I said, giving the other horses a morning once over. "Noah stopped by this morning and filled me in."

I walked back to the end stall we used as a tack room and sat in one of several tall, green director's chairs that were strategically placed in front of it. The chairs were great for sitting on, but they also kept other trainers from using that end of our aisle to get to the shower stalls, which were across from us, but partitioned by a cement block wall about five feet tall. Before you jump to conclusions and think I am mean, hear me out.

I'd discovered these stalls a few years ago and requested them whenever we showed at this venue. The absence of strange horses and another stable's activity on the opposite side of the aisle provided a peaceful, quiet setting during competitions. Plus, this aisle was wider than the others, which gave both horses and humans a little more breathing room.

In addition, these stalls were not occupied very much throughout the year. Because of that, the dirt floor was more level—horses had not had much opportunity to paw or dig in these stalls because they were usually unoccupied. Some trainers brought mats to put in their stalls, but I always thought that if God wanted horses to sleep on mats then our wild horses would be running on acres of rubber rather than on fields covered in prairie grass. So unless I knew a venue had stalls with cement floors, I left my mats at home.

While I loved the location, there were two main drawbacks. One, because there were horse showers across from us, the aisle could get wet if a horse was being bathed. Sometimes the dampness served to cool the area, but other times it made the aisle muggy. Two, and this is where my green chairs finally come back in, some trainers led their dripping wet animals past our tack room instead of using the walkway on the outside of the barn. For some reason, even though the horses had been scraped mostly dry, as soon as they walked past our tack room, seems like every horse would stop and shake off the rest of the water. It was like a thousand pound dog doing a big wet shake, and sprays of water invariably ended up on our tack, tack trunks, chairs, horses—and on any people who were in the aisle.

The chairs provided the perfect solution, as they called a friendly welcome to human visitors and, at the same time said "stay out" to wet horses. Besides, it was very easy for trainers to lead their horses on the walkway or down the other end of the aisle, and it didn't matter so much if part of our aisle or one of our stall fronts occasionally got a little damp.

I gave Jon the responsibility of hiring an unarmed security service, and told him I didn't care what the cost was as long as the firm guaranteed continuous twenty-four-hour protection. I'd call the owners about the expense later in the morning. It would have been nice to have armed protection, I thought, but Noah had said that due to state law, that would be impossible.

After a glance at my watch, I threw a saddle on Hillbilly Bob, an aged gelding I hoped not to embarrass myself on in the Sr. Western Pleasure class a few days hence, and headed for the coliseum. Classes were scheduled to begin at eight this morning and, knowing Noah, even with all the chaos the show would start on time. But it was now just six-thirty, which by my figuring, gave me a good forty-five minutes in which to familiarize Bob with the arena before show staff closed it to drag the surface smooth. I always made a point to find a relaxed time to acquaint each horse with the arena they would compete in and thought this was as good a time as any.

Bob and I rode slowly into the hushed coolness of the coliseum, and joined a dozen or so other competitors who were in various stages of workouts. Traditionally, the center of the arena was left either to the reining horses—so they could practice their dashes, spins, and spectacular sliding stops—or to the jumpers. During practice sessions like these, even if you worked quietly on the rail you had to keep a perpetual eye open for the stray jumper or slider. Bob and I took the rail counter-clockwise and eased into a slow jog.

I loved these early morning sessions. Sometimes, on the rare occasion I didn't have a horse to ride, I'd come down, sit in the stands, watch the competition, and evaluate the workouts. It was always quiet in the morning, and the acoustics of the huge coliseum deadened normal conversation so even if there were others around I got the impression of solitude.

When I rode, I always put everything I had into the horse. I knew the exact position of each leg and whether it was coming down hard or soft, the meaning of every flick of an ear, and whether the latest snort was a sign of relaxation or boredom. I created our own little world when I rode, tuning out all outside stimuli. Some people thought I was stuck up when I didn't answer their greetings in the arena, but the truth was I didn't hear them, and unless they posed a physical threat to our private little party, I didn't see them either.

That's why I totally missed seeing Mike Lansing fall, even though I was less than thirty feet away.

6

Bob and I had loosened up into an easy canter. Bob had recently developed a habit of tilting his nose to the outside of the ring, a position that left him slightly off balance. It could have been a soreness issue and I had Richard Valdez, a well-known equine massage therapist, coming out later in the day to evaluate Bob. In the meantime, we were working circles of medium size off the rail to stretch Bob's muscles and bring his nose around when I spied a man lying on the ground directly in front of me.

I pulled Bob up in a neat slide any reiner would be proud of and hopped off, keeping Bob's left rein tight in my hand. My concentration broken, I saw it wasn't just a man, but a group of people hovering around a man who lay in a tumbled heap.

"Boy what a spill, huh?" I turned to see Zach Avery standing next to me, an older gelding at his side. Zach looked as if he'd spent most of the night awake, as I'm sure he must have. Temptation was his baby. An ambulance is never far away at horse shows of this size and I looked up to see one lumbering across the arena toward us. Zach and I moved to make way.

"What happened?" I asked, concerned for the man I now saw to be Mike Lansing, the trainer who occupied the stalls behind the Zinners. "I was loping along and all of a sudden there he was."

"Don't see how you could have missed it," said Zach as he watched two female EMTs lift Mike onto a stretcher. "It was one of the worst spills I've ever seen."

Mike, Zach explained, had been working with his senior (in the horse show world any horse over the age of four) reining horse, Rabbit's Foot, when the front cinch on the saddle broke during a fast run. It looked, Zach said, like Mike tried to slow Rabbit down, but the former national champ took it as a cue to slide, and slide he did.

"Mike flew off right over the front and Rabbit bumped into him on the way down. Rabbit tripped, of course, after running over Mike and then fell on top of him. Crikey, it was awful."

We watched silently as one of Mike's older youth protégés came to collect a trembling Rabbit, and the ambulance, the youth kid, and the horse slowly left the ring together.

"You'd think Mike would have checked his equipment before he saddled up this morning, wouldn't you?" I asked Zach as he gave me a leg up on the ever-patient Bob. "Mike doesn't strike me as the type to be careless."

In fact, I thought Mike Lansing was very possibly the most thoroughly organized man I'd ever known. He was the type of guy who could wear a white long-sleeved shirt, give a horse a bath, and not get a drop of water or speck of dirt on him. The rest of us mortals usually looked like we'd been dragged through a mud pit after we finished bathing our four legged friends. Ultra cleanliness aside, Mike ran a tight ship, never forgot anything, had horses and students well prepped, and he used the best equipment available. The chance of him taking such a horrible fall due to broken tack was extremely low. Even so, I sighed, stranger things have happened.

"Hey, Zach," I called after his departing figure. He stopped and turned as Bob and I jogged up. "I was sorry to hear about Temptation."

Zach's dark eyes welled. "Thanks. He's really special," was all he managed to say before he turned and left the arena.

Inside our tack room I found a note from Jon saying he had taken Gigi for another round with the longe line and, in my cleverly blocked aisle, I found a large moon faced security guard who introduced himself as Ambrose. I tidied Bob up and wrote Jon an answering note that asked him not to forget to give Darcy a wake-up call at nine.

While we all had cell phones and texted back and forth a lot, I insisted that, unless it was an emergency, we work off of old fashioned notes when we were working with the horses. I had seen too many horses who had learned that when a cell phone rang or an incoming text dinged, their human would become distracted. Depending on the horse, he or she then either began to misbehave, or came to a screeching halt. Our tack room always had a dry erase board so we could post messages to each other. We had another on the outside of the door for messages to others, or for general reminders.

After I finished writing the note to Jon, I saluted Ambrose, who had the good grace to salute back, and I headed back to the coliseum to watch the beginning of the gelding halter classes. At most horse shows only one breed of horse is represented. At this event, all breeds the same age and sex competed against each other. Think of the major dog shows that air on Animal Planet. Same thing. Is this Paint horse a better representative of his breed than the Saddlebred is of his?

Armed with a couple of chocolate doughnuts and a thermos of iced hot chocolate, heavy on the ice, I settled myself halfway along the length of the arena and watched as the weanling geldings were led in.

In most halter, or conformation, classes, horses are led one-by-one straight to the judge at a walk, then away at a trot. It's important to travel straight to and away from the judge as the horse at this point is being evaluated on leg motion. Do the legs travel directly forward and back from the body, or is there some sideways movement in the swinging of the limbs?

If the horse is led in a curving path, or worse, a zigzag approach, the judge cannot correctly evaluate the horse. Some judges will not give the handler a second chance at approach and the horse is scored low, which effectively knocks it out of the competition.

Here, three judges were to judge each class and scores were averaged. Each judge was also an expert in a different breed type, so as to prevent bias toward a specific breed. It was a fair system of judging, but lengthy. Each horse now had to walk to a judge and trot away, then stop and wait for the next judge to turn around from viewing the previous horse's trotting motion.

The process was repeated until all three judges had seen each horse walk and trot. The horses were then lined up either head to tail around the perimeter of the arena, or side-by-side down the center for individual attention on body conformation. With sometimes upwards of thirty horses per class, even with computers sorting and tabulating each judge's scores, some classes took what seemed like forever.

Halter classes were the backbone of any breed exhibition. The winners set the standard for coming breeding seasons and the types of horses bred were directly attributable to the winners of classes at national and world championship competitions. Halter classes were not, however, very exciting to anyone outside the immediate industry—to spectators, for example. So halter classes were usually scheduled in the morning, which left evening classes for the final eliminations of the more visually stimulating reining, driving, and jumping classes. Preliminary rounds of western and English pleasure, trail, and timed events such as barrel racing filled most afternoons.

"I think Tony's black weanling has it hands down, don't you?" said a voice in my left ear. I chose to ignore both the comment and the voice. The voice, unfortunately wouldn't allow itself to go unacknowledged and moved into the seat next to me.

"Well," said Cam, "what do you think?"

"The black," I agreed. "It's by far the best entry out there."

Most breeders waited until the yearling or even two-year-old year to geld their colts, hoping their little beloveds would mature into the next super stud. Consequently, the current year gelding class was always small, as was this class of nine. I risked a sideways glance at Cam and noticed he was dressed for competition. Western cut tan dress slacks, crisp tan shirt, spotless tan Ariat boots, the obligatory leather belt fastened with a shiny sterling silver buckle, tailored tan vest and newly-blocked straw cowboy hat. For competition throughout this ten-day event, human competitors were to dress according to the rulebook of the breed of horse or discipline they were showing.

"What've you got today," I asked, "the two-year-old palomino?" Cam was well known for color coordinating his show attire with his horses. It was his signature style, and one that easily identified him from a distance to even the most obtuse of judges.

He nodded and casually leaned back snaking his right arm along the back of my seat. I edged away, but his hand caught my shoulder and pulled me to him.

"Shhh," he whispered. "I have something to tell you."

"I don't want to hear it."

"No, listen." The intensity in his voice was arresting. "I heard Mike Lansing's fall was not an accident. Someone cut part of his cinch."

I gaped at him in horror. "How do you know?"

"I overheard security talking outside the show office. They don't want anyone to know just yet, until show management can figure out if this ties in with the colic of the two colts. So don't say a word."

"But why would someone do a thing like that?" Harming others was something I'd never understood.

In response, Cam just shook his head and removed his arm to clap for Tony's black colt, the winner of the class.

Cat's Horse Tip #1

"Rubbing a bit of corn starch into a horse's white sock makes it sparkle."

7

I WAS HALF WAY BACK to our stalls when a bubbly older woman with short, spiky, electric-blue hair shrieked my name and came running down the main aisle of the barn that came before ours.

"Cat, darling!" she cried an instant before she enveloped me in a strong hug that flopped me from one side to the other.

It was Agnes, of course, Sally Blue's owner. I felt the sharp edge of Agnes's blue-tinted glasses poke me in my left shoulder, so I carefully extricated myself. The color of Agnes's hair and glasses were in honor of Sally. "What have I told you about running and yelling anywhere there are horses?" I asked.

"Why the same thing Lars told me," Agnes replied. "Don't. Run. Don't. Shriek. But I was excited to see you and forgot."

Before I could ask who Lars was, a huge dark hand extended itself from behind Agnes. I looked up, and up, to see a gigantic man with skin the color of chocolate leather. It wasn't just that he was tall or big, this guy was so fit you could see every bit of his massive bone structure. From his dress pants and cowboy boots to his matching vest he was dressed all in black. Only his teeth showed some color. Gold. The image, along with his tall, structured crew cut almost made me miss the fact that he wasn't wearing a shirt underneath his vest.

"Lars," said the man in a booming voice as he picked up my hand to shake it.

Lars, it turned out, was Agnes's new driver and bodyguard. In theory, she didn't need either. Well, there was that little incident last spring when Agnes rolled her car over the foot of an off-duty police officer in the parking lot of a Baskin Robbins. But even the officer agreed that anyone would have gotten excited about the two for one sale they had going on. He decided not to press charges after Agnes bought him two-dozen donuts and visited him in the hospital. Twice.

And the bodyguard thing was not to guard Agnes from danger, but to guard other people from Agnes. She tended to act first and think later. You'd think after seventy years on earth that she would have settled down some, but then again, maybe she had.

Lars and Agnes had driven in from Louisville, Kentucky, where Agnes lived. They'd made the nearly four-hour trip in record time partly by following an ambulance that was traveling close to ninety miles an hour.

"All of the other cars and trucks cleared right out of our way," said Agnes. "They probably thought we were with the ambulance."

Agnes had some experience with ambulances, as she'd been widowed by all three of her husbands. Not sure what that said about Agnes's choice in men—or her former spouses' ability to deal with her—but she now lovingly carried vials of all three of her dead husband's ashes around with her in her purse. She also talked regularly to the ashes, which wasn't so bad except that she recently told me that the ashes now spoke back to her.

All that aside, Agnes was one of my most loyal owners and in addition to Sally Blue, had a tall, elegant, chestnut mare with a lacy white blanket of white over her hips named Redgirl's Moon in my barn. "Reddi" excelled in English events and the six-year-old mare and I had recently placed second in Saddle Seat Pleasure at the Appaloosa nationals.

Saddle Seat was a class for horses with big trots and collected rocking chair canters. The seat was ridden in a flat English saddle and the rider wore an outfit similar to an old-fashioned formal man's business suit. It was the perfect class for Reddi, and she would have won it at the nationals if she hadn't been a hair too excited. Reddi's personality was a lot like her owner's.

On our way back to our stalls we veered off to visit Annie and Tony, to congratulate them on Tony's win that morning with his little black gelding. Annie, however, was the only human we found there. Hank, who was apparently visiting, dropped the latest in the series of never-ending sticks that he carried in his mouth and started in on a growling tug-of-war game with the Zinners' terrier, Mickey, and a barn towel. Over the din, Annie told us that Debra Dudley and Tony had just left to go to Tennessee Equine Hospital to check on Starmaker and Temptation.

"One of the veterinarians there told us Star was holding his own, but won't be out of the woods for a number of days yet," Annie said. "Dr. Carruthers has been great, too. She's not even a member of that practice, but she has answered a lot of Tony's and my questions about what to expect as Star recovers."

The worried look on Annie's face told me that while she was concerned about Star, she also wondered how in the world they would pay the vet bill, which was sure to be humungous. Just as with a human hospital, the longer a patient stayed, the higher the bill. I squeezed Annie's arm, called Hank away from Mickey and the towel, which was now in shreds, and Agnes, Lars, Hank, Hank's stick, and I walked the few aisles over to our stalls.

Cat's Horse Tip #2

"Horses raised in the wild can cover up to thirty miles a day grazing, so horses confined to stalls at shows need to get out for regular walks."

8

THE HEAT OF THE DAY was already making it uncomfortable, but Jon had all of the stall fans going and the big fan in the middle of the aisle had a huge chunk of ice in front of it. It was amazing how much that block of ice helped cool things off. I thought, not for the first time, that whoever decided to hold this event in Tennessee the first week in August had never been here during our very warm and humid summers. So far, daily highs had hovered in the upper eighties, a nice respite from the upper nineties we'd experienced the previous week.

Ambrose stood at parade rest at the end of our aisle, his watchful eyes following anyone who walked by. I hoped his evening replacement would be just as sharp.

Darcy had Petey tied in the aisle to the front of his stall. He was still wet from a bath and she was spraying ShowSheen across his body. ShowSheen added a special gloss to a horse's hair coat and also helped the hair repel dust and dirt. Darcy and Petey were competing in the older youth trail class that afternoon. It was one of their weaker events, as Darcy typically tried to rush Petey through the many obstacles they had to navigate in the class: a bridge, gate, jump, backing through poles, etcetera. All of the obstacles simulated items one might encounter on a trail ride, and horse and rider were scored on how smoothly they navigated each object. I needed to remind Darcy to breathe and to take her time.

"Oh, there's my Reddi. And Sally. There's my loves," Agnes cooed as Lars and Ambrose introduced themselves.

Most horses want to interact with kind humans who are familiar to them, and usually Sally seemed glad to see Agnes. But today she stood frozen in place, legs squared underneath her, head up, ears pricked forward in typical halter competition pose.

"Look, Cat darling. Sally is telling us that she is going to win her halter class. Isn't that right, sweetie?" Agnes added to Sally.

Darcy gave me a look and I knew I needed to redirect Agnes or Darcy would say something *she* wouldn't regret, and I would. Just then Sally spread her back legs, lifted her tail, and let loose a gushing flow of urine that splashed against the far stall wall. So much for the halter pose. Sally just had to pee.

I looked at my watch and suggested that Agnes and Lars get settled into their hotel rooms. Lars stuck out his fist with his knuckles pointed toward me and without thinking I reciprocated. After the bump fest he wrapped his arm around Agnes and piloted her off toward the parking lot. I hoped it would take them hours to check in and unpack. I loved Agnes, but found her most appealing in small doses.

Just after they left Jon came back with Gigi, who for once was calm and quiet. "She was so wound up that I took her over to the spa services area in the farthest barn to see if they had any ideas. They let me stand her on this huge vibrating metal plate and now she is ready for a nap," Jon said. "This plate thing is about four feet by ten and vibrates to beat the band. I stood on it with her and, man, my feet and back feel great! Normally they charge thirty dollars for a ten-minute session but they let us try it this first time for free."

I looked at the filly, who was as relaxed as I had ever seen her. "When you have time, go back over and set up an account with them. I'll add it to Mason's bill." I knew even if we took Gigi to the spa every day, that Mason would not quibble—if it helped Gigi stay in shape physically and mentally.

As Jon busied himself putting Gigi into her stall I checked the rest of our horses. Reddi and Bob were napping, but Wheeler, a chunky palomino gelding who sported a big white blanket filled with lots of spots, was nosing around his stall for any forgotten wisps of hay. That horse was always hungry.

Wheeler was owned by the Prentiss family—Sean and Tiffany, their eleven-year-old daughter Amanda, and identical twin seven-year-old sons whose names I could never remember. That might be because I didn't want to remember. The less I saw of those boys the better. In fact, I had banned the little hellions from my barn—from even getting out of their car on my property—after an unfortunate incident that involved a saddle, super glue, and one of the Carson girls from next door. Actually, the less said about that incident the better. The girl's father, the hunky country music star Keith Carson, had only decided not to sue after I promised to give said child weekly riding lessons until she was thirty-five.

Amanda was the rider in the Prentiss family and Tiffany was due to drop her off any minute. The young girl had only been riding with us for a few months, having switched from another trainer earlier in the year. Amanda had suffered a prenatal stroke and had weakness on her left side as a result. She was a good little rider, though, in western events where only one hand was used to steer the horse. We'd been working on several trail obstacles but she fumbled anything she had to do with her left hand—such as open a mailbox and take something out—often enough that her confidence was not where it should be. Today she was coming to support Darcy—and maybe learn a little something along the way.

Darcy finished grooming Petey, gathered her show outfit and walked up a few aisles to the large air-conditioned bathroom in the center of the barn. That's one thing about showing horses. No matter what class you entered you were doomed to wear long sleeves. In western classes, ladies usually wore a glittery Spandex top called a slinky. Pair it with long pants, suede or leather chaps, and a western hat and there was no getting around it, you were hot. No pun intended. The getup was difficult enough to get into in cooler weather and virtually impossible when your body was sweaty. Air-conditioned bathrooms were a godsend.

Amanda arrived, her strawberry blonde hair braided into two pigtails, just like Pippi Longstocking. I put her to work rubbing Petey's saddle, which Jon had just placed on Petey's back, with a soft cloth. When Darcy returned, she looked stunning in a black and silver slinky, gray western hat, and black chaps and boots. Her hair was done up "old-school" in a bun at the nape of her neck and held in place with a ton of bobby pins and a hair net or two.

We left Ambrose and Hank with the horses, and Jon, Amanda, and I walked with Darcy and Petey to the warm-up arena, which was across a small drive from the holding pen and the coliseum. Typically, riders practiced and loosened up their horses in the warm-up arena, then ten to fifteen minutes before the class was scheduled to enter the coliseum they moved to the holding pen, which was behind and attached to the coliseum. In a class where one rider at a time performed—such as reining, trail, Dressage, or jumping—the horse and rider moved to the holding pen when the fourth or fifth competitor ahead of them began their performance.

A few practice obstacles had been placed in the warm-up arena, but most of the competitors were either walking their horses along the rail, or getting buffed up by a trainer, parent, or groom. Trail class was not so physically taxing to a horse that he or she needed a lot of warm-up, and I think I mentioned that it already was pretty hot.

My cell phone rang and I dug it out of my pocket to look at the caller ID. It was my new boyfriend, a.k.a. Brent Giles. Brent was a small animal veterinarian that I had begun dating the previous spring. We were taking it slow, but our relationship had progressed to the endearment stage. I called him Honey-cakes and he called me Bumpkins. I knew that my name for him was far superior to his for me. Goes without saying, even though I just did.

"Hey Bumpkins, any word on Starmaker?"

Last night I had filled Brent in on the happenings of the previous day, but hadn't had time today to tell him about Temptation, Mike Lansing's fall, or Cam's assertion that the fall wasn't an accident. Actually, with Honeycakes, the less said about Cam the better. There was a little jealousy thing going on, even though there really was nothing to be jealous about. Cam was no better than pig doodie to me but Brent didn't seem to get that. And there was no point in bringing up Noah to Brent. At all.

"Star is holding his own," I said, making the decision not to tell Brent the rest right then. No need for him to worry. He and I had met during a little kidnapping and murder investigation I had been involved in. Ever since then Brent had been somewhat overprotective. My perspective anyway. Besides, Honeycakes was coming to the show in a few days to hang out. With any luck all of this would be cleared up by then.

I disconnected the call and nodded to Dr. Carruthers, who hurried past the warm-up arena with her vet bag in hand. No rest for the weary here. With four hundred horses on the grounds there would always be a "next" on her list.

Eventually Darcy and Petey moved to the holding pen and not too long after that her number was called as being "in the hole," meaning she would be the second rider to compete after the horse and rider combo that were currently entering the course. When they moved to the "on-deck" position I reminded Darcy to take her time and let Petey think about each obstacle, and Amanda and I left her next to the in-gate with Jon, who gave Petey's nose a last swipe with a little baby oil to make it glossier. Jon was better at the in-gate than I was. I tended to give my riders too many last minute reminders when the reality was, they were either ready or they weren't.

There were more than thirty competitors in the class and Darcy had one of the best rounds that she had ever had. She bobbled a little backing through the zigzag and Petey took a half step forward with one leg, but he didn't touch any of the poles. Petey also hesitated a fraction of a second before entering the water hazard and Darcy didn't ask for the stop quite soon enough after the lope to the mailbox, but all in all, a great ride. The judges thought so too, and when all was said and done an hour or so later, Darcy was placed fourth. I was stoked. For Darcy and Petey, that was amazing!

Jon had already gone back to our stalls to greet Richard Valdez for Hillbilly Bob's massage, and to do touch up clippings on Sally and Bob, who both had classes the next day. Jon was a whiz with a set of clippers—I had even admitted on occasion that he was better than I, but hopefully no one remembers that.

Presentation counts for a lot at shows like this, so each horse had to be turned out in the latest, most flattering style. If that meant long flowing manes, or manes pulled to a rigid three inches and laid over to one side of the neck with hair gel, each horse had better be clipped and styled according to the breed standard. From hair on top of the hooves, inside and around the edges of the ears, behind the ears, along the jawline, the eye and muzzle whiskers, to the fetlocks and more, not one stray hair (short or long) could be out of place.

Darcy, Petey, Amanda, and I started back to the barns—and our stalls—just as a swarm of jumpers crossed the drive between the holding pen and the first barn. They were headed to the warm-up arena for elimination rounds ahead of this evening's performance. I have to say, most of those horses were mammoth in size. We had entered the first barn when I remembered that Jon asked me to see if one of the vendors had some clear hoof polish. Someone had not put the cap on our last bottle tightly, and the polish had dried up. I am betting that the someone was yours truly.

I waved the others back to our stalls, while I dashed back inside and went up the stairs to the seating and vendor level of the coliseum, the mezzanine level. I found a vendor halfway along the long side of the arena that had the polish we needed and made my purchase. I had just turned to leave when a tall, elegant Dressage trainer walked by and I got caught up in a sneezing fit due to her perfume. What was it? Eau du Heavy Cleaning Fluid? Yuk. Not wanting to either wipe snot on my sleeve or walk the length of the arena to the ladies bathroom, I headed out a side door, to a stand of port-a-potties.

While I was hesitant to actually use a portable toilet, I knew I could grab a Kleenex and a spritz of hand sanitizer. That was one thing about Noah. Any show he ran had plenty of bathrooms, and if he had to set up the outdoor, portable kind they were always the best "plop johns" available, with sinks, mirrors, and room to move around.

It turned out that these were the trailer kind of port-a-potties: four potties to a trailer the size of a small construction office. Each potty had a set of metal steps with a handrail that led to a door. Well ventilated, every potty had its own light switch and didn't smell like the usual outdoor loo. If push came to shove, I might even be able to make traditional use of one of these . . . eventually.

I was not pleased, however, to see that the potty trailer was placed parallel to the road. A 45-degree angle was so much better. Noah and I had that conversation a number of years ago after an incident with a door blowing open when I was changing that allowed Mike Lansing's barn crew a full frontal view of . . . ah . . . well just about everything. The land here sloped, though, so there probably wasn't room to angle the line of potties. Besides, few people came this way so if a repeat incident happened, anyone seeing it was unlikely.

I went to the last potty (everyone knows the first potties in line are the most used and therefore the dirtiest) and trotted up the steps. I opened the door and had just moved my hand to turn on the light switch when I saw I wasn't alone. I saw the vet bag on the floor, then noticed Dr. Carruthers sitting on the potty, pants down around her ankles. Or, I saw what was left of Dr. Carruthers as she seemed to be missing a good portion of her head.

9

The rest of Friday's competition was postponed. Campus police searched the entire 154-acre facility, along with every vehicle, trailer, and tack room. From how the officers went through our things I think they were thorough, but if they found anything suspicious they didn't tell anyone about it.

The organizers of the show took a huge financial hit with the thousands of tickets for the evening performance that they had to refund, but they knew that solving Dr. Carruthers's murder came first. Now I sat by myself early the next morning, Saturday, near the top of Section 206. This morning's competition had also been postponed, pending the outcome of an owner and exhibitor meeting that Noah had called.

As I waited for the other trainers and some of the owners to arrive, I thought about yesterday's events. Dr. Carruthers was just the second dead body that I had ever seen, and as with the first, my initial reaction was to upchuck my breakfast. I sat on the pavement near the port-a-potties with my head between my knees trying to figure out what to do next. Call Noah? Call 911? My thoughts were swirling around so fast in my head that I couldn't get a handle on any of them.

"Cat? Are you okay?"

I had looked up to find Jon's brown eyes peering into mine. He thought I might have gotten waylaid after getting the hoof polish and went to find me. Once on the main level, he took the ramp that led to the VIP room and from that higher vantage point saw me go out the side door.

"Have you eaten today, Cat? Did the heat get to you?"

When we were at horse shows I often "forgot" to eat because we were so busy. But that morning I'd had iced hot chocolate and doughnuts, my typical show grounds "breakfast of champions." Later, I'd downed my favorite summer cooler, a mixture of orange juice and Sprite.

Jon must have noticed the remains of my breakfast on the ground and the open door to the port-a-potty because the next words I heard from him were "Uh-oh."

Before I knew it, campus police had secured the area with crime scene tape and a campus EMT had slapped a blood pressure cuff around my upper arm. Jon later told me that these were the people who showed up minutes after he called 911. We were, after all, on the grounds of a university.

When homicide cops from the Rutherford County Sheriff's Office arrived not too much later they did again what the campus guys had already done, and after an interminable number of questions and an all clear from the EMT, I was allowed to go back to our stalls.

It wasn't often that I chose not to spend time with my horses, but this was one time I made that choice. Horses pick up so easily on human emotion; for them it is a matter of survival. An angry human could turn his or her anger toward a horse. Or, a human who was unfocused could lead a horse into danger. I certainly didn't want to bring my shaky emotional state to horses who were then expected to compete with other high-level horses, so I turned everything over to Jon, gathered up Hank and his latest stick, a twig about a foot in length, and went back to the comfort of my hotel room.

Jon really was a rock and I didn't give him enough credit. He had been part of my team for almost four years, just showed up on my doorstep one day and quickly moved into the apartment I'd just had built over the barn. He was my backup and I trusted his judgment implicitly.

In my hotel room I curled up in bed with Hank, then called Brent. Honeycakes was on call through the weekend but I was able to give him the gist of what had happened. When he asked if I still had the pepper spray he had given me I told him I did. I had an aversion to guns and refused to have one in my house or barn, but felt comfortable with the spray. He knew better than to ask if I was going to pack up the horses and go home.

"I'll see what I can do to rearrange my schedule. I might be able to switch shifts with one of the other vets and come out on Sunday," Brent said.

"Thanks."

"You know, you could always go home, even for the night. You're less than ninety minutes away."

I supposed that I could, but then I would feel that I was abandoning my team even more than I was by hiding out here in my hotel room.

"Maybe another night," I said. "I miss you."

"Miss you, too."

I sighed, thinking of my Honeycakes. But, before I could recap Friday night further in my mind, Tony and Annie Zinner plopped down in the coliseum's seats on either side of me, followed by Jon, Agnes, and Lars, who sat in the row above me, and to my left.

"Where's Darcy?" I asked, panic rising into my throat. Everything that had happened over the past few days had made me unusually jumpy. And, finding Dr. Carruthers made me realize how much I loved my friends.

Jon started to reply but Tony gave him a look and Jon turned away. Tony then put his arm around me and pulled me to him in a one-armed hug. "Don't worry," he said. "You'll see."

"But—"

"No worries. Darcy is safe. Really, she is."

I was prevented from responding by the start of the meeting. Noah stood on the floor of the arena and, after he thanked all of us for attending, said, "The show organizers and I want to give you the latest news on the tragic events of the past few days, and get your input on the best way to proceed."

He had everyone's attention, including Agnes's.

"As you may have heard, Tony and Annie Zinner's yearling Appaloosa colt colicked badly Thursday afternoon."

Tony gave my shoulder another squeeze.

"Starmaker had surgery at Tennessee Equine Hospital in Thompson's Station, about an hour from here. The cause of the colic is, so far, unknown, but an independent lab is testing the contents of Starmaker's blood, saliva, urine, stomach, and intestine. As of this morning he is holding his own, and his medical team is hopeful about his recovery."

There was a smattering of applause from the audience that began to build. I joined in and soon the coliseum echoed with our clapping hands. Tony removed his arm from my shoulder and put his face into his hands, and it was my turn to put an arm around *his* shoulder.

Noah waited for the applause to die out, and then continued. "Early Friday morning Debra Dudley's yearling Arabian colt, Temptation, also colicked. He, too, is at Tennessee Equine Hospital and is recovering from surgery there."

I looked around the audience and spotted Debra toward the front left, in the section closest to the gate area where the horses came into the arena. The other half of the dynamic duo, Zach Avery, was nowhere to be seen, but a woman I recognized as another Arabian trainer gently patted Debra's back.

"Then," continued Noah, "Appaloosa and Quarter Horse trainer Mike Lansing sustained serious injuries when his saddle slipped on Rabbit, his reining horse, Friday morning during the warm-up here in the coliseum. "Mike's right leg is broken in three places, he has two broken ribs, a broken collarbone, and various other injuries. He is being cared for at Middle Tennessee Medical Center here in Murfreesboro, but will be transferred later today to Vanderbilt University Medical Center in Nashville for special orthopedic surgery."

Mike's wife, Judy, sat to our left and a few rows down. Her youth kids and their parents, including Darcy's rival Melanie Johnston, surrounded her.

"Finally, Appaloosa trainer Cat Enright discovered the body of our veterinarian, Dr. Linda Carruthers, yesterday afternoon."

I saw everyone's eyes swivel toward me and I slunk down into my seat. Finding a dead body was not something I wanted to be recognized for.

"Dr. Carruthers was in one of the port-a-potties just to the east of the coliseum when she was shot once in the head." Noah turned his head away from the microphone and rubbed his face. "We are working closely with MTSU campus and Rutherford County police, and also with management here at Tennessee Miller Coliseum, and I thank you for your cooperation with them.

"The question I have for you this morning comes from the organizers of the show. As your show manager, they want me to ask one question: Do you want to proceed with this competition? We have beefed up security and have encouraged you to hire your own security people, but neither the organizers nor I can guarantee your safety or the safety of your horses. This is your decision, so I'd like to hear from you."

Rustling and murmured conversation among the owners and trainers was just turning into a dull roar when a man popped up from a center seat on the top row.

"Well, hell no. I don't wanna stay, put horses in that kind of danger. You all be a bunch of crazy people if you go on with this here thing. That's all I gotta say."

I slunk farther down in my seat because the man who had popped up was Hill Henley. My neighbor two farms over, Hill was not respected by people who were involved with the Tennessee Walking Horse—his own breed—much less people from the general horse population.

"Mr. Henley," Noah said, "as much as I appreciate your input, have you been invited to compete at this show, or do you own one of the horses here? I don't recall your name on the list of owners, trainers, or exhibitors."

Hill had been appalled when he learned I was invited to compete . . . and he wasn't. Ever since, he had tried to worm his way in. How he found out about this meeting or got past security to get in, I have no idea.

"I'm one a them there bloggers," Hill said. "I tell people how it really is and the public has a right to know what's a goin' on here."

I snorted so hard at his words that orange juice and Sprite flew out my nose and onto the neck of a Dressage trainer who sat below me. She jumped up and turned around with an angry look on her face, but Annie swiftly offered her several clean napkins as I apologized.

Hill Henley was no more a blogger than I was a bright pink goldfish. He must have come up with a homemade press card that fooled a gatekeeper at the main entrance. Noah would have to deal with that sooner, rather than later.

The father of one of Mike Lansing's youth competitors stood up next. "Even though that man," he said pointing at Hill, "is not an official member of our group, I agree with him. My kids are too important for me to put them at risk. I'm taking my daughter and going home."

His daughter, a cute little blonde of about ten, burst into tears. But when her father picked her up and gently carried her out the door, a number of other parents followed suit.

"If I may say a few words?" asked Debra Dudley. "I understand parents not wanting their children to be here. I get that and believe for them, leaving is the right thing. So I vote that we cancel the youth classes, but go on with the rest of the show.

"I am one of the people with the most at stake here. My colt is one that is not doing well. But if we cancel this great event, then we may never find out who did this. That's important to me, and it should be to you as well. I, *we,* need to know who did this. We also may kill forever this incredible event that has brought horse people from all over the country together in a way that has never before been done. So who here is with me?"

Judy Lansing jumped up and began to clap, even though most of her youth kids had departed and her husband was in the hospital. The Dressage trainer in front of me was next, and a hunter/jumper rider in the front row stood up after her. Even Cam Clark, who was impeccably dressed in a monochromatic dark gray shirt, slacks, and vest—and who had been listening with his arms crossed and an uncharacteristic expression of sadness on his face—stood to applaud. After that, we were all on our feet. The show would go on.

As we clapped, Agnes tapped me on my left shoulder. "Did you bring your black trench coat?" she whispered.

Hmmm. Let me see. Black trench coat. August. Sweltering Tennessee weather. "No, Agnes, I don't believe I did."

Agnes had given the coat to me earlier this year when I was trying to keep myself from being arrested for murder and kidnapping. She thought the coat would help me dress the part of a detective, and thus help me solve the case. The coat did in fact come in handy, but not in the way Agnes intended.

Just then Darcy walked onto the arena floor and took the microphone from Noah. I was relieved to see that she was safe, but could not imagine what she was doing out there.

"If you can all, like, quiet down for a minute," Darcy said. The rest of the crowd must have been just as curious about Darcy as I was, as everyone settled back into their seats. Darcy introduced herself as part of a Youth Watch—similar to a neighborhood watch—that the organizers wanted to put together for the duration of the show.

"I spoke to show management before the meeting, and in the event the show continued, they wanted me to ask all of you, not just kids, to be alert and aware of who is around you, and also of what is going on. Question everyone you don't know. If you see something unusual, call Noah, call security, call 911. Use the buddy system and don't, like, go anywhere alone.

"We are all neighbors here. Within our own breeds we compete regularly at the same shows every weekend. That makes us family. I'm a youth kid, and I'm staying. Noah said any kids who want to stay can have their entries moved to the open or adult classes. So who's with me? Who's going to help Debra and Judy and the Zinners and the family of Dr. Carruthers put whoever did this behind bars?"

Darcy's voice had risen in both volume and enthusiasm as her spiel progressed. Maybe she had a bright future in politics ahead of her. By the time she finished she had the support of everyone who was still in the crowd. One of the Lansing's remaining youth kids, Melanie Johnston, even ran down the steps and hopped over the arena wall to run to Darcy. Will wonders never cease? They had been rivals since they were thirteen. Maybe there was a blessing in all of this and the tragedy would finally bring them together.

Cat's Horse Tip #3

"Just as with people, your facial expression alone may either be enough to drive your horse away from you, or invite him to you."

10

AFTER THE MEETING WAS OVER I apologized again to the Dressage trainer. I had certainly never intended to spit my orange juice mix all over her.

She considered me for a moment, then stuck out her hand. "Sloan Peters," she said.

Sloan was much taller than my 5'6" and had long, coal black hair that was pulled back into a sleek ponytail. Her makeup was impeccable and she wore an exclusive brand of riding breeches that I could only dream about.

As we talked, I realized that she was the same trainer I had passed just before I found Dr. Carruthers. Where I had been sitting for the meeting, air circulation had blown past me toward her, which blew her nauseous-scented perfume away from me. But now I could smell her in full force. What was she thinking?

We walked up the steps to the main level together, then headed toward the VIP room and the set of steps that would take us down to the arena level, and also to the barn area. I had intended to walk down with her, but I saw Jon and Tony near the concession stand so I said my goodbyes to Sloan and started to join them.

Something in their stance, however, stopped me. Jon was jabbing his finger toward Tony in a way that looked anything but friendly, and Tony's face looked as if it was carved from stone. What was going on, I wondered. This wouldn't do. The last thing we needed right now was to be angry at each other. We exhibitors, especially those exhibitors who were like family, needed to stay close until we knew who had killed Dr. Carruthers. My bet was that her murder was also tied to the colts' colic.

And Mike Lansing? Maybe his fall was just a bad accident. Cam said that Mike's cinch had been cut, but I knew enough to know that I could not always trust Cam to tell the truth. Only when I heard that fact from Noah would I believe it.

I had just started again toward Jon and Tony when Agnes swooped down out of nowhere.

"Cat, my precious. I am so glad the show will go on. Is Sally ready for her class this afternoon? Western pleasure? Oh, I do so love seeing Sally all gussied up in her western clothes. All that silver trim on the leather equipment! Now, what can I do to help? How about—"

Before I knew what had happened, Agnes had bustled me down the stairs and toward the barns. I took one last fleeting glance at Jon and Tony, who by this time seemed to have resolved their differences as they were standing together in the concession line. Very odd, but I had other things to worry about right now, and that was to help Sally bring home a blue ribbon.

That afternoon Jon and Darcy got Sally ready for her western pleasure class as I gussied myself up in the bathroom. That is the one thing I don't like about showing, but because both horse and rider need to look like superstars, I knew I had to make the effort.

This class would be a mix of Paints, Quarter Horses, and Appaloosas, with a few Arabians and other breeds mixed in. Walk, trot, canter along the rail on an absurdly loose rein. Over the years western pleasure had developed from a smooth-gaited, western-style horse that was "a pleasure to ride," to a horse with a tiny jog and very slow, rocking chair canter. One bobble, one pop of the nose, one swish of the tail, and it could be over. I had come to think of the class as a kind of performance art.

After the show meeting and before classes started I had led Sally into the arena and she balked just before the in-gate, pinned her ears, and made it clear that she didn't want to go in. I stood with her to let her become accustomed to the sights, sounds, and smells of the place. Then, when she refused to go in the second time I asked, I turned her around and backed her in. She snorted her displeasure and glared at me, but after that she went along willingly enough.

Now, as we entered the western pleasure class intentionally last, so as to separate ourselves from the other competitors, Sally hesitated. But once she saw all the other horses walking nicely on the rail, she decided to join them. Sometimes the herd instinct is a wonderful thing.

I have often said that geldings are steady and mares, when they are on, can be brilliant. Today, Sally was on. I knew going in that several of the Quarter Horses would be tough to beat. That's why I was thrilled beyond belief when Sally won the class.

Agnes was also just as thrilled. Because she tended to go overboard waving her blue pompoms when she cheered Sally on, Jon had instructed Lars to keep her away from the bigger crowd of people who sat to the left of the announcer's stand. Lars had found an isolated spot on the far side of the arena and had even been able to confiscate her pompoms during the class. Still, when the winner was announced, I heard Agnes's scream of delight all the way down to the arena floor.

Jon had also given Lars strict instructions to keep Agnes away from the out-gate. I am sure that he had visions of Agnes either being trampled by all of the horses and riders who were attempting to exit the arena, or that Agnes would cause all of the horses to fly backward into the arena when she ran up to Sally shrieking, arms and pompoms rotating like propellers. Lars knew that if Sally won, he and Agnes were to meet us in the corner of the holding pen where the show photographer had set up a nice little backdrop to take pictures of all the class winners. If Sally did not win, he and Agnes were to graciously and sedately go back to the Cat Enright Stables stalls.

All of that was beyond me, though, as I was giddy with success. Jon met me with a high five at the out-gate and we had only walked a few dozen yards when Jamie Jennings of *Horses in the Morning*, a daily online horse radio program asked for an interview. I don't remember what she asked or what I said, but as I handed her portable recorder back to her I waved at Glenn the Geek and Coach Jenn, Jamie's co-host and producer.

Glenn and Jenn were standing with a small group that included Noah, Hill Henley, Zach Avery, Sloan Peters, Cam, and several others, including Judy Lansing—who had been in our class, but who had not made the cut on the nice bay mare she had ridden. I thought about going over to them, as Jenn looked as if she wanted to say something, but Sally pinned her ears and made an ugly face at the group. Right then, Jon clucked at Sally and we went off, as my grandmother would have said, to have our "pitcher" made.

"Sally has been acting so odd lately," I said to Jon as we walked to the photo area. "Could she be coming into heat? She's not due until next week."

"She's probably picking up on all the tension here; lots of nervous people, lots of blue ribbons and money at stake."

"You don't think she's trying to tell us something, do you?" I said this only half in jest. Agnes and a lot of other people really did think Sally was psychic.

Jon just gave me a look. He apparently was not a believer.

Most win photos show the winning horse and rider flanked by the trainer, owner, and anyone else important to the horse's career, standing next to each other smiling into the camera with their arms at their sides. Agnes insisted that she hug Sally with one arm and shake her pompoms with the other. The photo also showed Agnes smiling so widely that you could see the fillings in her back molars, but at least everyone could see that she was happy.

I dismounted near our stalls where Agnes's celebration continued—with a lot more people. Darcy, who had been conspicuously absent from the win photo, had bolted back to the stalls after our win was announced so she could pull out all of the decorations and party food that Agnes had brought. Agnes claimed that the previous evening Sally had "told" her she was going to win, so today Agnes came to the show grounds fully prepared to celebrate.

Annie supervised Mickey and Hank as Darcy dumped a small bag of ruffled potato chips, original flavor, into a green feed bucket. It was Sally's favorite treat. But by the time I could think "colic potential," Sally had eaten all the chips. Oh, well. I resolved to keep a close eye on her.

Most of the trainers, owners, and support staff whom we knew were there—those who weren't, were prepping for classes of their own. Even Sloan Peters stopped by to offer her congratulations. With all the people moseying around our aisle, Ambrose was on red alert and seemed to have his eyes on everyone at once.

I had been standing most of this time on my tiptoes, so as not to damage the ends of my expensive suede chaps. That's another thing about show clothes, they are made for riding, and not for walking—or even standing. My chaps were so long that I would have tripped over them if I didn't roll them up, but then I risked rubbing the knap the wrong way and ruining them.

I excused myself to the tack room and replaced my heavy felt western hat with a new Sally Blue ball cap that Agnes had given me. I had just hung up my chaps when Bubba Henley burst into the stall and enveloped me in a bear hug. Well, it was as much of a bear hug as a ten-year-old boy could manage.

"I watched from up there in the stands an' you an' Sally rocked, man, you jus' rocked," said Bubba. He was so happy he slapped everything within reach as he repeated that last part over and over.

Bubba was what one might politely call pudgy, but he looked to have grown an inch or so in the past few months without adding any weight. It was a slight, but nice, improvement.

"I didn't even know you were here, Bubba. Hang around and I'll put you to work."

"Can't. Me and Dad, we're gatherin' info for that there blog he's writin', so I gotta move on along, but I jus' wanted to say you rocked, man."

And before I could ask him if he'd found anything interesting for his dad to write about, he was gone.

Cat's Horse Tip #4

"A horse knows from the second he sees you if you fall into the category of people who are dangerous, or if you are non-threatening. If only people were that perceptive."

11

AN HOUR OR SO LATER everyone had dispersed. Darcy had gone back to the coliseum to watch the tail end of the jumping, and Agnes and Lars took Agnes's purse to the Stones River Battlefield, which was only a few miles up the road. This part of Tennessee had seen a lot of battle during the "War of Northern Aggression" and Stones River was one of the major Civil War battle sites. Because Agnes carried vials of her dearly departed husbands' ashes in her purse, she thought maybe they could communicate with the soldiers who died on the battlefield—or something like that. In any case, it kept her busy.

I had changed into shorts and a tank top and had dumped much of the ice that was left over from the party into the large thermos I carried around with me during the summer months. I topped the ice off with a fresh mix of orange juice and Sprite and sat on a huge tack trunk rearranging assignments for the next few days. With the show moving forward, classes that had been postponed due to the death of Dr. Carruthers were now being worked back into the schedule. That meant some of the other classes had to be moved and I had to redo exercise, bathing, and other schedules for the coming week. It also turned out that even after the mass exodus of youth kids, there were still enough to hold youth classes, although most of the kids who stayed were older teens.

Hank had eaten one too many blue corn chips at the party and was asleep on his back in the corner of the tack room, his bloated tummy bright pick and pointed skyward. Jon was polishing silver trim on Gigi's leather show halter, as her class would be held the next morning. Even though we kept tack with silver on it in special bags, much as you would with heirloom silverware, our show silver never stayed shiny more than a few days.

"That was a nice party," I said. "I know Darcy and Agnes did most of the work, but I know you were in on it, too."

Jon grinned.

"I just wish Tony could have been there. And Debra," I added. "Have you heard anything? Any updates on the colts?"

Jon's grin faded.

"What?" I asked. "You've heard something. Tell me."

Jon gave me a level look before he said, "I didn't want to spoil your celebration, but Noah called during the party. He had hoped to be there but he had a call from Tony . . . and—"

"And what? Jon, the only way you'll spoil anything is if you *don't* tell me."

"And . . . Tony called to say Temptation died."

Tears sprang from my eyes and streamed down my face. Dagnabbit, Temptation wasn't even my horse. I had only even glimpsed him once. But I was saddened all the same. This shouldn't have happened. Yearling colts should not be living at an equine hospital and veterinarians should not have their last hurrah in a port-a-potty.

I slammed my clipboard down and stood up, all pumped up with nowhere to go. Hank, even though he was in dreamland, sensed something was wrong and woke up enough to wag himself over to me and lean against my calves. I sat back down and rubbed Hank's back.

"Sorry to be the bearer of bad news," Jon said, eyeing me cautiously. I came from a line of Irish people who were a wee bit on the emotional side and Jon had learned when I needed space and when I needed to talk. Today, talk won out.

"You can make it up to me by telling me what you and Tony were arguing about near the concession stand," I said. Now it was my turn to eye Jon. He and Tony had always been on edge around each other and I never understood it. Here were two of my favorite people, each like family to me, but around each other each was wound up tighter than an eight-day clock.

But instead of telling me what he and Tony had been talking about, Jon got up and walked out the door.

My jaw actually dropped when Jon left, but before I could close my mouth, Darcy bounded in with Amanda, Melanie, Bubba, and a tall, thin coffee-skinned kid with hair so short I thought he might have forgotten to shave his head this morning.

"You okay, Cat?" Darcy asked, and then continued without giving me a chance to answer. "This is Hunter." I assumed she meant the one person I did not know. "We've been 'observing' a few things around the show grounds that we thought we should report to a responsible adult."

"And that would be me?" I asked.

"Yes, Miz Enright," said Hunter. "We were going to talk to my dad but he has a horse ready to jump and doesn't like to be distracted before he goes in."

Hunter, it turned out, was the fourteen-year-old son of Reed Northbrook, an Olympic caliber trainer and rider. I have to say that the names of people who were associated with the English disciplines were much better than those of the rest of us. You just cannot compare Sloan, Reed, and Hunter, to Bubba, Darcy, Jon, Agnes, or Cat. Well, technically I was Mary Catherine, but still. However, the name Ambrose, I thought, catching a glimpse of our security guard as he passed by the door, had real potential.

"So then, what have you found out?"

The kids all began to talk at once and by the time I sorted out the information I had the following four observations:

One, Cam kissed Sloan in his tack room, even though she wore a rock as big as Gibraltar on her ring finger. Hadn't stopped him before, so no reason to think it was an issue for him now.

Two, Noah had grabbed a few hours of sleep in the show office between his own night patrols. He probably was taking all of this personally and wanted to leave no stone unturned.

"But what if that's all a front?" Amanda asked. "What if he just wants everyone to *think* that he cares?"

I assured Amanda that I had known Noah for many years and that he was the least likely person in the world to be part of a murder, or anything that would hurt a horse.

Three, they also found out that Mike Lansing wanted to begin selling arena maintenance equipment, such as the kind that smoothed out riding surfaces, but Judy was against it and the subject was a source of an ongoing disagreement between the two. No matter, I just could not picture Judy cutting her husband's cinch just because he wanted to start a little side business.

And finally, the biggest piece of news was about Debra Dudley. Bubba had discovered that Debra's husband's money came from naked baby photos. Not the pornographic kind of baby photos, but baby modeling. Debra's husband had been Baby Brandon. In the early 1970s adorable little Baby Brandon had posed for an ad for a diaper rash cream. That led to ads for everything from diapers to baby oil and before you could spit, endorsement deals and merchandising. The biggest of these was the Baby Brandon doll. For a few years, Baby Brandon gave Barbie a run for her money.

Long story short, Brandon's parents had invested the money well, and by the time Brandon turned twenty-one, he found himself a millionaire many times over. There was still an ongoing source of royalties and residuals, but that, according to Bubba (and who knew how he found this stuff out) was drying up, and Debra and her husband were in dire financial straits.

Hmmm. Would Brandon Dudley kill his own horse for the insurance money? There was sure to be a hefty policy on a colt that stunning. Could he have gotten Star to colic to deflect attention from Temptation? I had never met the man, but I knew I had to find out more about him.

"This is all great info," I said, "but are you sure it is true? No exaggerations?" This last comment I directed toward Bubba who had been known to tell a tall tale or two.

No, no, they all assured me. Every word was fact.

"So how, exactly, did you discover all of this information?" I asked.

"Kids can ask a lot of questions and adults don't think anything other than that we are pesky little kids," said Amanda. "Plus, we can hang out and adults talk as if we weren't even there."

I hadn't considered that, but it was true, I thought. What they told me was just as they had overheard it sitting behind people in the stands, or hanging out in the bathroom, or loitering near stalls. No one paid any attention to a kid.

"Bubba?" called a voice from the other side of the shower stalls. "Bubba, where the heck you got to now?"

Hill Henley wandered up our aisle and Bubba went out to greet his dad.

"I thought I tol' you to stay put by them big dumpster bins until I got done with my meetin'," said Hill. "You allus wander off, and it seems," he said taking in his surroundings for the first time, "that you allus wander to Miz Enright. You haven't been tellin' her anythin' about my meetin' now, have ya?"

"No, Dad, I—"

"You better be keepin' private things private, now."

Bubba did his best to placate his dad as Hill led his son toward the coliseum. At the end of the aisle, Bubba turned his head and gave a casual wave of his hand and I discreetly waved back.

When it came to Hill, my opinion had always been that it was better for him to keep his mouth shut and appear stupid than it was to open it and remove all doubt. What, I wondered, had been the nature of Hill's meeting, and just whom had he met with?

12

BY LATE AFTERNOON THE JUMPING was over and the Dressage preliminaries were being held. Dressage is a training method where the rider guides the horse through a series of complex maneuvers by slight movements of seat, hands, and legs. The history of Dressage traces back more than two thousand years and in fact, in French, it means something akin to training.

Agnes had asked me to sit with her while she watched the event, and I agreed. Even though she often tap-danced on my last nerve, she also made me smile. Agnes had a heart of gold and was a dear friend, and I had not had much time to spend with her since she arrived. Plus, when Sloan stopped by our celebration she was on her way to prep one of her horses for this event. My new friend had supported me, and now I wanted to do the same for her.

Jon had still not returned, but he was scheduled to feed soon, so I knew he'd be back. No matter how angry or upset he was, Jon always took care of his responsibilities. I left him a note that asked him to give Wheeler and Reddi their hay only, as Amanda and I were going to ride in the coliseum during the break between the afternoon and evening performances. Too much grain before exercise could give a horse a bit of colic—a word I hoped never to hear again any time soon. Then I locked the tack room door, waved at Ambrose, and walked toward the coliseum.

Hank, of course, started to follow but I explained to him, as I had many times before, that dogs were not allowed inside the coliseum. Besides, I told him that he needed to guard our horses. Hank wagged his tail, then went back to the end of our aisle to resume chewing on his stick. Even though Hank had some beagle in him—his other lineage was anyone's guess—he did not roam. If I told Hank to stay by the stalls, well, that's just what he would do. And I knew, too, if anyone he did not know tried to get into the tack room or open a stall door, Hank would let loose with such a howling that people would come running just to get him to shut up. He wasn't named after the country music legend Hank Williams for nothing.

I caught up with Agnes on the far side of the coliseum, near Section 220. Lars gave me a nod and bumped my hand as I sat down next to her, then disappeared into the vendor area. I smiled, because I knew Lars could use a few minutes away from his effervescent boss to decompress. Keeping up with Agnes must be like trying to herd cats.

Dressage competitions are divided into several levels, and this was a third level class, so we were being entertained with such advanced moves as half-passes and flying lead changes. The horses were judged on suppleness, rhythm, thoroughness, impulsion, straightness, and many other things that could be hard for a novice such as Agnes to discern.

"Cat, darling," Agnes said as she patted my knee. "This is all so thrilling! Why, these horses go sideways, and sometimes it looks as if they are dancing. Let's teach Sally to do this and enter her here next year."

I looked at the leggy Thoroughbred entries, and the tall Warmblood breeds such as Oldenburg, Holsteiner, and the Bavarian and Dutch Warmbloods, and tried to think how to explain to Agnes that I used a lot of basic Dressage in all of my training. At a stocky 15.2, however, Sally was not built to compete in Dressage in high levels of competition. I decided Agnes's cheerleader background might open her to a sports analogy.

"Agnes, have you ever played basketball?"

"Me? Goodness no. I'm too short, dear. I was head cheerleader my senior year in high school, though, and our basketball team went all the way to the state championships. But, my husband Seth's cousin played college ball. My, he was a looker."

I decided not to ask if Agnes was talking about Seth or his cousin.

"Well, see each of those horses?" I asked. "They are the equivalent of basketball players. Their legs are a lot longer than Sally's, and they carry their necks higher than Sally does. It would be wonderful to see Sally in a class like this, but it would be unfair to ask her to compete in something that she is not physically built to do."

Agnes didn't miss a beat. "Then what about polo?" she asked. "That Prince William plays polo and he is one handsome young man. I wouldn't mind getting a closer look at him. Do you think if Sally did polo that we'd get to meet the prince?"

"Ah, no," I said. "I think that would be a long shot."

Then it was my turn to pat Agnes on her knee.

Sloan did well enough to qualify for the final round of competition, which would be held the next day. She gave us a nod as she exited the arena and a yucky picture of her and Cam floated into my mind. Should I let her know what a dud muffin he really was? Or, should I leave well enough alone?

Before I could decide, Lars returned to take Agnes off to dinner and I headed back to our stalls to meet Amanda and tack Reddi. But first I made a little detour and stopped at the Zinner stalls to see how Starmaker was doing.

I found Annie picking manure out of the stall of a cute, two-year-old, bay leopard mare—a cousin to Star on her sire's side. As Annie moved droppings from her rake to a large muck bucket she told me that Tony hadn't returned from the equine hospital yet but Star was holding his own. Then she fainted dead away.

Cat's Horse Tip #5

"Many domestic horses (about a third) have myopia (near-sightedness), with few being far-sighted. Wild horses, however, are usually far-sighted."

13

ANNIE LANDED ON HER LEFT side in the stall's deep shavings. Holy crap. I didn't know if I should move the mare first or see to Annie. Maybe I should start CPR. But if I did that, would the mare panic and trample the both of us? Then again, if I moved the mare first I might take precious time away from my friend, time that she desperately needed.

I am not good in emergency situations. Not in the least bit. My brain turns into a mushy mess and no thought of any worth can get through. Fortunately, I heard voices on the backside of the stalls.

"Help," I shouted as I pulled out my phone. My hands were shaking so badly that I couldn't punch in 911. "Help!"

I heard the clank of a bucket as it hit the floor, then footsteps, and Judy Lansing and Melanie Johnston appeared. Judy did much better in dialing 911 than I did. Melanie found a halter and pulled the mare into the aisle as I fumbled to find Annie's pulse. Fluttery, weak, but it was there.

Even before the 911 responders could arrive, the EMTs, whose truck was parked near the entrance to the coliseum, showed up. By this time Annie was coming around and the shakiness in my legs and stomach was going away.

When something like this happens at a show, it's as if a vacuum sucks all the people from a two-hundred-yard radius into the area. Noah elbowed his way through the crowd and I saw Hunter's dad block gawkers from the open stall door.

I asked Melanie to take the mare for a walk and she nodded her head and headed for the outdoor ring. Another kid might have complained about missing all the excitement. I would have to remember to tell Judy how impressed I was with Melanie. And speaking of Judy, she not only called 911, she also called Tony. He was on his way back from the equine hospital in Thompson's Station and, after conferring with one of the EMTs, agreed to meet the ambulance at Middle Tennessee Medical Center, the local hospital in Murfreesboro.

I was glad they were taking Annie in. My friend was now waving off all the attention in true Annie style, but she didn't look good. As they loaded her onto a stretcher she searched the faces in the crowd of bystanders. When she got to mine, she held out her hand.

"Please take care of Mickey, will you? And if it's not too much trouble, can you throw the horses some hay? It's almost that time."

I nodded my head and was about to speak when Darcy jumped in. "I'll help, Miss Annie. We can feed grain, too. Isn't your feed chart in your tack room?"

Annie nodded, but the effort was almost too much for her and she closed her eyes. "Thank you," she whispered. Then the EMTs rolled her away.

I asked Darcy to find Melanie and the mare, and to bring them back.

"I'm on it. We can, like, take care of the feeding, too," she said looking at her watch. Isn't it time for you to meet Amanda?"

Amanda! I had forgotten about her. She had a class tomorrow and this would be her only opportunity to get into the coliseum with Wheeler. I was torn. Part of me wanted to be at the hospital with Annie, and part of me wanted to stay here and help feed the horses.

Darcy saw the indecision on my face. "Go," she said. "Tony's with Annie. Melanie and I have the horses. You take Mickey and find Amanda, and I will meet you later, at the hotel."

Reluctantly, I headed to our stalls.

Jon had Wheeler and Reddi tacked. He gave me a rueful grin and I smiled back. There was unfinished business between us, and between Jon and Tony, but now was not the time. Because horse shows are a hotbed of gossip, Jon already knew that Annie had fainted and had been transported. Without missing a beat he had stepped in, and I was grateful.

One of my goals with Amanda was to give independence to her riding, and also to her with Wheeler. But she was small, even for eleven, and due to the stroke she had suffered before she was born she had limited strength and movement on her left side. Because of that, she could not yet get the saddle or bridle on her horse. The key word here was "yet," for I believed that someday she would be able to do these tasks for herself. But, not today.

Jon carried our two-step portable mounting block to the end of the barn and placed it on the paved path that ran around the building. I gave Amanda a leg up, then climbed onto the block, put my foot into the stirrup, and swung my leg over Reddi.

There were vast differences between the western style saddle that Amanda had on Wheeler, and the English saddle seat gear I had on Reddi. The deep seat and the horn on the western saddle made Amanda feel more secure, and the one-armed style of reining allowed her to use her stronger right hand and arm to help steer. Most western riders held their reins in their left hand, which traditionally kept the right hand free to open gates or swing a rope. But, horse show rulebooks usually allowed a rider to use either their left hand or their right.

In addition, the slow western jog trot did not require Amanda to post, to rise up and down at the trot, as English riders did. Amanda's left leg was almost as strong as her right one, but not quite, and posting was tiring for her. Someday!

My saddle seat saddle was flat, with no hint of a horn. This style of riding favored big trots and horses that had a personality that was far more on edge than horses who excelled in western pleasure.

If I had been scheduled to ride another horse I might have switched gears and coached Amanda from a front row seat in the coliseum. Horses are so sensitive to the moods and emotions of humans that my shaky mental state and worry about Annie might confuse another horse. But Reddi loved drama. Any excuse to tense up, to be on the alert, and she was all about it; my shaky mind-set just gave her a reason. Reddi was the perfect saddle seat horse.

Amanda had competed last month at the Appaloosa youth nationals. It had been her first big show and her nerves had gotten the better of her. She made the cut and came back for the finals in her equitation class, a class judged on the rider's form and ability to ride the horse, but got the gate in everything else. That's why this preparatory ride was so important for her. Wheeler was an old pro. He had taken several youth riders to championships, so this was old hat to him. But Amanda needed some mental guidance if she was to be competitive here.

We started on the rail, side-by-side at the walk. I first asked Amanda to view everything she saw with a blue or purple haze because, as Agnes often said, blue was the color of champions. We then isolated vision, sight, and sound. Amanda discovered the parts of the arena that were cooler due to the circulation of the air conditioning, and how on the arena floor the sound became flat, yet still had a mild echo.

Then I walked her through her class: walk, trot, and canter. I asked her to breathe as she made her gait transitions, keep her shoulders relaxed, and steer clear of traffic as best she could. Then I reminded her that she was not competing against the other horses and riders; she was competing against herself. If she came out of the arena knowing that she had ridden better than she ever had before, then she had succeeded. A ribbon would just be icing on the cake.

During this time I had been letting Reddi take in the sights and sounds as well. She was smart, and I had found it was better to let her come to realization on her own, rather than me try to force it on her. Just by being in the arena, she learned on her own all that I'd had to tell Amanda. Mission accomplished.

Jon and Noah met us at the out-gate and I sent Amanda and Wheeler back to the stalls with Jon. I wanted to talk to

Noah, so I hopped off Reddi and gave her a calming pat as we walked. While it was good for Reddi to be "up" for her saddle seat class, she also had to know when it was time to calm down and be still.

At home I helped her understand that by taking her with me when I did chores around the farm. I often led her down the path to the water spigot by the front pasture and waited with Reddi as the trough filled. When I checked the fences for nail heads that had popped up, or for loose posts, Reddi was right there with me. Over time, she learned to be patient, although it was harder for her to do so here on the show grounds with so many sights, smells, and sounds to distract her. I lowered my body energy as I asked Noah about Annie.

"I spoke with Tony a few minutes ago," he said. "Annie's heart beat is irregular, not dangerously so, but they are going to run some tests and keep her overnight."

My stomach tightened and I blinked back tears. Annie was the closest thing I had to a mother, my own having died of breast cancer when I was nine. My dad went off the deep end after that and found solace in a bottle. Social services eventually uprooted me from our Chicago tenement apartment, and after that I was raised by my grandmother in a small town about a hundred miles west of Nashville. Grandma passed away close to eight years ago, and since then, Annie was the one I turned to whenever I needed "family." I couldn't imagine losing her. I also couldn't imagine what it would do to Tony.

"Do you think Annie getting sick is part of what is going on here?" I asked. "Dr. Carruthers' murder, the colics, Temptation, Mike Lansing's accident?"

"I hope not," said Noah, but his words didn't convince him any more than they did me.

"I heard," I said, stopping, and turning to look at Noah, "that Mike Lansing's girth did not break, that it was cut. Is that true?"

"There are many rumors, Cat. But that rumor . . . is true. My job here is to keep everyone safe. I just wish I knew how to do that."

I was mad, scared, and nervous all at same time, and knew Noah must feel the same way. The difference between Noah and me, though, was that I was just an exhibitor. Noah was the show's anchor. He was our rudder, our calm in the storm and it was important that he not give in to despair. Too many people counted on him.

"Hey Noah," I said as Reddi and I began to walk again. "What do horses fear the most?"

"I don't know, Cat. What?"

"Hay fever!"

Noah smiled and gave me a mock salute. Sometimes a little humor can make all the difference.

As we passed the lavatories in the first barn, women on the left and men on the right, Cam rushed out of the men's room and nearly bumped into Reddi. His timing was so "perfect" that I thought it might be contrived. Then I thought again. Surely Cam Clark did not wait in a barn bathroom on a chance that I might wander by.

"Sorry," Cam said, steadying himself on Reddi's neck, and then crossing in front of her to place a hand on my upper arm. I was struck again by his height—and his blue, blue eyes. I almost got lost in his gaze, but before I fell under his spell I shook myself. Whew. Close call. I had a steady boyfriend in Brent, but there always had been something about Cam that called to me, two-timing dirt bag that he was.

"Cat, I really do want to catch up with you. What about dinner? Tonight. Any night."

I remembered how Cam had publicly betrayed me and broken my heart, gee, less than a year ago.

"No way, Cam. And besides, what about Sloan?"

"Sloan?"

"Sloan, the married girl you were playing kissy face with just a few hours ago? Remember her, Cam?"

Before he could wipe the chagrined look off his face, Hill Henley stumbled out of the bathroom. Holy bells, what would that room spit out next? If Cam was my least favorite person on earth, Hill ran a close second. He was cheap, belligerent, and seriously needed to use a toothbrush. It went without saying that if dumb was dirt, Hill would cover about half an acre.

Thank goodness Reddi chose that moment to come to an end of her patience. She began to paw, and then dance in the aisle. It was the perfect excuse to leave the two losers behind. Not that I needed a reason.

Back in our aisle, Sally was busy kicking the back of her stall wall. Bam. Bam. Bam. The individual kicks rang out like gunshots. Jon came out of the tack room to glare at Sally and she went back to munching her hay. Some horses banged around in their stall out of boredom, but Sally had never been one to do that. I should probably check her legs before I went back to the hotel. Kicking could result in swelling.

Jon and I worked companionably getting the horses put to bed. Hank and Mickey played tag in the aisle as we filled water buckets, fluffed bedding, and checked every horse for the tiniest bump or scratch. When we were done we went into the tack room to be sure all of the equipment was ready for the next day's events.

As we organized saddles, bridles, and pads in the order we would need them, I said, "We still need to talk about what is going on with you and Tony. I could feel the hostility between you two at least thirty feet away, and whatever this, I am not going to allow it to affect our relationship with the Zinners."

Jon's silence was an answer in itself. It stretched on for what seemed like an eternity before he said, "We're different people. Not everyone gets along just because you want them to."

"But why, Jon? Why don't you get along?"

Jon finished hanging the last bridle, then made a notation on the next day's schedule on our dry erase board. Then, for the second time that day, he walked away from me.

I stared at his retreating figure and noted the aggression in my friend. It came out in a swagger that I had never seen before. I sighed, locked the tack room door, and with Hank and Mickey at my heels I headed for my truck.

Between Annie's health scare, Jon and Tony's circling of each other, all the problems at the show; and Noah, Cam, and Hill; it was hard for me to stay focused on my horses, riders, and the competition. But I had to. It was what my clients paid me to do and I owed them my full attention. If that wasn't enough, a bigger distraction was headed my way. Tomorrow, Honeycakes was coming to town.

Cat's Horse Tip #6

"Hay, the main food source for most horses, only contains about 11 percent water. In the wild, horses pick and choose grasses with high water content to keep from getting dehydrated."

14

I GROANED WHEN MY ALARM began to blare like a foghorn at five A.M. That was one thing about horse shows: every day began before dawn. Gigi's yearling halter class, the second of the morning, should go in about eight-thirty. Weanling fillies, this year's female foals, would go in right at eight and not take long, as there were not many weanlings entered at halter at this show.

First up was hair and makeup. Standard school of thought for the show ring was that women needed to slather on enough makeup to make their cheeks and lips look "rosy" from fifty yards away. I had never been a makeup kind of girl so when the blush on my right cheek ended up a little higher and rosier than on my left, I just stuck my tongue out at my reflection.

My hair was of far more concern to me. My mouse-brown curls were especially hard to tame in our very humid Tennessee summers, and my choices of hairstyles were limited by show tradition to a sleek ponytail, a long braid, or a fat bun at the nape of my neck. Sleek was obviously out, and my braid always turned into a frizzy mess, so I went with a bun that I could cover with a heavy hair net. About a thousand bobby pins later I added two silver studs to the lobes of my ears, and roused Hank and Mickey, who were both still snoring. Then I grabbed the show clothes I had organized down to my underwear and socks the night before, and drove with the sleepy dogs through the morning quiet to the Tennessee Miller Coliseum.

Over years of showing at the facility, I had learned that John C. "Tennessee" Miller had been quite a guy. He made his money in Alaskan oil, then along with his wife began to breed and show mules and Tennessee Walking Horses. When the couple died, there was a bequest in his will that directed Middle Tennessee State University to purchase land and build the equestrian facility. Since then, in addition to being a huge bonus to the university's horse science program, the facility had become *the* place for horse shows in the mid-south.

I signaled and turned into the long driveway as a thought popped into my brain. Maybe everything that had been going on at the show had to do with a rival facility. Maybe some scumbag of a person wanted the big shows to move somewhere else and had sabotaged the event to make that happen. I would ask Noah if the police had considered that angle whenever I saw him. He had been working such crazy hours that I didn't want to call or text him if he had found time to catch some sleep.

Plus, I had to stay focused on Gigi and her upcoming class. She loved Jon and we'd found she did better in the ring if he exercised, bathed, and groomed her before her competitions. That left me free to mentally transform myself into the commanding presence I needed to be to convince the judges that they were fools if they did not give the top ribbon to our filly. I also needed to be dynamic for Gigi, for she respected nothing less. She was a beautiful filly who was filled with charisma and presence, but standing still and posing with her ears forward was hard for her. She'd much rather gallop pell-mell around the arena and squeal. I'd take her over to the vibration plate, but that might make her too relaxed for her class.

It was six-thirty by the time I arrived at our stalls. I peeked around the corner of the nearest wash stall to see Jon scraping the last of the water off Gigi and, after a quick wave, began to feed the other horses. Reddi dived into her breakfast; and Wheeler, Bob, and Petey all waited respectfully for me to finish serving them before they took their first mouthful. That was normal for all of them. But Sally, usually an eager eater, used her body to block me from her feed bucket. That was odd. If Agnes was here she would say that Sally was using her body to predict some important future happening, but what that could be, I didn't have a clue.

"You want your food, you have to move," I said to Sally, looking directly into her left eye. "Seriously, if you want breakfast I have to be able to reach your bucket."

Sally blinked, then slowly backed away. I poured her grain but never broke eye contact with the mare. Was Sally psychic? Did she "know" things the rest of us didn't? Was she trying to communicate some important future event to me? Was she warning me of a specific danger? I didn't think so, but other people thought all of those things could be true.

I relaxed and patted her roany neck. "Eat up, big girl. We have a busy few days ahead." Feeding done, I hoisted my show clothes onto my shoulder and walked to the coliseum. Show management had just closed the arena to horses and riders who had used the hour or so of early morning riding to accustom themselves to the feel of the arena. Now the grounds crew was moving in a big tractor to drag the dirt footing into small, neat, smooth rows. If I had the opportunity, I liked to spend time on the arena floor on days that I competed to get a vibe for the space. Now I walked sixty or so feet into the arena, closed my eyes, and breathed. I felt the lumpy, un-dragged footing underneath my feet, and sensed the hum of the facility as vendors uncovered merchandise in their booths on the mezzanine level and concession stands opened for the day. After a minute I nodded to myself, turned, and walked to the barn bathroom to change.

Men in traditional western suits still dominated halter classes for Appaloosa and other stock-type horses. I'd had the choice of wearing a tailored gray western business suit, or a tight, showy navy stretch suit with a bit of tasteful silver bling on the yolk, collar, and cuffs. On the theory that I wasn't going to fit into the good old boy's club anyway, I went with the bling. I added navy cowboy boots and a matching western hat, and grinned at myself in the mirror. At home I took comedian Gilda Radner's approach to fashion: if it didn't itch, I wore it. But I had to admit that, with the right clothes, sometimes I looked pretty good.

By the time I returned to the stalls it was almost eight. Darcy was there, communing with Petey in his stall, and two big blonde men stood in the center of my aisle.

"Bumpkins!" the slimmer and slightly shorter of the two cried as he held his arms wide. Before I even knew what was happening I found myself melting into the comfort of Brent Giles. Honeycakes had arrived.

The larger man was Brent's younger brother Martin. I'd met Martin last winter when my neighbor, movie star Glenda Dupree, was murdered and our whiz-bang sheriff not only thought I'd killed her, but also that I'd kidnapped Bubba Henley. Martin was the county deputy who had convinced his boss otherwise. In the process he introduced me to his older brother, who was a small animal veterinarian in the nearby town of Clarksville.

I was glad Martin was here. He was built like a hefty trash bag with jug-ears, but his mind was razor sharp and his eyes missed nothing. Maybe he could figure out what was happening here at the show.

Just as I was thinking of staying in Brent's arms all day, the show announcer made the first call for yearling fillies. Time to go. I disengaged myself and stepped into the tack room to find my mojo. Then, properly psyched, I stepped out and took the glistening leather lead that Jon handed me. Darcy appeared with my in-gate bag of emergency supplies. Long ago I had learned that I never knew what I might need at the last minute, so the bag was stocked with such things as band aids, safety pins, duct tape, lip gloss, facial powder, earring backs, boot polish, lint rollers, and a host of other items that, true to Murphy's Law, I'd never need as long as I had them.

Jon carried Gigi's groom kit, which contained the equine version of my bag: fly spray, ShowSheen, baby oil, Vaseline, small scissors, mane comb and tail brush, hoof pick; and an assortment of rags, rubber bands, and ribbons.

In the warm-up arena I sized up the competition as Jon and Darcy fussed over Gigi and me. The Thoroughbred and the

Warmblood fillies were much taller, but possibly not as well conditioned. Zach Avery had a striking charcoal-colored Arabian filly with a silver mane and tail. She looked narrow through the chest, though, but that may be typical of the breed at that age. Hunter's dad had a whopping bay Oldenburg filly with an intelligent eye. There was a lot of good horseflesh here, but none with Gigi's presence and perfect build. Time would tell if the judges agreed with me.

The weanlings were coming out now. Cam held a yellow third place ribbon for his entry, and Judy Lansing's filly had a pink fifth place ribbon. Some of the yearlings were going in, but I held back. I wanted to be last. Gigi had the attention span of a gnat, so the less time she had to stand still the better. Plus, the judges might give her a little extra attention if they knew she was the last horse to be judged in the class. My philosophy was to bury mediocrity in the middle, and put excellence either first or last into the ring.

I tried to keep my mind focused as I led Gigi in an arrow-straight line to the first judge and trotted away just as straight, but Annie, Tony, and Starmaker were in the forefront of my mind. I hadn't admitted to myself before how worried I was about all of them, but I was. I really was. Out of necessity, I shoved my thoughts aside. I *had* to zone in on Gigi, or she would sense my lack of attention and start to goof off. This was an important competition, and a win here could be listed with pride in Gigi's credits for the rest of her career.

We were standing head to tail now, and the fifteen or so entries circled the floor of the arena. I focused on the three judges, sensed when one was looking our way, and turned my body to face her. The judges were using iPads to score, so it was hard to tell when they were done judging this round. In the old days you could see when the judges handed slips of paper with their choices to the ring steward and could let your horse relax a smidge until the next round. Today, I did not let Gigi out of presentation mode until I saw the three judges troop one by one to a small gate in the arena that led to a private seating area. This was the judge's stand, the place where judges sat between classes, or where they judged some classes, such as reining.

When the announcer read off the numbers of the eight horses who were to stay in the arena for additional judging, I didn't realize I was holding my breath until Gigi's number was called. I trotted Gigi to the center of the arena, then toward the gate so we would be at the far end of the line. If I could keep her facing the gate, and the holding pen beyond, then she might be interested in the activity there and look even more brilliant.

The judges buzzed around the top eight like busy bees and it took all of my attention to keep track of who was looking at what. One judge, a tall, older man who I knew had a hunter/jumper background, was quite thorough and looked closely at Gigi twice.

This time when the judges relaxed I knew they had made their final choices and a computer somewhere was combining their scores. Then the placings came and I got so nervous I thought I would faint. Gigi had an undefeated record of wins that I did not want to be broken here. And, even though Mason was Darcy's dad and a steadfast client, there was always the chance that if she didn't win, or place high, that he would move the filly to another trainer. Gigi was a difficult horse at times, but I had grown to love her and our barn would not be the same place without her.

The show only awarded six placings, so by the time there were just four of us left, I knew we had placed either first or second, or would receive no placing at all. I thought the announcer would never broadcast the second place winner, and when he did, it was Zach's silver filly.

There were not many spectators this early in the morning, maybe a hundred or so, but those who were in the seats were cheering and applauding so loudly for Zach that it was hard to hear the announcer. With all the noise, Gigi was beginning to dance at the end of the lead, something I tried to discourage, but she was already acting as if all the fuss was about her. And you know what? It was. Gigi jumped into the air when she was named champion yearling filly—and so did I.

Cat's Horse Tip #7

"To assess the fit of a web, nylon, or leather halter, the top of the noseband should fall several inches below the bony protrusion on the side of the horse's face, and only two or three of your fingers should fit between your horse and the noseband of the halter."

15

TWO WINS IN TWO DAYS, first Sally and now Gigi. That was huge for us, but we had no time to celebrate. Darcy and Amanda both had bareback equitation classes that afternoon and it was going to take all of us to get them ready.

I took Wheeler for a walk to loosen his muscles for Amanda's class. Even the fittest of horses got a little stiff standing in a stall all day, and to be honest, Wheeler wasn't all that fit. He was a chunky babysitter of a horse who knew how to do his job well, and as far as he was concerned, his job required a lot of food and very little exercise.

He went with me agreeably, though, and began to walk loosely and easily in a matter of minutes. When I got back, Darcy, Amanda, Melanie, Hunter, and Bubba were all talking to Jon.

"They have news," he said. Then he took Wheeler from me and led him back to his stall.

Bubba's was the first voice to rise above the others. "Me an' Hunter are part of the Youth Watch an' we volunteered to run errands for the show office," he said. "It was cool, we were like spies."

"We overheard something interesting, too," said Hunter. "Show management sent lots of samples of hay, shavings, feed, and water to be analyzed to see if any of it was poisoned."

"They're afraid of bein' sued," chimed Bubba. "They sure 'nuff want to know the supplies they sold on the grounds here ain't tainted."

Good for Noah, I thought. I doubted that anything would be wrong with the samples, but at least that could be ruled out.

"And *we* asked Cam Clark if we could sweep his aisle," said Melanie. "His stalls are behind Debra Dudley's so we went around the corner and swept hers too."

"We could tell Cam thought we wanted to do it because we had a crush on him," added Darcy. "And we're like, really? He's like, yucky old, but I'm glad we let him think that because we overheard lots of stuff."

"I heard Debra tell someone on the phone that the police think she is behind the colics because her family business is in trouble and Temptation was insured for a hundred and fifty thousand dollars," said Melanie.

"*I* heard it, too," said Darcy. "Then Cam told *me* that he'd thought from the beginning that Noah was in over his head managing the show. Oh, and Cam's got a guard 24/7 on his yearling because he's sure his colt will be targeted next."

"I was there, too, Darcy. I heard what Cam said, too," added Melanie.

The two girls shot hateful looks at each other. Before their differences escalated I suggested Darcy get ready for her class. Melanie, too. Since they were the same age, they always competed with each other.

"Thanks, all of you," I said before the kids disbursed. "That was great work. Any of this could be important information."

Darcy grabbed her clothes and stomped off to the bathroom to get dressed. I knew if she rode into her class in a mood like that she would set herself up to fail, so I followed.

"Here," I said as Darcy struggled with her long, thick hair. I grabbed a brush and began twisting her locks into a bun. She looked madder than a box of frogs. "So what is it with you and Melanie? What is this love-hate thing you have going on?"

Darcy glared at me, then gave a dramatic sigh. "I crowded her into the rail once *by mistake* when I first started showing. I was thirteen. I didn't mean to squeeze into her, but when I crowded her she had to drop back and she broke gait from the canter to the trot and didn't place. My inexperience made Melanie lose the class. Now Melanie crowds me whenever she can, or cuts me off. We're both just now realizing how immature our feud is, so we're trying to be friends. Sort of.

"I know it's important to win or lose a class on your own merits," she continued, "but that's hard when you don't know if someone is gunning for you or not. It adds a lot of extra stress."

Ah, the reason for the sigh. I now also knew why Darcy had taken a break from showing the year before. She was tired of the rivalry with Melanie.

"Well, I think Melanie wants to end the meanness as much as you do," I said. "If you smile and wish her a good ride before the class, I think she'll concentrate on herself and leave you alone."

"Maybe," Darcy answered. She looked stunning in her rust colored outfit. The uniform color from head to toe elongated her short body, perfectly matched her tack, set off her blonde hair, and provided good contrast when she was on Petey, who was dark.

I could feel Darcy's bad mood waning, and I complimented her on how well she jumped in to help when Annie fainted. A big part of a horse trainer's job is playing amateur counselor to his or her clients. It wasn't something I had planned on when I started in the business, and I wasn't all that sure how good I was at it, but I did my best. I knew if my clients did not go into a class feeling positive and focused, it was a guarantee that they would not do well.

As we walked back to our stalls I asked Darcy something that had been on my mind for a few days. "When you were sweeping Debra Dudley's aisle, did you happen to notice what any of her stall numbers were?"

Darcy thought for a moment, then her face brightened. "The one on the end was 116. Why?"

"I thought maybe someone wanted to get to Temptation, but got a stall number mixed up and got Star instead."

"What was Star's stall number?"

"Two hundred."

"Darn," she said.

"I know. Guess that would have been too easy."

Amanda's class was first and she rode as well as I had ever seen her. She came out of the ring with a big smile and a pink fifth place ribbon, and I knew the placing would do a lot to build her confidence.

Darcy ended up third. She could have won the class, but she had a little swing going on with her lower leg at the canter that I hadn't seen before. I'd ask her to stretch her lower leg down through her heel more next time and that should fix the issue. Melanie was right behind Darcy with a respectable fourth place ribbon and they rode out of the arena together, chatting like best friends. Teenagers. What else could I say?

Martin emerged from a corner outside the holding pen and began to walk with me. He was younger than I was by a few years, but had a nice, companionable silence about him. I had learned that while Martin didn't talk much, when he did, he usually had something worth saying.

"No security to speak of here," he said now. "Anyone can come in or out, but I 'spect you know that."

As we walked, he told me in neat, concise, words that the campus police were cooperating well with the county cops. "But they do that all the time," he said. "Not too many murders here on campus, but the university guys are holding their own."

I wasn't sure where Martin had gotten his information, but there was no doubt in my mind that it was accurate. He had also discovered that Dr. Carruthers suspected the yearlings were poisoned with a substance that was soluble in water, and had maybe been added to their feed. "She was supposed to have a tape recorded version of her notes. The tape recorder is missing, but the county cops found the written notes under the seat in her truck."

I wasn't sure if Noah knew all of this or not, so I added the information that the kids had given me earlier, then sent Martin in search of the show manager. As I watched him lumber away I thought that even though Martin looked like someone whose family tree didn't have any branches, he had more knowledge about human nature than just about anyone I had ever met. I was glad he was here, even if it was just for the day.

Brent treated me to lunch off the show grounds. This was a bigger thrill for me than you might imagine, because between the hot dogs, hamburgers, and nachos offered in the coliseum, I had already become tired of the choices. Jon made sure we always had healthy snacks in the tack room—fruit, and the gluten-free granola bars that I usually ate for lunch—but it was a real treat to have a sit-down meal in the middle of the day.

I could not have asked for better company. There was something about Brent that made me smile, and my heart lifted every time I saw him. We ended up at The Apple Tree, and in the midst of baked apple chicken, green beans, and corn bread with apple butter, Brent made his feelings very clear. He had two things he needed to get off his chest, and their names were Noah and Cam.

Brent always spoke quietly and this made his words more impactful to me than if he had shouted. As he had today, Brent had met up with me several times when I was on the road with the horses. And during those times he had met both Noah and Cam. We'd already had the talk about previous relationships, and I thought I had made it very clear that Noah was a friend and that Cam was as useless to me as a back pocket on a shirt.

Brent never mentioned the two unless we were at a horse show. I don't know if seeing them up close and in person made his jealousy rise to the surface, or if it was always bubbling close by, but this was a side of Honeycakes I knew we'd have to deal with together sooner rather than later, or our budding relationship would not survive.

"I am concerned because it is obvious that they both have strong feelings for you, and also because I get mixed signals from you about your commitment to our relationship," Brent said in a reasonable tone of voice.

I had a feeling we were in the middle of our first fight and I didn't have a clue how we got there. Maybe it had something to do with how the planets were aligned because there sure was a heap of tension surrounding this horse show. Darcy and Melanie, Jon and Tony, and to be honest, Cam and me. But that was all Cam. I felt like I was trapped between a dog and a fire hydrant.

I reminded Brent that we had both agreed to take our relationship slowly. My commitment to him on the level we were on now was not unwavering. Did I want to make it permanent? It was far too soon for me to tell. We'd been dating for less than five months. I tried, but my words to him were not nearly as calm as his words to me. Plus, he ignored my important words about us, and jumped straight to Noah and Cam.

"I don't see how you can be friends with someone you used to love, because some small part of you will always care about them in that way," Brent said.

"Do not put words in my mouth or feelings in my head," I hissed. By this time we were walking out the door of the restaurant, so only the people sitting at the table nearest the exit turned to stare at us. "Cam Clark is as helpful as a milk bucket under a bull. And Noah has become like a brother to me.

"You know what I do for a living. I haul horses all over the country. I travel a lot. I see the same people show after show, year after year. You knew that going in. There has to be some trust here and if you can't find it, then I don't know if we have a future together."

Brent looked as if he was going to reply, but instead he kicked the bumper of his truck and then slammed his fist into the fender. Only then did I burst into tears.

Cat's Horse Tip #8

"Horses do not look upon emotional people as competent leaders. Same probably goes for people."

16

THE TWO OF US PROBABLY looked like Darcy did when she was in a snit as we stomped around to our respective sides of the truck and got in. It occurred to me that this entire show was turning into a soap opera. All I wanted to do was advance my horses and riders through lessons learned from competition, but the enormity of the personal and professional drama that surrounded the event was getting in the way.

Three things were for sure. One, I needed to get a handle on my rolling emotions. Two, I needed the people around me to understand that they had to get along—at least in my presence. Three, I needed to feel safe in my environment and I sure did not feel safe at this horse show. There was a murderer floating around, for goodness sake, and people and horses were being hurt.

Then I looked at Brent. He was a good, kind, and very attractive man. I barely even noticed his protruding ears or Jay Leno-esque chin. In my mind, his features had long since melded together to make him my safe, dependable, huggable Honeycakes. That meant something, didn't it? I reached over and gave his hand a squeeze. He looked at me out of the corner of his eye, then gave me the barest of smiles. "Did we survive our first fight?" he asked.

"You know, I think we did."

There was a knee-deep group of people hanging around our stalls when we got back, and poor Ambrose looked overwhelmed trying to keep an eye on all of them. Not that anyone here would harm my horses or me. Agnes and Lars were there, Jon and Darcy, Martin and Tony, and the two dogs, Hank and Mickey.

I sent Brent off with Agnes and Lars to watch some of the reining preliminaries. Reining is a western discipline where horse and rider execute a series of fast runs, sliding stops, and mind-boggling spins. Brent actually liked Agnes, and I never saw a more unlikely friendship. Kooky out-there Agnes and staid, responsible Brent. Two of my favorite people and I was glad that they, at least, got along.

Darcy went back to the hotel for a little R&R, which left Jon and Tony. I gave the older man a hug and Mickey wagged his tail, happy to be reunited with his dad.

"How is Annie?"

"Better," he said. "She's much better. I think they'll release her tomorrow."

"Did they find out what was wrong?" Jon asked. Jon and Tony may have their differences, but Jon had always liked Annie.

Tony gave Jon a wary glance. I watched his face as he decided there was no hidden agenda in Jon's question. "Her blood pressure was unusually low, which they think caused both the fainting and the heart irregularity."

"Had her medication been adjusted recently?" I asked.

"As a matter of fact, it was," Tony said, "but two months ago. She began taking less, so if anything, her pressure should have spiked, not dropped." He shook his head and I patted him on his shoulder.

"While you both are here—"

"No, Cat," said Jon, standing. "Not now. Besides, I told you. Tony and I are different people. That's all there is, so just leave it. Please."

I looked at Tony. "Jon's right, honey," he said. "But here's the thing. We both love and care about you. I know, and I know Jon understands, that our differences are upsetting you. So I, for one, will do my best to get along. And maybe over time Jon and I can come to terms. Jon?"

Tony gave Jon a hard stare then stuck out his hand. Jon grasped it reluctantly. It was an awkward shake but I felt it was a huge step in the right direction. If only their words could match their future actions when it came to each other.

Jon left to go to my hotel room to take a nap. I knew he never slept well here in the barn, so he had a standing invitation for the use of my room during the day whenever he felt the need. The bags under his eyes told me that, today, he needed a nap.

I was setting out tack in preparation for a ride on Sally when two uniformed county patrol officers rounded the corner of my stalls. Noah and Martin were hot on their heels. As soon as they all stopped, Noah gave me a helpless look.

"It's okay," I said. "I was the one who found Dr. Carruthers's body and other than my initial statement, no one has talked to me yet. At least," I turned to the uniforms, "I think that's why you're here?"

Martin shook his head from his position behind the cops and I tried to understand what he wanted to say, but couldn't. Was he trying to warn me of something? I looked at Noah, who shrugged, then wiggled his fingers at me as he answered a squawk on his walkie-talkie. I kept one eye on Martin and the other on Ambrose as one of the two officers began to talk.

"You are Mary Catherine Enright?" he asked. He was the older of the two. He was about fifty and carried thirty more pounds than he needed to, but I had no doubt that if I made a break for it that he'd catch up with me before I got out of the barn. Not that I would try to run, really, other than the general idea of talking to police made me so nervous that I thought I might vomit.

I nodded. "Yes, but please, call me Cat."

He ignored my request. "Do you have a gun, Miss Enright?"

"A gun? No."

Jon, Tony, Brent, Martin, and even Agnes had all tried to get me to carry a gun after I was kidnapped last spring. But I couldn't do it, even with the promise that it could provide a humane end to one of my horses in case of a disastrous accident. No, for better or worse it wasn't in me and if I knew one thing about guns, it was that in the hands of the wrong person, they could be deadly. I was the wrong person.

"If you had a gun, ma'am, where would you keep it?"

Ma'am? When did people start calling me ma'am? Ma'am was for older people, or for five-year-olds to call their kindergarten teachers. I was neither old or up to supervising one five-year-old, much less an entire herd of them. My mind also had a bad habit of distracting me whenever I was presented with something unpleasant, such as talking to cops.

"I just said, I don't have a gun so I have no idea where I'd keep one, if I had one, so your question is irrelevant."

I caught a quick shake of Martin's head. Another weakness of mine is prattling on when I am nervous. I think if I keep talking, awkward situations will resolve themselves. Add to that my unintentional "habit" of pissing off authority figures. I needed to get a grip.

"This will probably be a lot more productive for all of us if I can sit down," I said. "Is that okay?"

The younger cop nodded. He, obviously, was going to play the role of the good guy. I offered them seats and the good cop pulled up a tall director's chair that matched the one I was now sitting in. Hank, worried, stood guard next to me, the remains of a stick at his feet. The "bad" cop remained standing, and Martin melted into the background behind him. I did understand that Martin wanted the police to forget that he was within my eyesight.

One question after the other, I walked the officers through my experience from the moment I arrived on the show grounds the previous Thursday. Every time my narrative began to wander, Martin jutted his chin to the left and I had the good sense to take notice and shut up.

I was just beginning to relax and get into my stride when the officers changed directions on me. Although I shouldn't have been, I was surprised that the emotional timing of these two was so perfect. They knew the exact instant I felt comfortable and intended to keep me off base. Goshdawg, but that was intimidating. I imagined both officers wearing big, round, red clown noses. That helped.

Now, when the good cop began to ask about the people at the show, I was not as nervous. First, I had no intention of giving anything but basic background information. I did not want my personal opinion of people to color their investigation. That I thought Mike and Judy Lansing's "perfect" marriage wasn't all that perfect should be no concern of theirs, should it? Second, my new visual of their noses made my inquisitors less frightening to me. We eventually trudged through everyone I knew and quite a few people I didn't before they finally packed up and left. Martin wasn't the only one who breathed a sigh of relief.

The police had asked their fill of questions, but I had a few of my own. Were the colics, accident, and murder related? Was anyone close to catching the person or persons involved? Other than asking questions, what, actually, was law enforcement doing to solve the case? And the most important question of all: Was I a suspect?

I had been a prime suspect in a murder/kidnapping a few months ago and the only two positive things about that experience were that I got to meet Brent and had gotten to know Bubba better. Bubba was a good kid at heart, but he needed boundaries and guidance. His dad was not about to provide either. Hill's priorities were skewed off the charts, so much so that I often thought that his driveway didn't go all the way to the road, if you catch my drift.

And holy horseshoes, here was Hill Henley himself coming around the corner. I wondered why Hill always showed up when other people I felt uncomfortable with were around? Homicide cops, for instance. There must be something to that "like attracts like" theory.

Martin eased out from the stall front he had been leaning on as Hill approached. He was not a fan of any member of the Henley clan, but then again, Hill was not an admirer of anyone connected with what he called "the law." Guess they were even.

"Afternoon, Hill," I said in hope that he was just passing through. No such luck.

"I seen them po-lice talkin' to ya," he said. "You a suspect? Warn't surprise me if'n ya were."

I looked for a tape recorder or a notepad. If Hill was the legitimate blogger that he claimed to be, you'd think he'd have one or the other handy. But no. No recording device, manual or digital, that I could see.

"The police are talking to every exhibitor on the grounds," said Martin quietly. "It was just Cat's turn."

"Humph," snorted Hill. "Wall, I hope you din't bamboozle them like you did the cops who investigated my boy's kidnapping. You had them all fouled up. Crazy po-lice anyway."

I had forgotten that Hill's mouth flopped more than a barn door in a windstorm.

"All fouled up?" I asked. "What are you talking about? Hill, have you forgotten that one of those cops is standing two feet away? An officer of the law who worked overtime, lost sleep over your missing son, and correctly solved the case while you were missing in action for almost three days? Have you forgotten that—"

It was probably a good thing that Martin came up behind me, put his arms around my waist and dragged me away from Hill. I was getting way too worked up.

"The officers were just gathering information, Hill," said Martin as I squirmed to free myself. "Have *you* talked to them yet? If not, I can put them in touch with you."

Martin knew that talking to the "po-lice" was the last thing Hill wanted to do. True to form, Hill muttered something about needing to find Bubba and scurried away.

Cat's Horse Tip #9

"Horses are able to form categories and generalize. They can differentiate between geometric shapes, such as triangles and circles, or move different breeds of dogs into specific classifications, just as people can."

17

MINUTES LATER, WHEN I WAS opening Sally's stall door, Darcy appeared in matching hot pink breeches and tank top. More and more, I was leaving riding and training decisions that involved Petey to Darcy, and I was glad that it looked like she was going to spend some time with him in the arena during the afternoon break. It would be good for them both, as they had a class tonight where they would be competing against Hillbilly Bob and me.

Brent, Agnes, and Lars returned from the reining preliminaries about the same time as Darcy arrived. I was always glad to see Brent, even now, after our little difference of opinion. But I have to admit that he was a big distraction. I was trying, not very successfully, to keep all of the negative events of the past few days out of my mind. I was also trying to focus on the many classes Cat Enright Stables still had to compete in, in the days ahead. Too much stuff floating around in my head made me lose track of everything, and today Brent was that one thing too many.

Then of course, there was Agnes. I always accommodated owner visits in the barn at home and at competitions. After all, owners were the ones who kept me fed and in business. But I always felt as if I had to entertain them, and truth be told, some owners could be both a time consumer and an energy drain. I'm not a great people person in the best of situations, and at shows I liked to be left alone to do my job, which was to win.

In the owner category, Agnes was special. Despite her "uniqueness," she was as loyal as anyone could be. She meant well, and I knew that when I needed a friend she would always be there.

"Oh, Cat darling! We saw the most amazing displays of riding, dear. Those horses ran at top speed, then sat down on their bottoms and ran with their front legs. Then the horses jumped up, whirled, ran the other way, and did the same thing—just like my cat Toodles does when he has an itchy bottom. Oh . . . you don't think all of those horses had itchy bottoms, do you? That would be terrible! I hope my poor, dear Sally doesn't—"

"As I explained to Agnes," intercepted Brent, "I have a limited knowledge of reining competitions, but as a small animal veterinarian, I am pretty certain that those horse's butts are just fine. It just *looked* like they were scratching them."

"Well, it was amazing all the same," said Agnes. "Cat, dear, what is Sally doing?"

I turned to look at the mare through the open stall door. In front of her were half a dozen or so golf ball-sized balls of dirt that she must have dug up from her stall floor. Now she picked one up in her mouth, then spat it out. That was the odd thing. Horses don't really spit things out of their mouth. A horse might drop something from her mouth, or open her mouth to let something fall out of it, but it really looked like Sally was spitting the ball out. Then she picked up another ball with her lips and did the same thing.

"She's trying to tell us something!" cried Agnes. "Oh, this is so exciting! My psychic darling has come through yet again!"

By this time Ambrose and Darcy had joined Agnes, Brent, and me in front of Sally's stall door. "Do you think she wants to play catch?" asked Ambrose.

I jumped at the sound of his voice. I wasn't certain that I had ever heard him speak before.

"Actually, eating dirt is a normal behavior for horses," said Brent. "It's a reaction to a bodily need. There probably is something in the dirt that Sally feels she is missing. Maybe," he said turning to me, "you should run some blood through the lab to be sure she is not low in a vitamin or mineral."

Sally spat another dirt clod out of her mouth. There was something about the intent and repetitive manner of her action, combined with the way she was focused on *us*, that made it so strange.

"Okay," I said as I closed Sally's stall front. "Show's over. Darcy's getting Petey. I see Ambrose is already back on the job. Agnes, Lars is here. Why don't you go back to the coliseum and Darcy and I will be right along. You can watch us ride. And Brent— "

I grabbed his arm and pulled him into the tack room where I planted a big kiss on his mouth. A minute later Brent wandered off a bit dazed to find Martin, and I tacked Sally Blue in her hunt seat gear.

Hunt seat was another form of English riding. The seat had a higher front and back than the saddle seat saddle. Plus, the front of the saddle made an arc toward the horse's shoulder and provided a comfortable place for the rider's knee, as hunt seat was ridden with a shorter stirrup than saddle seat.

Sally squirmed when I placed the saddle on her back, and reached back to nip at the right side of the saddle when I gently tightened the girth. That was another odd thing. Some horses were "girthy." They had been girthed too quickly and too tightly in the past and learned to hate the experience of the girth being tightened.

I had always gone slowly when tightening the girth and none of my horses had ever exhibited signs of girthiness. And, even if they had, they would have turned toward the person to nip, not to the other side.

Going around to Sally's right, I checked to be sure the pads or girth were not twisted. Everything looked fine. Sally gave me her "stupid look," which meant she thought I was dumb, not the other way around.

"I don't know, sweetie. Everything looks good to me."

Sally sighed, and walked with me to the mounting block.

Inside the arena I felt the coolness of the air conditioning on my bare arms. It dried the sweat on my arms into little beads and felt good. I watched Darcy as she let Petey warm up on a long, loose-reined walk. They looked good.

I pulled to the center to tighten my girth before we began trotting. I moved my lower left leg forward and reached down behind it to tighten the stretchy girth one hole. When we moved off, Sally pinned her ears. Ugh. I was getting so tired of her diva-like behavior. I used firm legs and my voice to move her forward. She sighed again, then walked on willingly.

I flexed Sally's head and neck to the left and right at the walk, and pushed her hips off the rail in both directions. When we began to trot to the left, she cocked her nose toward the center of the arena to give me another stupid stare with her left eye. I pulled her nose back to center and as soon as we went around a corner the saddle fell off.

Because I was sitting on the saddle, I fell too, flat on my back with my feet sticking up in the air, legs still wrapped around the saddle.

Noah had been standing near the gate, and as we were not too far away, he was the first to reach me. By this time I had rolled onto my left side and was simultaneously trying to extricate my feet from the stirrups, and catch my breath.

"Sally," was all I could manage to say, but Noah knew what I meant. Like many good horses, Sally had stopped when I came off and was standing nearby. Noah pulled the reins over Sally's head and came back to me. Cam and Zach had also come out from the gate area to help me disengage from the saddle. Darcy, Sloan, and Hunter's dad, Reed Northbrook, were all stopped nearby on their horses. It was more than common courtesy to stop your horse when someone had fallen off; it was a safety precaution that helped keep the downed rider from getting run over.

I was pretty sure I was okay, just had the wind knocked out of me, but for the second time since my arrival the event's EMTs arrived to check me out.

"Fine . . . wind." I said. And I heard Darcy tell Brent and Agnes, who must have run down the steps in the seating area to the first row, that I was going to be okay.

When I was able to stand, Zach carried my saddle to my stalls, as Noah led Sally. Cam began to assist me out of the arena and, for once, his hands did not feel inappropriate; they just felt supportive. But we hadn't taken a dozen steps before Brent arrived to move Cam out of the way. I liked to feel a little breathless around Brent, but this was not quite what I had in mind.

Back at the stalls I flexed and stretched before I sat on a trunk in the tack room. Noah settled Sally into her stall and removed her bridle before resuming his show management duties. Lars and Ambrose were watching Agnes flutter up and down the aisle as she communed with one of the dead husbands in her purse. It was how she calmed herself.

I knew I needed to get something anti-inflammatory, such as aspirin, down me, and Brent went to his truck to see if he had anything stronger than the over-the-counter Advil we had in our tack room first aid kit. I also needed a long soak in the tub in my hotel room, maybe even a trip to the vibration plate and a massage in the spa area here on the grounds, or I'd soon have some very stiff muscles. But, I had a hunt seat class tonight with Hillbilly Bob so I'd have to start with whatever Brent could find.

Plus, I needed to find out why my saddle had come off. Zach had draped the saddle over a portable saddle rack in our aisle and I got up to look at it. I first checked the girth. It was still attached to the saddle on the left side, the side that was most often used to tighten the saddle. It was the right side that was free, but the buckles were still attached to the billet straps, the two leather straps that went underneath the saddle's seat and were sewn to the inner workings of the saddle. On the right side of this saddle, the underside of the billet straps high up near the seat looked like they had been cut. It was only a matter of time before the remaining thin pieces of leather tore away.

I held the end of the girth in my hand and my stomach flip-flopped. All of the blood rushed out of my head and for a second I thought I was going to do an Annie and faint dead away. I sat down in a nearby director's chair.

"Ambrose?" I asked. "Do you have Noah Gregory's phone number? Would you call him please? Ask him to come here right away. Then call Jon and ask him to come as soon as he can."

Then I asked Lars to find my phone in the tack room and call Brent back to the stalls. And Darcy. Please, bring Darcy.

Cat's Horse Tip #10

"Check the tightness of a girth or cinch between the horse's legs, not on the horse's side, as the thickness of the saddle pad can give a false reading."

18

GRIM FACES SURROUNDED ME. EVEN before I was done explaining about the girth, billets, and the saddle, Noah had the police on the phone. The university guys showed up in record time and took my precious Steuben brand saddle into evidence.

"This can't have happened," said Jon while running his fingers through his short, dark hair. "Ambrose or one of his counter parts is here all the time. *I'm* here. And when I'm not, or Cat's not, the tack room is locked."

"When was the last time you used the saddle, ma'am?" Ma'am again. I was twenty-nine. Maybe I needed to do something with my hair. The words came from a young, eager-faced cop. He looked as if he had been on the force for all of two minutes, but his question was a good one. When had I last used my hunt seat saddle?

"Not since I arrived on the show grounds," I said. "Possibly last Tuesday, at home. We loaded Wednesday and drove in on Thursday."

The cop looked at me and I knew what he was thinking. The billets could have been cut at home. Unlikely, but possible. Or, more possible but still unthinkable, was that they had been cut shortly after our arrival, possibly at the same time as Mike Lansing's cinch. I shuddered. Mike had serious injuries. It could just as easily have been me lying there in the hospital as Mike.

"You two the only ones with the combination to the tack room lock?" the young guy asked, pointing first to Jon, and then to me.

"I have it," Darcy said.

"I have it, too," added Noah, then he explained as the cop lasered in on him. "Cat and I have been good friends for many years. She gave it to me some time ago, when I was managing another show. Jon got food poisoning and was back at the hotel for much of the competition. I helped out some.

"It's the same lock, isn't it?" Noah asked me.

I nodded. It was an unusual green, clover-shaped padlock, one my dad gave me years ago. One of the only things he had ever given me.

Brent and Martin stood on the fringe of the group, observing. Martin was aware of the cop, but his eyes were watching everyone else. Brent's eyes were on me. When he heard that Noah had a key to my tack room he humphed, turned, and walked away. I did not have time to address his jealousy now. I looked at Martin and he gave me a half smile and a nod. It would be okay. He'd talk to Brent.

"Isn't it possible," I asked, "that someone could have crawled over the wall of the tack room from another stall?"

The cop looked around. Gigi was next to the tack room, and a cute Haflinger was behind it. There was an aisle to the front and on the left. Some trainers had decorative fabric coverings for their tack rooms that included two sides and the top. We just had the side coverings, because a cover prevented airflow and trapped too much heat.

"Maybe," he said.

The campus cop then eyed Jon, and then Noah. No way. No possible way that either of these two men had a hand in this. The idea was unfathomable. The cop snapped his notebook closed and said to me, "Get a new lock. We'll be in touch." Then he walked away.

I was at a loss. In addition to my muscles feeling sore, I felt violated. Someone had been in my tack room with the specific intent to harm me. Until now, all of the events swirling around the competition had been concerning, heartbreaking even, but peripheral. This directly affected me, was about me, was about hurting me. I was furious, but I needed to channel my anger. There was a class to prepare for.

"Our immediate challenge," I said to the group still assembled around me, "is that I have no saddle for tonight's competition. We either need to buy one or borrow one."

The hunt seat saddle the police had taken away was a top of the line Steuben that had cost several thousand dollars. It could be repaired, but not in time for tonight's class, and certainly not while it sat on an evidence shelf.

The best thing about the saddle was that it had the uncanny ability to fit 90 percent of my horses. Getting a good saddle fit can be a trainer's nightmare. If you consider that a trainer might bring five or six horses to a show, then ride each of those horses in classes that required a hunt seat, saddle seat, western, or even a Dressage saddle—and that each saddle had to fit each horse—that could add up to a lot of saddles.

Saddles had to fit the horse through the shoulder, not be so tight as to cause discomfort, or so loose as to rock on the horse's back and cause a safety issue for the rider. The saddle also had to clear the horse's withers, the bony protrusion at the base of the horse's neck, by several inches. It had to fit so that the seat was level for the rider and so it provided even coverage and pressure on the horses back. If any one of these things (along with several others) did not happen, then the saddle did not fit and neither the horse nor the rider could perform at top level.

Finding a saddle that fit Bob was going to be tough. Like a lot of older horses, he was not perfectly symmetrical left to right. The right side of his body was slightly rounder than the left, had more muscle. He also had a large cecal swing. The cecum is an internal organ that sits to the right of many of the horse's other organs. It is the equine equivalent of the appendix, but in the horse it is necessary to digestion. Basically, the equine cecum is a fermentation and breakdown vat for digestion of tough carbohydrates, such as hay. Food can stay in the cecum for up to seven hours, so if the horse has eaten a lot of hay, the cecum will expand the right side of the horse's mid section. When you see a horse walking toward you, you can see his belly swing from left to right. With a horse with a big "cecal swing," the right side of the horse's belly is larger than the left. That was Bob.

Jon headed to the vendor booths to see of any of the tack shops there had anything that might fit, and Noah began to canvas the exhibitors for spare hunt seat saddles. Before too long I had a dozen saddles stacked up on various racks in my aisle. Darcy helped sort through them.

"If we don't find anything, I can scratch Petey and you can use my saddle on Bob tonight," she said.

My jaw dropped so far at her offer that I almost had to pull my chin back into my face. Her words were extremely generous.

"I mean," she continued, "Bob's owner is a loyal client. Plus, he's an orthopedic doctor and you seem to need his services regularly. Wouldn't want to mess that up."

Darcy was right that Bob's owner was loyal. Doc Williams had been my first client and had patched me up over the years if not regularly, then at least several times. And, I knew he was planning to come watch his horse compete this evening.

While Darcy's thought was kind, it was not feasible. In addition to Bob's cecal swing, Petey was a tall, angular horse, while Bob was mid-sized and square. Even my Steuben had not fit Petey and I knew her saddle would not fit Bob.

After we had tried on all of the saddles we were down to two, a synthetic Wintec all-purpose English saddle that Mike Lansing had thrown into the trailer in case he needed to school one of his horses in the rain, and a nice Pessoa that Reed Northbrook apparently had lying around. I was dying to try the Pessoa, as they were top jumping saddles, but it was a little too narrow at the top of the shoulder for Bob and a little too wide in the lower part of the shoulder. The Wintec fit better, but was darker in color and did not match Bob's bridle—an important factor in top-level competition. Presentation was key.

I looked at the Pessoa, sighed, and went with the Wintec. Darcy sent Agnes and Lars to the local mall to find both dark brown and black shoe polish so we could darken Bob's bridle. Between the two colors, we should be able to mix a temporary shade onto the leather to get a match.

I walked to the Lansing's stalls to thank Judy for the saddle and found her sitting alone in her tack room. She looked utterly exhausted.

"How is Mike doing?" I asked.

"Good," she said, brightening some. "His surgery went well. He will be out of competition for several months, of course, but he hopes to be back on show grounds in a few days. That's probably optimistic, but it motivates him. How are you?"

"Sore. I'm going to try out that vibration plate, and see if I can get a massage. I know I was lucky. The fall brought home to me that someone really is gunning for us. To be honest, it scares me to death."

Judy nodded. "Whoever it is knows what he or she is doing. I just wish Noah or the police, or someone would figure out what this person's agenda is so we could take more precautions."

"You ever think about packing up and going home?"

"No," she said. "I'm not going to let some sicko scare me out of my livelihood. Besides, Mike doesn't need to travel just yet. I've been spending nights at the hospital with him and I can tell that he is still in a lot of pain."

No wonder Judy looked so tired.

"Judy, please let us help you. I have a good crew here. We can walk horses, feed, whatever you need. If I can't do it I'll find someone who can."

"Thanks Cat. I'll let you know."

I knew she would never ask. Judy was a do-it-yourself kind of woman. I vowed to talk to Darcy and Melanie to see if they, and Hunter and Bubba, could ease Judy's load.

On the way back to our stalls I ran into Noah.

"Just the person I was looking for," he said as he fell into step with me. "A few days ago you said Cam Clark told you Mike's cinch had been tampered with. How did he know that?"

I thought back. "He said he overheard security talking outside the show office."

"Security, as in our student security?" Noah asked. "Or as in an exhibitor's hired outside security?"

"I don't know."

"I'll ask him. The last thing I need is our kids shooting off their mouths about stuff they do not need to discuss publicly."

I watched Noah walk off and for the first time in my life I wondered if his questions had hidden meaning. Could Noah possibly be the one with the agenda? Reality was, someone tried to hurt me, attempted to kill me. No one knew I planned to ride Sally that afternoon. No one except my barn crew—and Noah. It was public knowledge that I was riding in an evening class with Bob, because it was listed on the entry board outside the show office and also in the show program.

Did someone intend for me to fall off in the middle of a crowded class? If so, the damages would have been far worse. I could easily have been trampled, and other horses and riders could have fallen when they stumbled over me, or swerved to get out of my way. Or, did the timing of my fall not matter? Was it just the fall itself that was important? I didn't have a clue.

I should be afraid, I thought. In fact, I should pack up and go home. But I knew I wouldn't. First, I was too stubborn. I had come to compete, and compete I would. Second, this new show was important to the horse industry. There really was an unheard of level of cooperation and camaraderie between breed affiliations and discipline. Third, in addition to being honored that I was invited to compete, I wanted to support Noah. And fourth, there was the promise of a twenty-thousand dollar bonus if one of my horses or I had the most points throughout the competition.

I knew it was a long shot, but we were doing well so far, and my barn badly needed a new roof. Most of any bonus money would go to the owner of the horse if the horse won it, but my contracts with my owners stipulated that I received a share. Finally, like Debra, I was afraid if we all dispersed, that we would never find out who was behind this, or why.

No. I had no time to be afraid. We all just needed to be extra cautious.

Cat's Horse Tip #11

"A horse behaves toward you exactly as you behave toward him."

19

I EASED MY STIFFENING MUSCLES over to the spa and waited in a short line for a turn on the vibration plate. Jon and Gigi were just ahead of me, and Sloan Peters and Coach Jenn were in front of them.

"Want to step on with us?" asked Jon.

"Sure, if it's okay with the spa. Will Gigi mind?"

"No, she almost falls asleep. Maybe you can get a massage after. Richard might have a spot open, as I just heard Sloan reschedule her appointment."

One thing about Richard Valdez was that he was amazing with both horses and riders. I caught his eye and made a hand motion, and just like that I was booked into Sloan's former spot.

I have to say, I liked the vibration plate so much that I asked about ordering one for the barn. Ten minutes on that thing and

I was as loose as a goose. In fact, I was so relaxed by the time I got to Richard's table that I almost fell asleep. Okay, so maybe I did fall asleep. I normally do not drool during a massage. I booked another appointment with Richard for the following day and walked part way back to my stalls with Jenn, producer at the Horse Radio Network.

"You okay after your fall?" she asked.

I didn't wonder how Jenn knew. Plus, Jenn was media. It was her job to know.

"Yeah, getting a bit stiff, but if I keep moving I'll be fine."

"Maybe after this event is over you can guest on *Horses in the Morning* and we can talk about what to do after a fall. I'm sure you've had your share."

I agreed that I had, then added, "Maybe Richard can join me. We can cover it from both angles."

"Excellent idea," said Jenn and she reversed direction to talk to Richard about the idea.

Brent met me in the aisle with a box of apple doughnuts, the plain, old-fashioned kind with none of that gooey or sugary stuff on top that ruins them. There was also a small tub of apple butter to dip the doughnuts in. It was the perfect peace offering. "I'm sorry," he whispered as he kissed my cheek. "My jealousy is messing us up. I'm working on it."

I would have replied but my mouth was stuffed with the remains of warm, greasy dough.

Darcy and I met in the bathroom with our wardrobe bags and makeup kits. With many students it was awkward to compete together, and I tried to schedule classes so that it rarely happened. That wasn't the case with Darcy, however. She knew down to her core that the true competition was with herself. If I placed ahead of her, well, she knew if it wasn't me it would be someone else. She did not take it personally, as other riders or their parents might.

I thought her dad, Mason Whitcomb, might come see her ride. I had even emailed and texted him reminders, but the only reply I had gotten was a cryptic, TELL DARCE 2 HAVE FUN. He was a wealthy, loving, but often-absent parent who gave money rather than his personal time or attention. Still, Darcy didn't seem to mind. We all understood that Mason would be there when it really mattered.

Darcy's mother was another matter. She was currently living in Europe and had just married husband number four—or was it five—, a minor Bulgarian prince. She was obsessed with fashion and didn't want anyone to know that she could have a daughter as old as seventeen. Mommy swept into town several times a year to drag Darcy into designer stores and fancy restaurants. Darcy liked the attention, but seemed to be just as glad to see her mother go. I was pretty sure they Skyped regularly, though, so the relationship remained stronger than one might think.

Darcy wore traditional canary colored breeches, a snowy white shirt and stock tie, black knee-length boots, and a black coat accented by a delicate gold stock pin and gold studs in her ears. She topped it with a black velvet hunt cap over her blonde bun.

I was in taupe breeches, ivory shirt, and chocolate boots, jacket and cap. Those colors better suited the rich bay tones of Bob's coat, and while not as crisp in contrast, were on the more unusual side. Hunt seat attire was strictly regulated, even on the flat in the show ring, and the colors allowed were conservative and few.

I reminded Darcy to sit back at the walk and let the reins slide through her fingers. Petey had a long, strong, working walk that could compete with the tall Thoroughbreds and Warmbloods that would be in the class. Those breeds had the free athletic build needed for this competition. Bob however, was much shorter and squatter, and would have to stand out on the preciseness of his gait transitions and his unfailing sense of duty.

Bob was a horse who was resigned to perfection. He rarely bobbled a nose or swished a tail inside an arena; he was that dedicated to doing his best. When flashy, brilliant horses (or more often their riders) made a mistake, Bob was there with plodding regularity and often picked up a ribbon by default.

Fortunately, one of the judges for this class was a Quarter Horse judge whom I had met several times, so the deck would not be stacked completely against the stock horses. Of the other two judges, one was an internationally known hunter/jumper guy and the other a Dressage gold medalist.

At the in-gate Darcy angled her way to the front of the line and entered first, and I squeezed in right behind her. Petey always looked especially perky when entering an empty arena and I hoped the judges would take note. As Bob was one of the shorter horses in the class, I pulled about fifteen off the rail. Being closer to the judges would make us look taller, and we would not be hidden by the giants who were passing us nearer to the rail. I was glad it was cool in the arena, because in the holding pen I had observed that Agnes's shoe polish was starting to run off Bob's bridle and onto his face.

Despite the negative press the show was generating, or maybe because of it, the stands were filled with spectators, which brightened Bob up some. He took pride in his abilities and even though he was a modest horse, he secretly liked to show off—as long as he didn't think anyone would notice him doing it.

We walked, trotted, and cantered both ways, then lined up in the center of the ring. When all was said and done Darcy walked out of the gate with a pink fifth place ribbon, and I was right behind her with a sixth. I wondered if our placings would have been reversed if she had followed me into the arena, instead of me her.

Jon and Tony met us at the out-gate, as did Doc Williams. Doc was one of a few who not only knew I didn't like to be interrupted before a class; he also respected my feelings.

"You guys were awesome," he said enthusiastically. I also did not have many owners who were ecstatic over a sixth place ribbon. But that was Doc. "Hey," he added, "heard you had a fall. You okay?"

"Yeah," I smiled, because I was.

"If that changes, let me know. I'll squeeze you in. No need for an x-ray or anything then? MRI?"

"No Doc, but thanks."

We moved into the flurry of activity that came both after a class and at the end of the day. Several times I caught Tony looking at me. But, there were horses to walk and feed, water buckets to fill, legs to wrap, and bedding to fluff. I let Doc walk and care for Bob. Doc wasn't a horseman by any sense of the word, but I knew Bob would bring Doc back to the stalls in one piece.

After Doc left we moved to Tony's stalls and did the same for his horses. Hank stayed with Ambrose and our horses, but Mickey followed us to his show home. Agnes and Lars had not joined us, because the next morning at dawn she was going to sail down a zip line at a local adventure attraction, and needed her rest. Lars rolled his eyes as he led Agnes, giddy with excitement, to the parking lot. That man must have the patience of Job.

When we were done Tony pulled me aside, and I waved Jon, Doc, Brent, Martin, and Darcy on their way. "I'll catch up with you in a minute," I called. Then I turned to Tony. "You've been itching to say something all evening, so don't torture yourself any longer. What is it?"

Tony sat on a bale of hay in his tack room and rested his forearms on his thighs. Mickey moved to sit between Tony's legs. Tony patted the dog and looked about as sad as a person could look. "We are a little closer to finding out what happened to Star and Temptation—and to Annie," he said in a low voice.

"And?"

"All three had a very high amount of tannic acid in their urine."

"Tannic acid? What's that?" I was confused and intrigued at the same time.

"It's what makes your stomach upset if you drink too much coffee."

"So Temptation died from an overdose of coffee?"

"No. Well, I don't think so. I got a call from a veterinarian at Tennessee Equine Hospital this afternoon who gave me the results of testing they did on both colts. Just after that I got a call from Annie who said her doctor at the hospital told her basically the same thing. It probably wasn't coffee, though."

Tony explained that tannic acid is found in many foods and that it was a very concentrated form of it that had killed Temptation, and sidelined Annie and Star.

"But that means someone intentionally tried to hurt Annie," I said, new horror washing over me. "Tony, we have to go. We all have to pack up and go home. A competition is not worth this kind of risk. You and Annie are too important to me. Come on."

It was amazing how quickly my mind had flip-flopped. Hours previously I had resolved to stay the course and see the competition through to the end. But now, all I wanted to do was leave. All I wanted was to go home, lock the door, and snuggle into my down comforter. I tugged at Tony's arm, but he tugged right back.

"No," said Tony. "I am not going to let some sociopath run me off. I am not going to be afraid for the rest of my life that someone is going to hurt me, or you, or Annie. I'm going to stay here and help Noah, the police, and whoever else will help us find out who is doing this. If we leave now, it may never stop. None of us will ever feel safe."

I felt deflated. Tony was right. Only while everyone was gathered here, together at this show, could we find out who—and why.

"Okay," I said finally, "so it wasn't coffee. How did Annie and the horses get the tannic acid?"

"The vet thinks it was in a powdered form that was added to their water."

"Must have been mixed with something that tasted good then, or the horses wouldn't have given it the time of day. Flavored electrolytes maybe. Or sugar?"

"Annie thinks it was in her iced tea. She said it tasted funny but just thought it was a bad batch. She got it from the fountain at that convenience store up the street from the hotel."

"Has anyone contacted the convenience store?" I asked.

"I'm sure the police have by now. But the tannic acid was probably added later. Annie had been sipping on it for most of the day, you know. She'd put her drink down, go work a horse, then come back to it. Anyone could have slipped something into her cup."

I thought for a minute then asked how tannic acid worked.

"I don't have specifics, but the vet told me that in heavy doses it can make your stomach very upset, hence the colic, and it can also lower your blood pressure. That's why Annie fainted and why Dr. Carruthers thought for a moment there that Star was gone. His blood pressure was so low he might as well have been."

I thought again. "Who knows that Annie has high blood pressure? With the combination of medication to lower it plus the tannic acid, it could have killed her."

Tears leaked from Tony's eyes. "I know."

I put my arms around him as he sobbed out all of his fear.

"I wanted to talk to you privately, and only you," Tony said when he was done, "because you are the one person here at this show who I know could not be behind this. The only one."

"But you can't suspect Darcy, or Agnes, or Jon, or—"

"Everyone *except* you," he said. "I suspect everyone but you. Agnes, probably not, but what do we know of Lars? Anything we tell her will go straight to him."

"But they didn't arrive until after Star got sick," I reminded him.

"Well, maybe not them, but it could be anyone. That's why you cannot tell a soul. I have to trust you with this information, so please respect my request, no, my insistence, that it remain between just us."

I looked him in the eye. "Of course. I won't tell anyone."

"Not even Brent. Or that brother of his. The cop. Not yet."

"I promise. I won't."

I left Tony in his tack room and hurried back to our stalls. I had been gone far longer than I intended. I had been afraid that everyone would have left me to get something to eat, but they were all chatting like old friends. I looked at them, this group of people who were my friends. Could they? Would they? No. It was impossible. Wasn't it?

Hank greeted me with a short, fat stick in his mouth and I pasted on a smile as I joined my little group. Minutes later I walked Martin and Brent to Brent's truck. The Giles brothers had to head home, as both were on duty in the morning—Martin in Ashland City with the sheriff's department, and Brent in Clarksville at the vet clinic. It had been a long day and it seemed as if they had been there forever.

"Before you and Honeycakes here do the mushy face thing, I wanted to let you know I spent most of the day asking questions and listening," Martin said in his slow drawl.

"I know and I am so grateful," I said. "Were you able to pick up on anything?"

"Maybe," he said. "But what's most relevant is that the cops, campus and county, are grasping at straws. They have lots of leads and are following them orderly like, just as they should. But if they had to arrest someone, they'd go for your boy, Noah."

"Noah!"

"Yes'm. He's the one with the most opportunity. They've done background checks on the key players here and found that Noah has had a bit of trouble with gambling losses. Online stuff. Mostly sports. They think he could either be taking a payoff from someone to sabotage the show, or have taken out a large illegal bet, maybe even a private bet, on the results of the yearling stallion class. Maybe he just wants to hedge his bet a little."

"No, Martin," I said as I grabbed Brent's hand. "The police are way off base. Noah is not the one."

"You may be right. Don't go after me, I'm just the messenger, but that's what they're thinking."

I had no idea that Noah gambled, but even though we were old friends, we were no longer as close as we once were. Life had pulled us away from each other. So what if Noah gambled? That did not mean he was a murderer. Then Tony's words popped into my brain. Trust no one. Not even Noah. I sighed and leaned into Brent.

"You're exhausted, Bumpkins," he said, giving me a peck on the forehead. "Why don't you go back to the hotel and take a long soak in the tub? I'll call you tomorrow."

Before I knew it, he and Martin had driven away and I was standing alone in the middle of the parking lot. In addition to missing out on the mushy face thing, I felt as if everything I knew to be true had just tilted sideways.

Cat's Horse Tip #12

"Many horses will not drink water that tastes unusual to them, so trainers mask the taste at shows by mixing electrolytes, sports drinks, or molasses into the water."

20

I MUST HAVE BEEN EXHAUSTED, for I slept like a log. Early Monday morning I arrived at the barn stiff and sore, but refreshed and in good spirits only to find Jon and Tony were arguing—again. To add to the chaos, Hank was howling.

"Once more, Jon and I are having a difference of opinion," said Tony. I couldn't remember when I had seen such tension in the man. "But this time we're arguing about you."

"Tony thinks we need to adopt that buddy system Darcy talked about at the meeting. He thinks that you—that none of us—need to be on the grounds alone," said Jon. "But it's not practical. Who's going to volunteer to sleep in the tack room with me, for example? And, there aren't enough of us. What if we're at the in-gate and need something at the stalls? We can't all run back here or we'll miss the class. It's just not a good idea."

"And getting killed is?" yelled Tony.

Before Jon could jump back in, I held up my hands. "Can't you two even share an idea without having a shouting match?"

To their credit, both men looked chagrined. By this time Darcy was there, so I suggested that Jon and Tony each run their thoughts calmly by her. Then I went into the tack room to bang my head against the wall. Darcy's voice drifted in as she said she liked Tony's idea, but that Jon was right, too. Wow, our little girl was turning into a diplomat. Whoever would have thought?

"Maybe" Darcy said, "people could buddy-up voluntarily. At least it would slow the killer down, or make him think before he—or she—acted again. It might even keep the killer from hurting someone else."

When Darcy trotted off to present the idea to Noah, I came out of the tack room to pat Hank and to establish peace.

"I'm not doing another thing until you two shake hands," I said.

Jon and Tony both glared at me, then at each other. But when I held my ground Tony reluctantly extended his hand, and Jon, just as reluctantly, shook it. Briefly. It was interesting that Tony always seemed to be the one who made the first effort. Maybe rather than try to figure out what it was between them through Jon, I should talk to Tony. Before I could think more about that, though, Darcy came bounding back and the loudspeaker clicked on with a reminder announcement about the voluntary buddy system.

"Noah said he hadn't followed up on it after the meeting, but it was a good idea regardless of what was going on. Anyone could get hurt or need help at any time," she said.

A muscle in Jon's jaw popped, a sure sign that he was angry, but we had no time for that. We all had a busy day of classes ahead. Jon needed to get Wheeler ready for Amanda's showmanship class, and Darcy and I needed to prep Petey for her class.

Showmanship at halter is judged on the handler's ability to present the horse from the ground. Both horse and handler have to be impeccably turned out, and the handler has to be able to lead the horse in a straight line, and sometimes in a pattern of circles, turns, serpentines, and backing posted by the judge(s) before the class. Every move needs to be executed with precision and smoothness while the handler exhibits poise, confidence, and correct body posture.

The handler also has to be able to set the horse up with the horse's four legs perfectly square underneath his body, and be acutely aware of where the judge is—and which horse he or she is looking at. When the judge comes to inspect the horse, the handler has to move around the horse so he or she does not get in the way of the judge's inspection. The handler also has to position herself so she can maintain eye contact with the judge, if needed.

Showmanship was perfect for Darcy's sense of the dramatic, but because she was short and Petey was tall, she had to be creative about where she positioned herself. Farther from the horse gave her a better visual of the judge, but could also be considered a safety issue. Amanda did not have that problem, as she and Wheeler were a better physical match, but Amanda really had to dig deep to find enough inner confidence to pull off a showmanship win.

Jon and I busied ourselves in the barn and finally escorted Amanda and Wheeler to the main arena, followed by Darcy. Here's where we were a little short on staff. Ideally, a Cat Enright Stables staff person would have stayed with Petey after his bath to be sure that he did not roll in the nice comfy shavings that bedded his stall. But Jon needed to be near the in- and out-gates and I needed to watch the class from the stands. Darcy, whose showmanship class immediately followed Amanda's, needed to watch at least some of Amanda's class so she could see which horses and handlers were getting the most attention. A competitor could learn a lot about how to present herself in the show ring by watching the judges.

I might have roped in Agnes and Lars, but they were doing their zip line thing. Amanda's family, of course, wanted to watch her compete and besides, I didn't want the troublesome twins anywhere near my stalls. That left Ambrose, the least horsey person on the grounds, to keep Petey entertained until Darcy could get back to collect him. It was way beyond his job description, but I knew he'd give it his best. Besides, Hank would help.

Jon and I pumped Amanda up at the in-gate, then Darcy and I walked up the stairs into the stands. Or we tried to. Debra Dudley, tears streaming down her face, almost bowled us over as she flew down the same set of stairs. Sloan Peters and Reed Northbrook, who were imploring Debra to wait for them, followed—as did Bubba.

I turned to Darcy, concerned, but she whirled me back around and gently pushed me toward the next step. "Later. You need to watch Amanda, and I need to figure out what is going to impress the judges," she said.

Darcy was right. Amanda was my only concern at this moment. Performing all of the class requirements with ease was necessary to win, but competitors also knew that judging was subjective. One judge might like a handler with flair and mojo, another might prefer a more natural presentation. In these next few minutes Darcy hoped to learn enough about the judges so she could fine-tune her approach to the competition.

Because of her pre-natal stroke, Amanda had difficulty holding the length of her leather lead in her weakened left hand, so she used one that was shorter than average. It gave her less to manage but she still had nightmares that she would drop it. Amanda and I had done a lot of visualization exercises together that led her through the competition with the lead line firmly held. I prayed that the sessions would pay off.

I saw Amanda's family on the other side of the arena and waved. When it was Amanda's turn to work the pattern she and Wheeler did so without flaw, although the performance was also without flair. Not that Amanda didn't contribute, but Wheeler understood his job so well that once he knew the move he was supposed to do, he did it without much help from his handler. The judges might fault her for that—if they picked up on it.

"See the English judge over there? The one wearing breeches?" Darcy asked. "I think Petey and I will do well with him. He's taking a second look at the horses who trotted faster during their pattern."

Darcy was right. I had been so focused on Amanda, I had missed that.

"Good catch," I said, easing to a standing position. My back and ribs were still sore from the fall. "You should probably get Petey. I'll meet you in the holding pen after Jon and I meet Amanda at the out-gate."

When the class was over Amanda met Jon and me with a huge grin and a fourth place ribbon. She was most proud, though, that she had kept hold of the lead in her left hand. I gave her a hug and sent her back to the stalls with Jon. Then I went to the warm-up arena to give Darcy and Petey a final dusting. When Judy Lansing finished the same task with Melanie, I moseyed on over.

"Where's your safety buddy?" Judy asked.

"I guess that would be Darcy," I said. "Jon is over at the stalls. We're going to follow the buddy rule as much as we can, but. . . ."

"Same here. I love the concept, but we can't always put it in play."

Darcy and Melanie each moved through the in-gate, and Judy and I moved into the stands. Melanie looked fabulous in a light blue western suit with a cropped jacket. Her copper chestnut mare was in show mode and I knew they would be tough to beat—until Melanie stumbled at the trot. For a second I thought Melanie was going to fall flat on her face, but she righted herself and kept going.

"Ooohh, what a shame," I said to Judy. And it was, but inside my mind I was doing wheelies. I wished I could be more empathetic, but I so wanted Darcy to do well that I'd take any small gift that helped us along.

When the class lined up and the non-placing horses and handlers were excused, Judy and I went to the out-gate. Despite the stumble, Melanie was still in contention, but not for long. She exited in tears with a sixth place ribbon. In the show business, I have learned that sometimes life happens. It is what you do with it that counts. I hoped Judy could turn the stumble into a positive life lesson for Melanie.

Fifth, fourth, third. Darcy was hanging in there. I held my breath and felt, more than saw, a presence next to me. I turned to find Reed staring intently at the remaining two exhibitors. Only then did I realize that the other competitor still in contention was his son, Hunter.

"In second place, and reserve champion in the older youth showmanship is . . ."

The silence seemed to drag on forever. If they didn't announce the placing soon my brain would die of oxygen starvation.

". . . number 725, Darcy Whitcomb."

Reed jumped unto the air and let out a whoop as my breath released in a whoosh. I hadn't paid any attention to Hunter's performance, but he must have done well. Another day, another judge and the placings could easily have been reversed. The most important thing was that Darcy and Petey had both performed very, very well. It was my turn to be proud.

Cat's Horse Tip #13

"Backing tip: When standing, be aware of which front leg the horse has the most weight on, then ask the horse to move the other leg back. Works from the ground or under saddle."

21

WE HAD A BREAK BEFORE our next set of classes, so I walked over to the Dudley stalls. I was concerned about Debra's abrupt descent on the coliseum stairs and wondered if she had received more news about Temptation's death. I arrived to find Debra collapsed into Zach's chest, and Zach's arms around her.

"Those imbecile policemen have implied that Debra had something to do with Temptation's demise," Zach said. "I mean, seriously? It's impossible."

"Then that hateful Sloan Peters and Reed Northbrook began asking questions," sniffed Debra. "Why had my husband and I filed bankruptcy? Why did we put our farm up for sale? It's none of their business."

Hmmm. Looked as if Reed and Sloan were running their own investigation. If the information was true, it was just more proof that Debra Dudley and her husband were in an ominous financial position. A woman I didn't know, but who looked a lot like Debra, hurried up the aisle and Debra transferred her tearful embrace from Zach to the newcomer.

Zach beckoned to me with his index finger and we walked out of the barn and into the blazing sun near the outdoor practice arena.

"People are blowing things out of proportion," he said as we watched a dozen or so riders exercise their horses. "Debra hoped to keep things quiet, but you'll find out soon enough. Brandon has been diagnosed with multiple sclerosis. It was their tragedy to share publicly when and how they wished, but it came out in the news today, so the decision has been made for them. They've lost control of it."

"I'm sorry for them, Zach, but how does that come into play here?"

"That's right, you wouldn't know. Brandon did a lot of work on the farm, and also still modeled and made a lot of personal appearances, mostly overseas. He's still a huge star in Japan. With MS he will have to slow down, which means less income coming in. The Dudleys are downsizing. That's why the farm is for sale. We're still breeding and showing, just more selectively than we have been."

"And the bankruptcy?"

"A stupid business investment."

I walked away pondering Zach's words. Just how much would an influx of a hundred fifty thou help the Dudleys? Depending on the depth of their financial troubles it could mean everything, or it could be a single drop in a very big bucket.

I heard Agnes before I saw her. I also heard the clatter of what sounded like our director's chairs falling over so I half-walked, half-ran the remaining few yards to our stalls. Agnes was sitting on the ground surrounded by pompoms, her blue glasses knocked askew. Our chairs had indeed been knocked over but before I had time to say anything, Ambrose had righted them and Lars had helped Agnes to her feet.

"What happened here?" I asked.

"Miss Agnes was, uh, showing us her new cheer for her, um, horse," said Lars looking everywhere except at Agnes. Was his mouth working to hide a smile?

"Oh yes, darling," said Agnes. "It came to me this morning as I flew through the sky, tethered only by ropes and a tiny, tiny seat. Oh, and the nicest young man with his hair cut into a bright blue Mohawk helped strap me in. I know Sally telepathically sent that young man to me. Sally Blue. I have blue hair. The young man had blue hair. It's obvious, isn't it dear?"

Yep, as clear as mud.

"Anyway, while I was whizzing through the air, words popped right into my brain. You want to know the best part?"

Boy howdy, I couldn't wait.

"The words all arrived together. Not one by one, but together. Isn't that amazing?"

I nodded my head. For once I was speechless.

"You want to hear them?"

I gathered my thoughts together, and with them, some words, but I addressed them to Lars instead of to Agnes. "Do we have a choice?" I asked.

"No, ma'am. But the experience is worth it. Unforgettable, actually."

"Okay then, Agnes. I can't wait."

"Yippee!" Agnes moved the chairs back against the stall walls, gathered her pompoms, then put her feet together and her hands on her hips. I imagined her as a girl, more than fifty years ago, and a genuine smile came to my lips. Actually, I *couldn't* wait. I had a feeling I was going to enjoy the next few minutes very much.

"Hey everyone. Listen up!" said Agnes in a voice that was more suited to the football field than a horse barn.

You might be good at the canter,
You might have beautiful tack,
But when it comes to Sally Blue,
You might as well step back
Say what?
You might as well step back
Go Sally Blue!

Agnes's words were accompanied by an assortment of jumps and arm movements that brought all the horses to the front of their stalls. I didn't blame them, for this was something not to be missed. For her big finish, in time to the words "Go Sally Blue!" Agnes attempted a cartwheel but only got her legs a foot or so off of the ground. Then she landed in a heap on the floor of the aisle, sitting with her legs splayed out in front of her, arms and pompoms raised into the air. Victory.

For the second time in as many minutes I was speechless, so I began to clap. I turned to Ambrose to indicate that he should clap, too. Lars was right. Agnes just gave an unforgettable performance. And, it was something I desperately needed. I had been so caught up in keeping my horses and crew safe, and trying to compete effectively, that my nerves were worn raw.

I gave Agnes a huge hug and tried to help her rise from the floor of the aisle. Eventually Lars pitched in, and together we heaved Agnes more or less into a standing position.

"That was . . . amazing, Agnes," said Jon from the door of the tack room. He must have been in there all along. I was glad he hadn't missed what was sure to be the highlight of the day. "Very inspiring, actually. But we've got to get Cat, Sally, and Bob ready for their classes. Maybe you should grab some lunch before finding a good seat in the stands?"

Agnes and Lars took the hint and the rest of us at Cat Enright Stables got back to work.

The trail class was all about precision and smoothness. It was also about approach. Should the water hazard be approached dead center, or a little to the left? And if a rider initially decided on left, but all the previous competitors also went left, then the footing could be bad and a last minute switch in thinking was necessary. Depending on the competition, one bobble could knock a horse and rider out of the placings.

I gathered my show clothes, a flashy royal blue ensemble that would work for both Sally's trail class and Bob's senior western pleasure class, and brought them to the coliseum so I could change. It would also give me the opportunity to look at the positioning of the obstacles. The course had been posted yesterday, so I knew the route we needed to take, but seeing what color, for example, the poles on the small jump were, or the width between the poles on the backing obstacle, helped a lot.

Horses see differently than humans do. The current school of thought is that horses do not see reds and oranges very well.

If that was the case, then obstacles of that color might be difficult for a horse to see.

The size of an obstacle was also critical. Was the tent we had to pass a small green pup tent, or was it a shiny, white, ten-by-ten party tent with balloons, streamers, and a fan?

After I changed into everything but my chaps, I went down to the in-gate to get a better look. I hadn't been there two seconds before Cam slung an arm over my shoulder. I just as quickly slung it off.

"Which horse do you have in this?" he asked with a nod toward the obstacles. "Oh, wait. The incomparable Sally Blue, isn't it? I saw the, ah . . . cheer. Impressive."

I grinned. Dear Agnes. What would I do without her?

"You?" I asked Cam.

"Mike Lansing's junior mare. Quarter Horse. Owned by that oil guy in Dallas."

"Judy asked you to ride Mike's horse?" I couldn't believe that. Like me, Judy had little use for Cam Clark.

"No," said Cam. "The owner did."

Ah. That explained a lot. While Mike was in the hospital trying to mend, Cam was busy hustling his owners. A trainer's owners were sacrosanct. It was an unwritten rule that one trainer did not solicit the owners of another. I had little confidence that the oil guy in Dallas sought Cam out on his own.

Cam saw the look on my face. "Awww. Come on, Cat. The horse was there for the asking. Really, she was, and Mike couldn't ride it."

"But I bet Mike had someone in mind who could."

"Well, I got there first," Cam said. "You snooze you lose."

I didn't need to get angry at that moment, so instead, I left to get Sally.

During a trail class I normally position my horse as close to the in-gate as I can. That way we both can watch the competitors who go ahead of us. I never take for granted what a horse can learn by watching.

Today, however, I needed to use that time loosening up. In college I needed a non-equestrian physical education credit and had taken yoga. While I didn't keep up with it, I remembered some basic moves and used those, along with the motion of Sally's walk, to ease my muscles into a less painful frame. Then we stopped in the center of the warm-up arena and I did a quick visualization of the course, and of Sally and me completing it flawlessly.

And you know what? That's about what we did. Sally completed each obstacle perfectly, if slowly. When we pivoted inside a square laid out on the ground with poles, Sally's movement was consistent and rhythmic, but painfully slow. I didn't want to rush her and risk a less than perfect go, so we glided around the course like a herd of turtles. In fact, it was almost like she navigated the entire course in slow motion. I knew we had done well, but had no idea how well our competition had done.

When the placings were given, the announcer first called the top six horses back into the ring. We were one of the six called. Cam was another, as was Sloan Peters. That surprised me, as Dressage horses are usually not schooled in trail obstacles. Good for her for doing something to keep her horse's mind fresh. After the bottom three horses had been placed, it was the three of us that were left.

"Go Sally," I heard Agnes yell from the stands. Then, almost as loudly, I heard Lars shush her.

I didn't like to wish bad things on anyone. Okay, there were a few people and one of them was next to me on a dazzling

Quarter Horse mare. I didn't care if I won the class or not, just as long as Cam did not place ahead of me. My feelings were so strong that I looked at the rivalry between Darcy and Melanie in a new light. Maybe I could be the teensiest bit more sympathetic in that area. But until then I hoped with all I had that I would come out of the ring with a higher score than Cam.

The third place winner was announced. Sloan. Cam rode over, and instead of the usual handshake, which was the normal public show of solidarity and sportsmanship between the top two competitors, Cam leaned in to kiss me on the cheek. Or, he tried to. Sally did a quick sideways move that left Cam hanging off the side of his saddle. For a second there I thought he was going to fall. Then he righted himself. Darn.

I wish I could say that we won the class, but sometimes things do not end up as you had hoped. Later, when the score sheets were posted, Cam and the mare had scored a half point higher than we had. A lousy half point. Maybe I should have pushed Sally more, taken the risk. Unfortunately, we cannot go back in time. I would have fully embraced a do-over, however, one in which both Sally and I had stepped up our game.

I had little time for wishful thinking, though. Bob's senior western pleasure class was immediately after the junior trail. Darcy had tacked and warmed up Bob for me so all I had to do was hop off Sally and onto Bob.

Doc Williams couldn't make the performance, but I wished he could have been there. The competition must have been close, because the judges had us do more than the usual walk, trot, and lope in both directions. We changed direction three times and went from the walk, to the lope, to the trot, to the lope, to the trot, then reversed at the trot. As the commands went on—and on—my confidence grew stronger. Delays like these usually worked in our favor. Bob was not flashy. He was not beautiful, but he was precise. In most cases, sooner or later each of the other horses would make a mistake, but not Bob. And that's what happened here.

As Bob, Jon, Darcy, and I posed for the win picture, I gave Bob a hearty pat. He loved competing, loved the attention, and I was glad I could be part of his journey. I was also grateful for Jon and Darcy, for without either of them, we would not have won the class. Nor would we have been so close to a win with Sally in trail. I was fortunate to have these wonderful people in my life and realized, maybe for the first time, what a lucky person I was.

Cat's Horse Tip #14

"If a normally sensible horse refuses a jump or trail obstacle, it might be unsafe, or it might be that she cannot see it properly."

22

TUESDAY WAS AN "OFF" DAY at the show and no classes were scheduled. Management had wisely decided that exhibitors would need a break half way through the competition, and they were right. The end result was that I had the luxury of sleeping in until the amazingly late hour of seven A.M.

Because the show was just ninety minutes from home, Darcy, Annie, and I were using the day to head home to Ashland City, do laundry, re-stock our supply of snacks, and decompress. Annie said she felt fine but I thought she still looked peaked. She'd just been released from the hospital yesterday. A nap in the quiet of my guest room might be just the thing for her.

During any other event I would have roped another trainer into watching our horses and taken Jon with us, but given the circumstances, he was adamant that he stay. "If something is going to happen, today is the day," said Jon. "It will happen when everyone is relaxed and off their guard."

Sorry to say, I thought he was right.

We decided to bring Reddi and Gigi with us. Both had classes later in the week, but both were rowdy young ladies and I thought they would enjoy some turn out time. It would be too hot for them in the sun, but I had a covered arena and round pen. We hooked up the trailer, loaded the horses, and set off on our girls' day out.

My rig was an older green Ford one ton pick-up with a crew cab and more than a few dings. My trailer was a six-horse diagonal haul gooseneck, which meant the horses stood at an angle, instead of facing forward, and the trailer attached to the truck's bed, rather than to its bumper. The front of the trailer had a small space to carry equipment and while I dreamed of a new truck and a trailer with full living quarters, I got where I needed to go with the rig I had.

I was glad that Agnes and Lars had gone back to Louisville so she could water her plants. Only she, apparently, had the right touch for them to thrive. Otherwise I would have felt obligated to invite her and, as much as I loved Agnes, if she came along none of us would have been able to relax. Having Agnes around was like standing in a room full of rabbits; I never knew where she'd go or what she'd do. She and Lars would return to Murfreesboro on Thursday, for Sally's next class. In the meantime, I was glad I didn't have to worry about her.

We sailed up I-24 at the tail end of the morning rush hour, then bumped over to I-440 around the south end of Nashville, hopped onto I-40, and exited on Charlotte Pike on the west side of town. That led to a quick right and before I knew it, we were turning off River Road to home sweet home.

I'd purchased the twenty acres, farmhouse, and old tobacco barn with money I inherited after my grandmother passed away. That was about seven years ago. Since then, I'd patched the roof (well, actually, Jon had) and had an apartment built over some of the stalls that Jon now called home. I'd added a covered arena and spiffed up the house some, but I had a long way to go. The twenty-thousand dollar bonus for being the top trainer at the show would go a long way toward keeping fences mended and holes out of the driveway. I didn't dare hope that I would win the prize, but so far I was in the running. Fingers crossed.

We were unloaded by ten A.M. Darcy turned Gigi loose in the covered arena while I led Reddi into the round pen. The two enclosures were within close sight and proximity, which meant that between them, the girls could form a herd. Having a herd was critical to horses for they lived by the motto of "safety in numbers."

I had a strict rule about not putting hay into any area where we might ride. This was for several reasons. The first was because the leftover wisps of hay always got mixed up into the footing and could cause a safety hazard. Two, it just looked bad, and three, I wanted the horses to have clearly defined ideas about eating/relaxing areas and exercise/training areas.

Today, though, the mental wellbeing of the horses was more important than the condition of the footing, so I ignored my own rule and threw each girl a flake of hay next to their buckets of water. Gigi was too busy running, bucking, and yes, farting, to care about the hay, so maybe I would not have to worry about the arena. Reddi trotted around a few times and kicked out a time or two, then settled down to watch Gigi. I have to say, watching our little yearling have fun was pretty entertaining.

When Darcy and I got back to the truck, Annie was already busy sorting laundry. We'd piled all of our clothes together, and jeans and casual clothes went into the washer in the barn while whites and more delicate fabrics were left for the washer inside the house.

The washer/dryer set in the barn was a new addition for Cat Enright Stables. We had badly needed a place to wash blankets, barn towels, polo wraps, and even English pads, so when I saw an ad for a washer and dryer on Craigslist and realized the seller was just across the Cumberland River from us in Ashland City, I dipped into my meager savings and snapped them right up. It was a luxury, but boy, the set sure came in handy.

When we got to the house, I showed Annie my office slash guestroom and said she could do whatever she wanted, but I was taking a nap. Darcy was already snoring across the hall in her room. Showing horses really was exhausting and as soon as I lay down on my bed I went out like a light. When my phone alarm sounded at two minutes after two, I had to drag myself from the depths of a sound slumber. It was like swimming into consciousness. Whew. I could have slept until morning.

Between the three of us we checked on the horses and got the newly washed clothes moved from the washers into the dryers. We were all quite hungry, so I sent Darcy up the road a few miles to the Riverside Restaurant. When I was away at shows I did not leave the kind of food you could eat without cooking in the house, because it always spoiled by the time I returned.

The Riverside didn't do take-out, but Brent and Martin's cousin Sissy worked there, and she always made an exception for anyone from our barn. I watched Darcy as she drove Jon's ancient Datsun down our long drive to make sure she didn't peel out and spin gravel where the driveway met River Road. Besides the fact that Jon's tires couldn't take much of that, it meant one of us would have to rake the gravel back into place. This time she drove sedately and I breathed a sigh of relief. With Darcy, I just never knew.

While we waited for Darcy's return—and the food—Annie and I settled at my kitchen table. I made us large iced coffees with instant coffee, hot chocolate mix, powdered creamer, and all the ice I had in my freezer. My opinion was that just about every beverage in the world was improved by a dash of hot chocolate. Iced coffee was just one of them.

Of course when we finally sat at my grandmother's butcher-block table, the show was the only topic of discussion. Who had killed Temptation and Dr. Carruthers? Who had put Annie in the hospital and damaged Mike's cinch and my girth? Who had hurt Star and was sabotaging the show?

"My money is on Debra Dudley," said Annie. "She's got the motive, the means, and the opportunity. She and Brandon are in dire financial straits with no hope of help in sight—except for Temptation's insurance policy."

"Seriously?" I asked. "You really think Debra could murder her own horse?" I didn't have a clue as to who the murderer could be and I was interested to hear Annie's reasoning.

"Sure. She has a certain level of lifestyle she needs to maintain, not just because she's used to it, but also because in some circles Brandon Dudley is a big star. She doesn't want anyone to think that Brandon squandered all that money, which it sounds like he did."

I pondered Annie's words for a minute, then asked, "If it *wasn't* Debra, who do you think it would be?"

"I know where you are going with that," said Annie as she reached over to squeeze my hand. "As much as I know you'd like it to be Cam, I don't see it that way. Cam is a cad and his personality is too weak for him to be a killer. It would be too much trouble for him. My goodness, he even gets the youth kids to sweep his barn aisle."

"Or Sloan Peters," I muttered.

"Now Cat, you chose to end things with the man. And it was a wise choice, too, if I may say so."

"I think you just did."

"Then leave him to his own devices and put your hard feelings aside. You deserve better, and I think," she said with another squeeze of my hand, "that you may have found it."

I smiled as I thought of Honeycakes. We had some issues to work through, but I thought we'd be okay. Then the door slammed and I jumped as thoughts of Brent were replaced with the smells of mouthwatering Southern cooking.

Darcy heaved bag after bag of food onto the table. Wonderful, warm, fragrant food of the kind I hadn't seen in at least a week. My stomach rumbled and my virtuous thoughts of a salad flew right out of my head as I gazed at piles of redneck fish tacos, catfish sandwiches, sweet potato fries, fried okra, sweet tea, and my favorite, blackberry wine cake.

All talk ceased as we chowed down. I couldn't believe how hungry I had been. When we got to the blackberry wine cake, Annie picked up where we had left off.

"Speaking of Sloan Peters, what do we know of her?" Annie asked.

"Or Hunter's dad?" Darcy chimed in.

"Not much with regard to either," I said, "although Reed Northbrook has represented the United States in the Olympics. But, there is someone I know very well who I could envision doing this, someone none of us has considered."

Darcy and Annie both looked at me with identical blank stares on their faces.

"Well, c'mon," said Annie finally. "Who?"

I looked out the east window of my kitchen and across the front lawn of Fairbanks, the Civil War era mansion where I had found the body of my neighbor, former film star Glenda Dupree. Then I moved my gaze all the way to the mobile home on the other side. The home of Hill and Bubba Henley.

"Hill?" Darcy asked. "You think Hill Henley is behind all of this? I know he's gutter slime, but why? Why would he kill Dr. Carruthers?"

"Because he wasn't invited to compete." The idea had popped into my brain fully formed. Even better, it made sense. "Hill was so outraged when he realized that I had been invited (and he hadn't) that I wouldn't put anything past him, even retaliation that included murder."

"Let me see if I understand," said Darcy, wiping her plate clean with her fork. "Hill is targeting people at random around the show because he's mad that he's not there as a competitor? You know, I can actually see that."

I filled Annie in on Hilly Henley's lesser qualities: his neglect of Bubba, his womanizing, his dishonesty, and his questionable intelligence. I could have told her about the time he got out of his truck at the end of his driveway near the road, put his truck in neutral, ran behind the truck and positioned himself down on the ground just in time for the truck to run over his legs, but I didn't. Hill then claimed that a passing car had hit him, but unfortunately for him I had seen the entire incident from my front porch.

Hill filed for permanent disability, but all he ended up with was a gigantic hospital bill. Yes, the more I thought about it, the more I thought that Hill could be our man. I reached for my phone, although I wasn't sure if I was going to call Noah, Martin, Brent, or one of the campus cops with my thoughts. Annie interrupted my reach.

"I'm not saying Hill isn't behind this, but let's give your idea a little more thought on the way back to the show," she said. "It's getting late and shouldn't we try to get through Nashville before the rush hour?"

A glance at my watch showed it was already past three-thirty. Yikes, we needed to hustle.

Darcy gathered the food, bags, plates and the like and put them in the trash can outside. Then she and Annie gathered and folded our clothes while I went out to wrap Reddi's and Gigi's legs.

The girls looked good and I was glad that we had brought them with us. Gigi especially had needed to be a horse for a few hours and she loaded into the trailer with much less tension than when she had exited it.

I locked up the house, loaded the laundry, our purses, and us into the truck, and began the trek back to Murfreesboro.

Cat's Horse Tip #15

"To raise or lower your horse's energy, breathe in rhythm with him, then gradually breathe slightly faster or slower, depending on whether you want an increase or decrease."

23

IT WAS HALF PAST FOUR by the time we pulled out of the driveway and turned left on River Road. I could see the road for quite a way in both directions so I didn't stop at the end of the drive. There was a slight rise and if I stopped with the big, heavy rig, I knew I'd spin gravel, so instead I eased onto the pavement.

I looked at my watch again. Holy cow. We were on target to hit Nashville during the peak of afternoon traffic. If I was driving a car I'd hurry up, try to get ahead of the rush, but there was no hurrying when you had horses behind you. Sudden starts and stops were hard on the horses' legs, and even taking a curve the tiniest bit too fast could knock them off balance. Plus, River Road was curvy, so slow and easy was the only way to go.

"I've been thinking about Hill," said Darcy between chomps on her bubble gum, which today was a horrid shade of vomit green. "He definitely could have done it. But, what if it's someone we don't even know? I mean, like there are hundreds of people competing, and then there are the vendors. It might be someone like that."

We rolled through a green light where River Road met Charlotte Pike near the Walmart. It was only a half-mile or so to I-40, and I scraped through each of the four intersections before the entrance ramp just as each of the traffic lights turned yellow. All right, so the last one might have been red by the time the trailer hit the intersection, but I was not going to slam on the brakes and risk the girls stumbling to keep their balance.

"You are absolutely right Darcy," said Annie. "I think the only thing we can do is rule out the people that we know positively, definitely are not involved."

"You, Cat, and me," said Darcy.

"Tony, Jon, Noah, Agnes, and Lars," added Annie.

There wasn't too much traffic on I-40 so far. We had to travel up and down a series of hills before we reached Nashville, and the weight of the horses and the trailer behind us going down the first hill pushed the speedometer to just above the sixty-five mile an hour speed limit. I wasn't worried about a ticket, though, as the upcoming hill would soon have us straining to stay above fifty.

"Ambrose," I said. "He wasn't even around when Star and Temptation got sick."

"Bubba?" Annie asked.

I considered the name. "Doubtful, but not impossible. If Hill is involved he could have convinced Bubba to play a part. I hope Bubba is not involved, but he has been known to play pranks on other people, pranks that he doesn't realize could have serious consequences."

I recalled the time last February when Bubba had stood at the end of his driveway and batted rocks at passing cars. "Bubba is not good at thinking things through." Some people thought Bubba was one fry short of a Happy Meal, but I was sure that his years of neglect and lack of a positive role model were more to blame. Our local country music super star, Keith Carson, lived next door to me and had taken Bubba under his wing. But, Keith was gone a lot and had four kids of his own to give attention to when he was home.

Speaking of Keith, he was performing at the show's exhibitor party the next evening. I must admit, I have a bit of a crush on the man. Okay, I have it bad. What I didn't understand though, was that Brent knew how I felt about Keith and didn't give a whit. In fact, he thought it was funny. But when it came to Noah or Cam, he got all pissy. Men. I'd never understand them.

We crested the top of the hill that led to the exits for Briley Parkway and White Bridge Road. A quarter mile in front of us down the hill lay a sea of cars, and none of them were moving. Hot doodie. I tapped the brakes but nothing happened, so I pressed harder. The brake pedal went all the way to the floor.

Instinctively, I moved the truck from drive into a lower gear. The truck jolted and I winced, thinking about the horses in the back. Annie, who was sitting beside me, turned to look at me. What she saw on my face must have scared her because all she said was, "emergency flashers."

I fumbled for the switch, but couldn't find it. All I knew was that I must stop the truck and trailer before we plowed into the mass of cars just ahead.

"No brakes," I said, as Annie found the switch and the flashers came on. Unfortunately, with all of the cars in front of us at a standstill, drivers to our rear might think the flashers were precautionary, rather than an indication of a real emergency.

"Darcy," I called, "buckle up. We have no brakes." Darcy had a bad habit of riding without her seat belt.

"What?"

"Listen up. We have no brakes. We're going too fast for me to downshift again. Annie and Darcy, roll down your windows, see if you can get that blue car to our right to drop back so I can move over."

We were in the center lane. The next exit was the Fifty-First Avenue ramp, which angled down, but we might be able to squeeze by the cars that were stopped in front of the exit if I could get over to the shoulder.

Annie and Darcy rolled their windows down and began yelling, and motioning with their arms, while I stomped on the brake pedal again. Nothing. I began to ease to the right amid a cacophony of honking horns, mine included. Then I took my left hand off the steering wheel long enough to flash my lights at the cars in front of me. Not that there was anywhere they could go.

I moved the truck onto the shoulder, and even with the downshift we were rolling at just under fifty miles an hour. But ahead, the shoulder narrowed to half the width of the rig. There was no way we could squeeze between the guardrail and the car that was stopped just next to it. Damn!

I kept honking, and flashing the lights. I was close enough to see that on the other side of the guardrail there was a huge cement support column for the overpass above. The column was as big as a silo. Decision time. Hit the guardrail and possibly smash into the cement column? Lots of damage to horses, vehicle, and people. Or, hit the car to our left and possibly the cars in front of it as we barreled through the narrow gap.

"Do something!" cried Darcy.

Gee. What a good idea.

"Hang on!" I yelled.

I took a risk and downshifted the automatic transmission another gear. The engine whined and the truck jolted, and even though we slowed to about forty, the weight of the horses and trailer kept pushing us.

I have no idea what happened next, but somehow the cars in the lane nearest the narrow shoulder inched forward and to the left enough that we could squeak through. We rolled up a small hill to the Fifty-First Avenue ramp. Only going about thirty now. I never realized how scary thirty miles an hour could be.

We picked up speed again going down the shoulder of the crowded exit ramp. Other drivers were trying to exit the freeway to get out of the traffic jam, so the ramp was almost as crowded as the freeway. Darcy and Annie began to shout and wave again, hanging as far outside the vehicle as they could and still remain buckled in.

The exit ramp merged with a frontage road to our right, and ahead, maybe four hundred feet, was a stoplight. To my horror, it was red. Sweat trickled down my back as I watched cars from the cross street drive through the intersection. I thought of Reddi and Gigi. I would be heartbroken if they got hurt. And Annie. Dear, sweet Annie did not need this kind of stress so soon after her ordeal. My heart lurched as I thought of Darcy and tears began to fall down my face.

I had no time to be terrified. Instead, I gripped the steering wheel harder. Amazingly, the drivers on the frontage road seemed to be paying attention to Annie and Darcy, for those cars had stopped. And, as the exit ramp widened to meet the road, a clear path formed between the intersection and us. I drove right down it. The light was still red, but the cars moving through the intersection from the cross street were no longer nose to tail.

We hit the intersection at thirty-seven miles per hour. I looked to my left and was horrified to see a bright red sedan barreling toward us. I could see the driver, a man, talking on his cell phone, oblivious to the huge rig that was crossing in front of him. This was it, I thought. The sedan would barrel into us. I prayed that no one would be badly hurt.

Just as I braced myself for the impact I heard a screech of brakes as the man stopped his car just inches from us. Then we whizzed past him and drifted to a stop on a strip of grass a block away.

Cat's Horse Tip #16

"The first horse trailers are thought to be horse-drawn horse ambulances for fire departments. The trailers took wounded but savable horses from the scenes of accidents (which were common then) to the veterinarian at the firehouse."

24

NONE OF US SAID A word. I still had the steering wheel in a vice grip and could not get my fingers to loosen up. My breath came in shaky gasps and I saw hundreds of tiny, colored spots dance in front of my eyes.

Annie was the first to realize I was about to faint and began barking out orders. "Cat, put your head on the seat down here. Darcy, you go check on the horses." Then she reached over, took the key out of the ignition, and turned off the truck. The silence was deafening.

Within seconds of lying down, my head cleared and my breathing returned to normal. I was even sitting back up by the time Darcy appeared at the passenger window.

"They're both okay, I think," she said. "But they are rattling around in there. I'm going to go back and stay with them."

"Good," I said. Internally, I heaved a sigh of relief. No one, not a person or a horse, was hurt. It was a miracle. "Be sure to open all of the windows and vents, but leave the back door closed for now. If you open it the girls will think it is time to unload.

"Darcy," I added. "Did you hear me?"

"Keep the back door closed. Open windows and vents."

Darcy said the words as if she was speaking to a simpleton. Good. Things were getting back to normal.

When we were alone, Annie turned to me and asked, "What happened?"

"I have no idea. My truck is older, obviously, but I keep it maintained. I just pushed the brake pedal and nothing was there." I wiped more tears from my cheeks.

"We're all fine. That's the important thing," said Annie. "The next step is to figure out what to do."

I heaved a sigh of relief that sensible Annie was with me, rather than, say, effusive and emotional Agnes. That would have been a nightmare.

"We need a big truck with a gooseneck hitch," I said.

"Well, as luck would have it, Tony and I happen to have one of those," Annie replied.

I couldn't believe how calm Annie seemed when she stepped out of the truck to call her husband. I wanted to check on Darcy and the horses, but I needed a few more minutes to get my sea legs back. I took a few deep breaths.

All I could hear of the call were snatches of Annie's side of the conversation, and the tone and volume of her voice made their way into my brain more clearly than her words.

After what seemed like an eon, Annie stepped back into the truck.

"Tony was sitting with Jon and a few others in front of your stalls," she said. "Sounded like those huge fans you have in your aisle were keeping a lot of people cool."

Good for Jon, I thought. With so many people there, chances of an accident happening to one of my horses or my crew were very slim. And, I was glad that Jon and Tony could stand to be in the same aisle with each other, even if it took the cool breeze of a fan to make it happen.

"Tony is on his way, but all I knew was to tell him to take I-24 east, toward Nashville. You need to call him with directions," Annie said. "Oh, and you'll need to call Jon, too. Jon is, understandably, very worried.

I gave the cross streets to Tony over the phone, along with directions.

"Do you have GPS on your phone or in your truck?" I asked.

"Both."

"If you plug in the cross streets it might help route you through traffic, although it seems to be thinning now."

The freeway roar had dropped by a noticeable number of decibels, and the volume of traffic on the frontage road next to us was almost residential. It made me mad, though, that not one of the hundreds of cars that had passed us, had stopped to see if we needed help. In Ashland City, less than thirty miles away, we'd have started a traffic jam with all of the people who *did* offer to help. Big difference between city people and country folk.

My next call was to Jon.

"What happened?" he asked before I could even say hello. I could hear his footfalls as he paced, presumably up and down our aisle.

"I don't know. The truck was serviced a few weeks ago. It's never had trouble. You know that. Then we headed down the hill on I-40, right by the White Bridge Road exit. There was a traffic jam ahead. Cars were at a standstill. I put my foot on the brake and nothing happened, then I pushed harder and the pedal went all the way to the floor."

I realized I was crying again. We could all have been killed. After assuring Jon that everyone, horses included, were okay, he asked what I was going to do with the truck.

"Ironically, we stopped right next to an auto repair shop," I said, "but their sign says they only work on import autos. I think I should take the truck up to Sadler Car Care, the place on Fifty-First and Charlotte. We've had it serviced there before and they put new brakes on, what, last fall?"

"Something like that. But how will you get the truck there, Cat? You have no brakes, remember?"

"The shop is only a few blocks away. If I drive in low gear very slowly I should be okay."

"No, it's too dangerous. We should get it towed. I, ah, don't suppose you filled out that membership to AAA that's been on your desk for months?"

I shook my head, even though Jon couldn't see me. It didn't matter anyway. The question was rhetorical. Jon knew I hadn't.

"Jon, I've got to go. Tony is calling in."

Darcy and I had just unloaded Gigi and Reddi when Tony's truck appeared from a corner behind us. I was glad to see the familiar gray Chevy, as both girls were skittish due to the near-crash and the unfamiliar, noisy surroundings. Gigi in particular was quite bug-eyed. My mood darkened, however, as soon as I saw that Tony had brought someone with him. Cam.

Rats! Of all the people to bring. The only person lower on my list would have been Hill Henley. While Tony hugged Annie and made sure she truly was okay, I handed Gigi's lead to Cam.

"Don't let go—under any circumstance."

Then I busied myself with the business of unhooking my truck from the trailer. When I moved to get into the truck to pull it away, however, Tony disengaged himself from Annie and stepped in instead. I was perfectly capable of putting the truck in gear and tapping the gas gently to let it roll forward, but I know Tony wanted, needed, to help. He had almost lost Annie twice in the last few days. He needed to do something constructive.

After pulling ahead, Tony put my truck in park, then got into his vehicle as I directed him through the process of backing his truck underneath the gooseneck of my trailer. As soon as the hitch was secured, Darcy and Cam loaded the girls, who both seemed eager to get back into the relative safety of the trailer. If only they knew how close they had come to injury. On second thought, no, I was glad they didn't.

Only then did the arguing begin. Tony, Cam, and I all felt we should be the one to drive the truck the several blocks to the service station. I didn't want Cam to do it because I didn't trust him not to be a showboat and end up crashing into something. I didn't want Tony to do it because I loved him and Annie, and did not want to risk him getting hurt. After several minutes of heated discussion, I just got into my truck and locked the doors. It was as simple as that.

Tony and Annie got into their truck but Cam insisted on walking a hundred or so feet ahead of my truck and me, to be sure other cars did not get in the way. After some visible indecision, Darcy joined Cam. I was going to have to talk to that girl. What was she thinking?

I hate to say it, but having Cam and Darcy in front of me helped. A lot. They were able to stop some traffic and direct other vehicles around me. It was a tense few blocks, but in the end, we all ended up safely at the car care center. They were closed by this time, of course. It was almost seven. But I left a note on their door and hid the key to the truck. I'd call them first thing in the morning.

My next challenge was where to sit inside Tony's truck. Tony and Annie had the club seats up front, which left Cam, Darcy, and now me, in the back. It was not practical for Cam, at six-foot-one, to sit in the center of the bench seat, and one look at Darcy said volumes about her opinion on the matter, so we ended up with Darcy behind Tony, me in the center, and Cam behind Annie.

We hadn't even hit the freeway before Cam slung his left arm across the back of the seat and pulled me closer to him. I was about to say something when Annie turned around and squeezed my hand. If the squeeze was a little too hard, well, that was just Annie's way of telling me to hold my Irish temper—at least until we got the horses back into their stalls on the show grounds.

I wasn't perfect during the trip, but I did my best.

Cat's Horse Tip #17

"A horse's successes and failures are a good reflection of her human's ability."

25

ON THE DRIVE BACK, ANNIE and Tony discussed every detail of the incident. The way they held hands was touching and I wondered if Brent and I would ever have that kind of care and concern for one another.

I didn't, however, want to relive one of the most harrowing few minutes of my life quite so soon, so I turned to Darcy. She was scooched as close to the door as she could get without falling out, as if Cam had the plague and I, by virtue of sitting next to Cam, was also contagious. That left Cam and me to make small talk. Wow, my favorite thing: having polite conversation with a guy who had publicly humiliated me.

Cam squeezed my shoulder again and I tried to fling his arm back across the seat, but he just held on tighter. I put my head into my hands in frustration.

"You hanging in there, Kitten?" he asked.

"You *know* I never liked that name," I said. "In fact, pretty much everything about you irritates me."

"Now, Cat," said Tony. "Cam was kind enough to take time to help. The least you could do is be decent to him."

Tony's words reprimanded me, but I looked into the rear-view mirror and saw the twinkle in his eye. I couldn't believe it. Tony was *enjoying* my discomfort.

"It's only, like, another forty minutes until we get there," said Darcy.

I made a sound that was half-way between a laugh and a whimper.

It turned out that once Cam reclaimed his arm, the ride wasn't all bad. We began to discuss the new equine grooming products that were on the market and the discussion then moved to equine ulcer treatments, the best makes of saddles, and alternative beddings for stalls.

It was typical chatter for horse people, and for that I was grateful. I needed normalcy. I realized that I did not want to continually look over my shoulder, or be on the lookout for someone or something that was out of place.

Until now, I hadn't realized what a toll the events of the competition had put on me. When we turned off I-24 and spent about ten seconds on I-840 before exiting to Thompson Lane, I blew out some air. I needed to relax.

"Hey," I said quietly to Cam. "I haven't meant to be rude. Guess I'm more wound up than I thought. You, ah . . . you did a nice thing, coming to help."

Sorry to say, but I'm not sure I would have done the same for him. In fact, I am pretty certain if our situations had been reversed that I would have left him stranded. I didn't like what that said about me. Maybe Brent was right and I did have unresolved feelings for Cam—and for Noah. Maybe he had picked up on something with regard to those two that I wasn't aware of, as compared to my schoolgirl crush on Keith Carson.

No. I dug deeper. My feelings for Noah were definitely of friendship, and for Cam, well, I was still just plain mad. He was one of those people you bring into your life, then when they abuse your trust, you want to kick them out and not ever bring them back in.

Unfortunately, I had to see Cam regularly at horse shows, even if he did live several states away. For the first time I realized I was waiting for an apology that would never come, because it wasn't in the man to give. I was going to have to get past my anger another way. I didn't know what way that was just yet, but I'd figure it out.

"You sure that place you left the truck will do right by you?" he asked.

"Sadler Car Care? Yeah. I've had the truck in there before. They're good people."

I almost added, "unlike other people I know." But I didn't, because I was trying to get past his betrayal. And, I realized that I was no longer as mad at Cam as a mule chewing on a bumblebee, as my grandmother would have said. Instead I was . . . confused. No, disappointed. Okay, both.

"Good," said Cam before I had time to think further. "I had the oil changed in my truck today and I'm always leery of dealing with strangers. I hope they did a good job, but I won't really know until my truck either starts losing oil, or doesn't."

I was saved from having to reply as we had pulled up next to our barn. I was greeted with hugs from Jon and Noah, who had been awaiting our arrival. Hank greeted me carrying a stick the size of a large cigar. I looked around. No trees were anywhere close by. Where did Hank keep finding these sticks? I reached down to give him a pat and his tail began to wag so fast I thought he might fall over. It was a good thing that he was built low to the ground.

While Jon and Darcy unloaded the girls, Noah pulled me aside.

"The police have taken Debra Dudley in for questioning."

"You're serious?"

"Very. They left about an hour ago. It doesn't mean they are going to arrest her, but it could lead to that."

I was stunned by the news. I just couldn't see Debra as a killer. Then again, what did a killer look like? It wasn't as if there was a standard physical description for the job.

Cam headed our direction and Noah pulled me farther down the aisle.

"It's not a secret, but I want to respect Debra's privacy, so don't say anything." Noah glanced at Cam. "The news will break fast enough by itself."

I nodded, then turned away when Jon asked me a question about the wraps on Gigi's legs. "Let's leave them on for a while," I said. "The trip might have put extra strain on her legs. Maybe the wraps will prevent swelling."

"Then I'll hose her legs later this evening, and re-wrap after," said Jon as he joined Tony and Annie to return my trailer to the facility's massive, and full, parking lot.

Re-parking the trailer in its original spot on the grounds was going to be tough. I hoped they could manage it because it was in a location that was convenient to our stalls. If we needed something, the trailer was a short walk away, versus fifty acres away. When I had parked the trailer last Thursday, there were no trailers on either side. Now, our spot was crowded on three sides: left, right, and rear. It had been tricky to pull the trailer out this morning without scraping any of the other rigs. Doing it in reverse would be even tougher.

Noah picked up where Jon left off and helped Darcy fill water buckets. I had already started in their direction when Cam touched my arm.

"Can I interest you in dinner?" he asked. "Anywhere you like."

I smiled. A year ago my heart would have done a happy dance. But today? Today I really had no interest.

"Sorry Cam, I already have plans."

I didn't, but he didn't have to know that.

"Maybe I can join you."

"Not tonight, Cam. Sorry." Noah jumped in to rescue me. "Cat and I are having dinner to re-hash old times. You know, we met as students here. Lots of great memories."

Cam nodded, checked his watch, and said a hasty goodnight. Probably wanted to find another female companion before the evening got too late. My bet was that the lady's first name began with the letter *S*.

Noah and I actually did go to dinner.

"I haven't eaten a meal off the grounds since I got here," he said. "I know you may have other plans, but I'd love to go to The Apple Tree and eat something other than a burger."

We found ready parking and both ordered apple salads. I'd had the feeling for a number of hours that I had eaten one too many sweet potato fries that afternoon. Counteracting it with a lot of green stuff might help my stomach. Or maybe my stomach was protesting the fact its life had almost ended earlier today.

We were waiting for our meal when Noah said, "I spoke with the lead investigator today and he gave me some news."

"This is separate from Debra being taken in?"

"Yes. I may be compromising the investigation, as I was sworn to secrecy, but I have to tell someone. You're the only person I trust."

I looked into his worried, turquoise eyes and nodded for him to continue.

"The investigator didn't give me information outright, but by the questions he asked I could easily put two and two together," he said.

Noah stopped talking as a pale young waitress with blonde eyebrows and pitch-black hair placed huge bowls of greenery on our table. Mine was topped with salmon, onions, dill, tomatoes, and feta cheese. Noah's had steak strips, bacon crumbles, mushrooms, ginger, and avocado. My salad looked good, but Noah's looked better. Why do I always want whatever the other people at my table are eating?

"Anyway," continued Noah after we'd both had our first mouthful. "Reed Northbrook has some big financial obligations that he apparently can't meet. He lost his main sponsor earlier this year and there was thought that he'd pick up some of Rory Swenson's clients, but that didn't happen."

In decades past, Rory had ridden on countless US Olympic teams, but he had died last winter at the ripe old age of ninety-two. He'd still been teaching and training, sometimes from his power wheelchair outside the arena, but mostly via Skype or video.

"But," I took a sip of water, "none of the horses that were hurt were competing in any of Reed's events."

"I know. Not sure how it all fits unless he was going for the leading trainer bonus and tried to wipe out competition."

I pondered that while I ate a bite of salmon.

"Then," said Noah, "there's Sloan Peters. She's in the middle of a messy divorce."

"That might explain the ongoing game of sucky-face that she's playing with Cam," I said.

Noah gave me a look.

"What?"

Noah shook his head, then continued. "A lot of the English riders, like Reed and Sloan, have corporate sponsors. Otherwise they could not afford to compete. Well, Sloan's sponsorship is with a soft drink company. And guess who the CEO is?"

"Her husband?"

"Close. Her soon to be ex-brother-in-law. The husband's an attorney."

"Not good," I said. "From Sloan's perspective anyway."

"Then, the reason Mike Lansing wants to start a side business is that his dad had a stroke a few months back. He needs to go into long-term assisted living, but the kind of facility the dad's insurance will cover is apparently pretty crappy. Mike wants to either bring his dad home and help pay for home health care, or put his dad in a better facility."

"Either could be expensive," I said.

When my grandmother passed away she'd had a massive heart attack and, boom, she was gone. While it was traumatic for me, at least Grandma had been spared a nursing home and declining health—and the expense and indignity that came with both.

"Absolutely," agreed Noah. "And, the list of financial woes go on. Just about everyone at the show seems to be in trouble. Including you."

I dropped my fork.

"Me!"

"According to the police. First off, you drive a truck that is almost old enough to go to college—"

"Come on, Noah. It's thirteen. It's not that old."

"And you need a new roof on your barn."

"Who told the police that?"

"It's common knowledge, Cat. You talk about it all the time."

Well, maybe I did.

"Then there are the Zinners," said Noah.

"No. Absolutely not."

I must have used my "outdoor" voice, as some of the other diners turned to stare. I dropped my voice to a stage whisper.

"No. Tony and Annie may not be at the top of this game. They may have a barn that is in about the same shape as mine, but listen to me. They. Did. Not. Do. This."

"Cat, ease up. You're preaching to the choir. I'm just telling you what information the police have."

I put down my fork and pinched the bridge of my nose. Nothing made sense, and I just wanted to go home.

"There is one other person," Noah said, signaling for the check.

"I'll get it Noah. It's my turn."

Noah and I were only able to get together for dinner about once a year, even though we saw each other regularly at shows.

"You can get the next two," he said. "The police also know that Cam has blown through his trust fund."

I shared Annie's thoughts about Cam with Noah, that Cam was dishonorable, but weak.

"She's right," said Noah. "But those traits on their own don't mean someone is or is not capable of killing."

Noah held the door for me as we left. I didn't even have a doggie bag, something I almost always leave a restaurant with. Noah drove me to the hotel. Since my truck was out of commission, I'd have to arrange an early morning ride to the event with Darcy.

"Thanks for sharing," I said. "From the perspective of the police, it really could be any one of us, couldn't it?"

As I watched Noah drove away I wondered two things. Why had Noah not been included in the long list of people the police suspected? And, why had I not shared with Noah my strong suspicions about Hill Henley?

I took a hot bath to soothe my nerves and called Brent before I went to sleep. We talked about his day and mine, except I omitted the part about almost being killed.

Was it because I didn't want Honeycakes to worry? Or, was it because I was losing trust in the people around me? I thought about that after we'd said goodnight. I was even beginning to suspect Noah, my friend, my confidant, my pal. Noah couldn't be involved. Could he?

Even though I was exhausted, I tossed and turned for several hours before I fell into an uneasy sleep. I almost wished I had stayed awake, for I had a terrible nightmare. In my dream,

Sally and I were on a beautiful forested trail. We were headed downhill and there were trees and woods to our left. To the right was a cliff edge that fell hundreds of feet to an arid desert.

As we rode, Debra Dudley jumped out of a tree and pushed me off Sally and I fell, terrified, all the way down to the desert floor. Or at least that's where I would have landed if I hadn't half roused myself before I went splat. When I fell back to sleep, the same dream began again. Only this time it was Jon who pushed me out of the saddle.

The dream repeated itself over and over. The only difference was that each time I fell, a new person pushed me over the edge. By morning, each of my friends, and most of my acquaintances, had taken a turn. When I finally woke, my heart was pounding and I was cold with sweat.

Cat's Horse Tip #18

"What might be irritating behavior to you, could be your horse's way of letting you know of her concern or enthusiasm. Once you acknowledge what she is trying to tell you, the behavior should stop."

26

THE NEXT MORNING MY BACK was stiffer than an old board, so Darcy and I took Reddi and Gigi to the spa. If we were stiff from the lack of truck brakes, they must be, too. Plus, I had not yet fully recovered from my fall off Sally. We each stayed on the vibration plates for a full fifteen minutes. Whatever the price, being able to move my neck and shoulders was well worth it.

Despite my dream from the night before, I was looking forward to today. Amanda and Darcy both had western equitation classes, Bob had his trail class, and tonight I'd get to see that hunky Keith Carson.

Darcy went to get us some breakfast, and I began my morning inspection of the other horses. I had learned long ago that the number of ways a twelve hundred pound horse could find to injure him- or herself was astounding. Constant vigilance did not prevent injuries, but quick discovery sure made the healing process quicker.

My good spirits were dashed, however, at nine A.M. when a mechanic from Sadler Car Care called. I had left a message the night before and had hoped the fix would be simple enough that I could get my truck back today.

Turned out that the timing of the repair wasn't the issue. It was the cause.

"You've got a couple of holes in your braking system," said Dee. Dee was actually Delores, a trim Hispanic woman who was maybe in her late thirties. She had worked on my truck before and seemed to know her stuff.

"What do you mean, holes?" I asked.

"You've got two holes, one each in both your front and rear brake lines. Have you been driving in your pasture? Drive over some heavy brush?"

"No." My heart was starting to pound and I felt the blood rush from my head. I needed to sit down.

"Then the only other possibility, in my opinion, is that the holes were intentionally put there. Got any enemies?"

Apparently I did.

Jon found me sitting, stunned, on a trunk in the tack room and took charge.

He called Noah, who called the campus cops, who called cops in Nashville, who sent a team to look at my truck. That chain of events could have taken several days, but today it was accomplished in less than ninety minutes. That might be because Nashville's West Station precinct was two blocks away from the service station. Or, it could be that the campus guys put some pressure on Nashville. In either case, it looked as if my brakes were part of a murder investigation.

I had been worried, too, about my transmission. When Dee called to say the police had taken numerous pictures, dusted everything they needed to, and cleared the truck for repair, I asked her to give the truck a thorough going over. All the downshifting at high speeds might, I thought, have damaged something, and if the brakes had been sabotaged, then something else might have been, too.

"Will do," she said.

As soon as I hung up, Noah and Jon came into the tack room with grim faces.

"Is Darcy back yet?" Jon asked.

When I shook my head, Jon made eye contact with Noah.

"I just spoke with the lead investigator," Noah said. "He wants to keep the brake thing between the three of us, not tell anyone else at the show."

"Not tell them my truck lost its brakes, or not tell them someone did it?" I asked. "Because just about everyone here knows about our wild ride yesterday."

"That it was intentional," said Noah. "He doesn't want anyone to know."

"Who doesn't want anyone to know what?" said Darcy, lugging in a huge bag of breakfast burritos from a local restaurant, along with two large containers of orange juice from Walmart.

"Ah . . . Mike Lansing doesn't want anyone to know how much pain he's really in," said Noah. "It's a guy thing. Macho man and all that."

I wondered about the fact that Noah had lied so easily, and hated that recent events caused me to question the integrity and motives of one of my closest friends.

Amanda showed up in time to help get Wheeler ready. Normally all of my show students would be fully integrated into the preparation process, but Amanda's mom always ran late, and when Mom and Amanda arrived the twins were always in tow. So, I cut Amanda a little slack.

Amanda was nervous about her equitation class because the class was judged on the rider—the rider's form and position, and how well he or she rode the horse. Amanda, in fact, became so nervous in the warm-up arena that she began to cry.

"Deep breaths, kiddo," I said, patting her knee. "Big deep breaths. You don't want Wheeler to get nervous, too, do you?"

She shook her head and snuffed her nose. I dug into our gate bag and pulled out a Kleenex.

"You want to scratch?" I asked. "You don't have to compete."

I held my breath as I hoped Amanda would not call my bluff. I'd never force her to ride, as some other trainers might, but I knew I'd be disappointed if she bailed out of the class.

"I'm good," Amanda said nodding her head. "I'm okay. I want to do this."

I listened as she talked herself back into the competition. The "psychologist" part of being a riding instructor was knowing how far to push students in the name of personal growth, and when to know the student was too overwhelmed to have any possible chance of success. Amanda just had a case of pre-show jitters. I came from the school of thought that if a competitor didn't get at least a little bit nervous, she would not have enough edge to be at her best. Since she had begun to breathe again, Amanda was right in the zone.

I left Amanda with Jon, and Darcy caught up with me in the seating area. She was boldly dressed almost entirely in red, but her slinky top had strategically placed black side panels that were slimming to the eye. I knew that when she got on Petey, she'd also be wearing red suede chaps that featured a black leather strip along the back of the leg that made her thighs look narrower.

The horses and riders in Amanda's class entered counter-clockwise at the walk. The judges were looking for things such as a vertical rider alignment of the rider's shoulder, hip and heel, and evenness from left to right. Amanda tended to hunch her weaker left shoulder and had to consciously work to keep it level with her right one.

Presentation and turnout was also a factor, and every entry here looked like a superstar. There would be a short pattern that had to be ridden individually and Amanda and I had gone over it in detail. With a horse as experienced as Wheeler, I knew she had the potential to do well. Whether she actually would or not was up to her.

Amanda looked good, but so did a young lady on a small bay Tennessee Walking Horse gelding. She had the form and the riding skills down pat, and it also looked as if she had a ton of confidence to go with it. The girl on the Haflinger stalled behind us also looked formidable.

I wanted to concentrate on Amanda and her ride, but my mind could only think of the fact that someone had tried to kill Annie, Darcy, and me. In fact, thoughts were flopping so fast in inside my head that I couldn't grasp onto any of them.

When Darcy got up to get Petey ready for her class, I gave her a hug.

"You look beautiful," I said.

At first Darcy looked embarrassed, then she grinned and hugged me before she bolted for the barn.

Amanda and Wheeler did well on the pattern, but I was not surprised when the rider on the Tennessee Walker came out with the blue ribbon. A cute little girl with red hair who was riding a red and white Paint was second, and I was thrilled with Amanda's third. She was, too, and seeing her smile was the biggest reward I'd had in days. The girl on the Haflinger placed fourth.

In the next class, Darcy and Petey were impressive, if I do say so myself. Petey's build was a bit too tall and thin for western events and he had to collect and balance himself, and shorten his stride, to be competitive. Because equitation classes are all about the rider (in theory) maybe Petey's build worked to Darcy's advantage. She had to work harder to get Peter's Pride looking and moving like a western horse. The judges may have recognized that because she won her class. I was so proud of both of them that I didn't even realize I was crying.

"Hey, congrats!" Zach Avery crossed the holding pen near the photographer's backdrop at the win picture area to join us.

"Thanks." I debated whether or not to bring up his boss, and decided on a generic, "How's Debra?"

"Good. You know she had nothing to do with anything that has gone on here," he said firmly, "don't you?"

I had never seen Zach as defensive as he was now. But before I could comment, the photographer's assistant pulled me toward Darcy, Petey, and the backdrop. I had to go.

"Tell Debra . . . tell her I said hi," I said.

Then I took my place, looked into the camera, and smiled.

My cell phone chimed just when I started to walk back to our stalls.

"Transmission's fine," said Dee, "as is everything else on your truck. I wish our other customers would take as good care of their older vehicles as you do this one. We're just finishing up, you can pick it up in an hour.

I looked at my watch. Holy Toledo. It was two o'clock. "You still open until six?" I asked.

Dee said that she was.

"If I can't get there, I'll send someone."

I gave Dee my credit card number and tried to figure out how I'd pick up my truck. Bob's trail class should begin a little after three and might go until five. I didn't have to have my truck that evening, but I did not like to rely on others for rides to and from the hotel and show grounds.

I would have pondered my problem longer, but when I rounded the corner to our stalls, I found two uniformed police officers from Rutherford County standing in front of my tack room. I should have known they'd show up eventually. I wanted to help them, but now was not the ideal time.

"What can I do for you gentlemen?" I asked.

This was a different set of cops than the ones I had spoken to previously. Jon had helped Amanda untack Wheeler and put him into his stall, and she and her family were waiting for a debrief from me. "I know we need to chat, but I'm kind of busy right now. Can you come back this evening?"

"Now would be better, ma'am," the older, shorter officer said. He was also pudgy. I couldn't read his nametag, but it might have read OFFICER D. O. NUT.

"Then I'll have to talk as I work. I have to be on a horse in less than an hour."

The older cop looked around nervously. He obviously was not a "county mountie," although Rutherford County did have a very good mounted patrol unit.

"Yes, ma'am," he said.

At horse shows I sometimes kept the stall doors open and used web stall fronts. These were simply a set of nylon straps that were sewn together and secured by snaps to the open stall at about the height of the horse's chest. This allowed the horse, in this case Sally, to stick her head and neck out into the aisle. The now open stall front allowed her to feel less confined and more part of the herd that was our stable unit.

Sally had taken a keen interest in the older officer and angled her body so it was almost parallel to the stall aisle, then she edged her head into the aisle along the officer's back and rested her chin on the officer's far shoulder. He jumped about a foot and moved to the center of the aisle.

I tried to hide my smile, but don't think I quite managed it. Before I talked with any police officer, however, I hugged and congratulated Amanda as quickly as I could. Not because the cops were waiting, but because Amanda's brothers had started to play spaceman in the aisle. We were all getting bombarded with the dancing red light and staccato gun noise of two toy lasers, accompanied by shrieks of delight when an invisible target had been assassinated.

To top it off, Hank began to howl one long "aarrrrroooo" of sorrow after another. I looked to Amanda's mother for help, but she was deep into a phone conversation and seemed oblivious to the commotion. Ambrose had covered his ears with his hands.

"Those boys," the younger cop asked, a glint in his eye. "Want me to arrest 'em?"

"Sure," I said.

I watched as he cop-walked up to the boys. Even I was intimidated, although I hadn't done anything wrong. The boys looked up at the young officer with matching pairs of round, blue eyes. At first it looked as if the junior cop had everything under control, but then the boys looked at each other and opened fire on him. The yelling that ensued from all three, along with a series of ear-splitting growling, howling, barks from Hank, was not pretty.

The pudgy cop and I watched for a few seconds, then he said, "Guess I'd better go in and hep my boy there."

I have to say, all it took to get the twins' attention was one piercing blow of the officer's whistle, a stern look, and then it was over. The boys were sitting cross-legged on the floor of the aisle facing a stall wall, and their mother was getting a long overdue lecture on parenting.

Whew. The sudden silence made my ears ring. The horses shuffled in their stalls, then Darcy, Petey, and Jon arrived. Too bad they had missed all the fun.

"I got hung up doing a *Horses in the Morning* interview," said Darcy looking at the boys and giving the cops a thumbs up. "I never know what to say during interviews. So, where did you go?"

I told her that Dee had called and I had to make arrangements about the truck. The truck! I had forgotten about it.

Jon must have seen the panic on my face. "If you and Darcy can handle Bob's trail class, I'll find a ride into Nashville and get the truck," he said.

Relief washed over me. Jon always had my back and I don't think I was ever appreciative enough. I nodded my head in agreement. It was all I could manage at the moment.

Jon put the bags of hamburgers and fries that he had gotten for our lunch on a tack trunk and Hank raised his head and sniffed appreciatively.

"I can't eat a thing," I told him. "You can have mine."

Hank instantly was transformed into the happiest dog in the world. If only people could appreciate the little things, as dogs did.

I gathered Bob's tack and began to hang it on a portable saddle rack that Jon placed in the aisle. Amanda and her family had left, thank goodness, and the police had also departed after an emergency call. I was sure their departure was temporary, though the timing was good. I could better deal with them later on.

I checked the stalls and all of the horses seemed to be dozing. Yep, a nap is just what I would have chosen after a visit from the twins. But, I did not have that luxury. Bob and a trail course were on my agenda instead.

I don't know where Bob and I placed, but it wasn't in the top six. I felt bad for Bob, and for Doc Williams too, because 100 percent of the fault in our not placing was mine. I judged the poles wrong and encouraged Bob to stretch his stride in walking through a series of them when he should have shortened it. Poor guy, he always wanted to do the right thing and I sensed his confusion. He was right and I was wrong, and he did not know what to do. In the end he decided to do just as I asked, and we ticked two of them.

In the U-shaped back through I again misdirected Bob, and while we didn't hit anything, our back through was anything but smooth. At another show those bobbles might not have meant so much, but here the competition was so stiff that they knocked us completely out of the placings.

"You're too hard on yourself," Darcy said back at the stalls.

I thought it ironic that she was placating me after a poor showing, when for years I had done the same for her. But I was also a little bit proud. The girl was growing up.

"I mean, like, you've had a lot on your mind lately, the colts colicking, Dr. Carruthers, Mike, Annie, your fall from Reddi, the truck. You can't do and be everything to everyone, you know."

I smiled. Darcy was right. I did the best I could under the circumstances I had been dealt and couldn't ask for more. Besides, in just about three hours I could gaze to my heart's content at the handsomest man in the world, Keith Carson. Hot dawg!

Cat's Horse Tip #19

"Horses use ear position, neck and head height, movement, foot stomping and tail swishing, among other things, to communicate."

27

DARCY AND I WENT BACK to the hotel to gussy up. The exhibitor party was an event that was dying out at many of the major shows. The parties started out decades ago as a way to socialize and have some fun in the middle of a long competition. But more recently, many of the shows didn't see the need because most of the exhibitors stopped coming. That's because showing is a livelihood for many trainers and instructors. The last thing they need is to stay out late and drink one too many margaritas before an early morning class with a client's horse.

I was glad, however, that Noah and the show management decided to have a party at this competition. My excitement about Keith Carson aside, many of us from the different breeds and associations still did not know each other. I hoped the party would be a nice way for everyone to meet each other.

I showered, then tamed my hair into something that did not look like a bird's nest. I had saved my favorite pair of dress up Wrangler Jeans for the party, and swapped out my boots for a pair of leather Ariat clogs. The party was going to be held in a space that usually served as the holding pen, and I didn't think they'd either remove or cover the dirt footing just for the party. So, no sandals for me. I'd let other women look good while they got dirt between their toes and bits of horse poop trapped up under the soles of their feet.

I topped my jeans and clogs with a shimmery sleeveless blouse that pretty much matched the color of Noah's eyes, and daubed on some makeup. Done. Darcy always took much longer than I did to get ready but today I was impatient to get going. I called and texted her several times with no response before I began to get worried. Usually she answered quickly. What if something had happened to her? What if the killer was in her room right now? Our buddy system had gone by the wayside and I felt Darcy could be in real danger.

I grabbed my purse, phone, and room key, and dashed down the hall to Darcy's room, where I proceeded to bang on the door. Darcy opened the door with her hair wrapped around enormous hot rollers and a puzzled expression on her face.

"Holy crap, you're all right," I said, hugging her.

"Why wouldn't I be?"

"Because I've called and texted several times and you didn't answer."

Only then did I become aware that her shower was running and that steam was pouring from underneath the closed bathroom door.

"I know what you're thinking and no, I don't have company and no, you are not interrupting anything."

I didn't know if that's what I had been thinking or not, but the fact that Darcy thought it was somehow unsettling.

"My jeans were wrinkled and I'm not great with an iron," she said, going into the bathroom to shut off the hot water. She returned with a pair of damp, but wrinkle free jeans.

"I just don't want to be too late for the party," I said, hiding my relief under practicality.

"You just can't wait to see Keith-y, can you?" teased Darcy.

Fact of the matter was, she was right. Even though Keith lived next door to me, I rarely saw the man. His wife, Carole, was a friend of mine but I rarely saw her either, unless I was giving her or one of her kids a riding lesson. Different people, different lives.

I do admit, however, to one episode of extensive brush trimming along our mutual property line on a day when Keith was hosing off his boat wearing nothing but his swim trunks. Surprising how much those bushes needed trimming.

Once Darcy and I finally made it back to the Miller Coliseum I first went to our stalls to feed the horses. I had hoped that Jon would be back in time to do it, but he had texted me that the truck was fine, but traffic was slow. Darcy and I each donned one of the many long sleeved blue denim shirts that Jon often wore and put them on over our nice blouses. Nothing like a piece of hay to snag fine fabric. We fed and watered the horses, then took off the shirts. Before we walked through the series of barns toward the warm-up arena we put our purses in a tack trunk, locked it, then locked the tack room door.

The walk took me longer than I anticipated, though, because we were stopped on the way to the party by Captain Donut and his younger partner.

"Now?" I asked.

"Yes, ma'am. If you don't mind," the young cop said.

I sighed. I would never get to see Keith. I sent Darcy on ahead and told her I'd be along shortly.

"You are not a suspect, ma'am, but we'd like to ask you some questions privately."

"You are *not* taking me down to the station or wherever it was that you took Debra Dudley. There is somewhere I need to be." At the party, looking at Keith.

"We won't keep you long; just a few questions."

Those were famous last words if I ever heard them, but I walked with the officers out the side of the barn to a patrol car. I was more mad than nervous, but I didn't mind talking to them. In fact, I wanted to talk to them, answer their questions . . . but now? Now was a worse time than this afternoon.

I sat down in the backseat of the patrol car and sighed again. This time an eye roll of dramatic proportion accompanied my sigh. Good thing neither of the cops saw it. Didn't want them to think I was uncooperative or anything, but come on. Tonight was my night to live inside my schoolgirl crush. I realized I was disappointed and tired, and gave myself an attitude adjustment. This would go quicker if I cooperated. I just hoped no one saw me being hauled off by the police.

Both officers settled into the front, then turned to look at me. The only other time I had been inside a police car was when I rode around with Martin when we were trying to find Bubba after he went missing. That was last February. From what I could tell, this patrol car didn't look much different from Martin's, except that there were a few more gadgets on the dash.

"We, uh, wanted to speak out of earshot of anyone else on the grounds because we wanted to ask you about your truck brakes," said the older cop.

That made sense. Noah said the investigators wanted to keep private the fact that someone had tampered with my brakes. I gave them all the details I could think of, then added, "The only time the truck was unattended was between eleven and two, when we were all napping."

"You're sure both Miz Zinner and Miz Whitcomb were napping all that time?"

"Yes . . . well, I guess no, because I was sleeping. One of them could have gotten up. You'd have to ask them."

"We will," said the younger officer snapping shut his notebook and opening his door.

"Wait, you don't think either of them had anything to do with this? That's absurd."

"We don't think anything, Miz Enright," said Officer Donut. "We just gather information and turn it in to the homicide boys."

I blew out a breath. Now was not the time to pick a fight. The younger cop opened my door and I stepped out.

"I hope you find this person soon," I said. "We're all on edge and I hope I didn't come across as rude. I didn't mean to be."

I walked back into the barn as soon as both officers hustled away. Apparently they were not going to hunt Annie and Darcy down for interviews right this second. I brushed any invisible traces of "cop" off my jeans, then finally walked to the party.

I knew the show's ground crew had a lot to do in a short time to transform the space from a horse holding pen to a party place with a stage, but they had done a miraculous job. Dozens of tall, round café tables were draped in long white tablecloths. White bistro chairs were placed around the tables and shorter chairs were arranged into a number of conversational seating areas.

Twenty or so tall columns of blue, silver, and white balloons streamed upward ten feet or more, and danced in a breeze made by the many oscillating fans that were placed around the area. Small spotlights were hidden near the base of the balloons and interesting, moving patterns were created as the lights shone through them.

More than a hundred people were already there, dressed in attire that ranged from traditional barn clothes to business suits and summer dresses. A few people were even in shorts. At the far end was the stage. Behind it, the areas to the left and right were cordoned off with curtains, but there were a few people on the stage itself who appeared to be checking cords, microphones, and the placements of instruments. I knew Keith was performing here with a scaled down version of his band, a step up from "unplugged."

I also knew that I was the reason he was here at all. When Noah was first hired to manage the show, due to my proximity to Nashville and a hoard of talented artists, he asked me for suggestions for entertainment for the party. You *know* which man was at the top of my list. Fortunately, the event was on a Wednesday, a day when Keith was not typically booked.

I felt a tap on my shoulder and I whirled around. I couldn't believe I was so jumpy. Turned out that the tap was from Noah and my legs became shaky with relief. If I had one wish, it was that the killer be found this very second. I couldn't remember when I had ever been more balled up with nerves.

"I've been looking for you," Noah said. "Keith was hoping you could go backstage for a few minutes before his show."

"Really?" I tried not to let my sudden giddiness show. Keith wanted to see *me*. Happy dance!

Noah's all-access pass allowed us to pick our way over sound and light cables, through the backstage area and onto Keith's bus, which was parked just outside one of the building's large sliding doors.

I'd been on Keith's bus several times, once when he performed at a large community picnic in Ashland City, and another time when Carole gave Darcy, Bubba, and me a tour of the vehicle. Each time that I walked up the bus's stairs and into the front living area I was amazed at the opulence. Leather couch and booth-style seats, marble table and counter top, stainless steel refrigerator and microwave, large flat screen TV, and Berber carpeting took up most of the space.

Keith walked toward us from the rear of the bus and enveloped me in a huge hug. That was the thing about my obsession with Keith Carson, there was no sexual chemistry. I wasn't attracted to the man himself, so much as I was a picture of him. He was just so gosh darn handsome.

"How's my favorite neighbor?" Keith asked.

"Good," I said. "We're doing pretty well in the competition. Is Carole here?"

"No, she and the kids are visiting her mom this week."

Drat, an entire week with Keith home alone and I wasn't even there to enjoy it. Okay. Even I could see that this little obsession of mine was too much. I needed to back off.

For the first time that day I thought of Brent. It was not unusual for us to go several days without talking, as we both had busy schedules. Now I wished very much that he was here, but I hadn't invited him. Not because I didn't want to spend time with him, but because many weeks ago, when Jon and I began to finalize plans for the show, I knew I did not need the extreme distraction Honeycakes would provide. My loss.

A man I knew to be Keith's tour manager climbed into the bus. "Thirty minutes," he said.

I nodded, and said to Keith, "We'll get out of your way, but I'm really glad you're here. Everyone is excited to see you."

Me, too. I was more excited than Hank was with a new stick.

Back at the party I mingled with Annie and Tony, who had just returned from a day spent with Star.

"This is the first time we could see a glimmer of Star's personality, rather than just a very sick horse," said Annie. "Until I saw that, I wasn't sold on the idea that he could recover."

"And now?" I asked.

"Definitely."

Annie smiled, then left to get a snack so I talked to Judy, and then to Melanie and Darcy, who were once again BFFs.

"Bubba is glued to the stage waiting for Keith, so we're following Hill Henley," Darcy whispered into my ear.

I looked at the girls. "Do not get separated. Do you understand me?"

Both Darcy and Melanie nodded.

"I'm serious. Better yet, find Hunter and ask him to join you." I scanned the room. "Look, there he is, over by the door. Three of you will be safer than two."

I watched as the girls made the connection, then I waved at Sloan and Reed as I flitted past them to make small talk with Debra and Zach. The (not-so) dynamic couple was off in a corner by themselves.

"No one wants to talk to us," said Zach. "They are all convinced that we killed—"

"That I killed," said Debra. "No one thinks you killed anyone, Zach."

"Well maybe they should, because I'm just mad enough to."

"You know you don't mean that," Debra said almost casually. "But other people might take you seriously."

I looked at Zach and wondered if I was one of them. Could Zach be the killer? I moved on, and introduced myself to several people I had seen around, but had not yet met. Just as Keith was about to go on, I saw Jon and Cam in the drink line, and walked through the crowd to them.

"I was getting worried," I said to Jon.

"Traffic," he said. "But Cam was nice enough to follow me back, just in case anything happened to the truck."

"I don't understand," I said, looking at both their faces.

"Cam gave me the ride into Nashville," Jon said.

Wow, two nice things from the guy in two days. I thanked Cam and was surprised when I realized I was sincere.

"No problem," he said.

Jon pointed to my cup. "Orange juice and Sprite?"

I nodded. He knew me well.

Jon ordered a lemonade for himself, a beer for Cam and, the OJ and Sprite for me. I wasn't above enjoying a beer or a glass of wine at times, but never at horse shows. I had a strict "no alcohol" policy for my entire crew at events. I never wanted a client to be able to say I lost a class because I had been drinking the night before, or that an injury had happened to one of the horses because my crew had imbibed one too many.

The first few notes of Keith's first song rang out and I went to the back of the room to watch. No front row groupie action for me. I wanted to enjoy looking at my idea of perfection in peace.

After a while, I began to walk around so I could enjoy the view from different angles. I lingered for a while near Jon, who was still talking with Cam, then squeezed playfully between Annie and Tony. Despite the many fans that were moving air around, it was warm, and several times people brought me a drink. I was grateful for both the people and the beverages. I moved one final time and stopped next to Sloan and Judy.

"He's pretty good, isn't he?" said Reed with a nod toward Keith. I hadn't realized Reed was on my other side. "I didn't think I'd be keen on a country music show, but I am enjoying this very much."

Just then Keith ended his next to last song. But before he kicked off the notes for his finale, he handed his guitar off to a roadie and stepped back up to the microphone.

"I'd like to thank y'all for being a great audience," said Keith. "My wife and two of my kids ride some, and I'd like to give a shout out to their riding instructor, who is here tonight. Y'all might know Cat Enright. She's our next-door neighbor and a good friend to my family. So Cat, this last song is for you."

Keith then swung into his signature song, a song he knew was one of my favorites. I didn't have time to enjoy it though, because when Keith mentioned he was my neighbor, it was as if everyone in the room was drawn into my orbit. That's the way it is. Everyone wants a piece of celebrity, and for many at the party the way to scratch their itch was to hobnob with the celebrity's neighbor. I met more people in the next ten minutes than I had during the previous week.

As the crowd thinned, Jon handed my truck keys to me and said he was going to take a shower. While not four-star quality, the showers in the barn bathrooms were clean and perfectly adequate. I felt a little funky using them, but Jon had never seemed to mind.

"He's my neighbor too, ya know," said Hill Henley, approaching in his usual quarrelsome manner. That man could start an argument in an empty house. "Why'd that superstar jus' mention you? That's what I wanna know. Why you an' not me?"

I stepped back. Personal space was not something Hill had ever learned about and he always strayed a little too far into mine. It made me uncomfortable. What also made me uncomfortable was that Hill was still the top suspect on my list. He also smelled. I couldn't say that he was as drunk as a skunk, but the wavering beer bottle in his right hand indicated that he was in a state of some impairment.

"I don't know why he didn't include you, Hill. Why don't you ask Keith?"

"Damn shootin' I'm a gonna ask him. Mr. Fancy Britches goes and opens his mouth an' never mentions his ol' pal Hill. Somethin' the matter with that boy."

Hill weaved off in the direction of the stage and I made a hurried escape.

Back at our stalls, Ambrose's evening replacement said he needed a bathroom break. While I waited for him to return, I called Darcy to tell her I had my truck and would drive back to the hotel on my own. Then I gave her another admonishment to stay with Melanie and Hunter as I filled the horses' water buckets. After that, I don't remember a thing.

28

I RARELY WAKE UP DISORIENTED, but when I opened my eyes I could not figure out where I was. It dawned on me first that I was not in my bed, either at home or in the motel. In fact, I wasn't in any kind of bed at all. I knew that for sure, but that was about all my sluggish brain could understand.

My arms and legs, I noticed idly, were sprawled every which way and I slowly rearranged them. Then I realized that wherever I was, it was quite dark. I looked around and saw stars and thought I might have banged my head. Then I realized that it really was stars that I was seeing. I was outside.

But I wasn't, really. I reached out and my hand touched a wall. A cool wall. Metal. I tried to sit up, but could not find anything solid beneath me. Every time I pushed with a hand or an elbow, my limb sunk as if I was in a large vat of pudding.

I blinked and looked around again. I couldn't tell how big my enclosure was, only that the walls were tall—much taller than I was. I rolled to my right, toward the wall my hand had touched. Maybe I could find a door, a handle, something to grasp so I could sit up. I hadn't yet considered the possibility of standing.

When I rolled, my face followed my body and fluid leaked into the right side of my mouth. Holy doo doo, I was in a huge pile of manure. And not just any pile, I was in one of the tall metal containers that show management used to dump all of the soiled bedding from the stalls.

I remembered seeing the enormous tan bins. There were a dozen or so throughout the show grounds. Each was about seven feet tall, and maybe six feet wide and twelve long.

As soon as I realized where I was, odor rolled into my brain like a tidal wave. I don't know why I hadn't smelled the acrid urine or the muddy poop earlier. I also hadn't realized bugs were in here. *Lots* of bugs. Tiny gnats, large horse flies, and something that felt like—oh crap—worms. Panicked, I scrambled around trying to find a foothold so I could right myself. I must have looked like I was in the middle of a mud-wrestling match, except the only person I was fighting was myself.

I spit urine-soaked shavings and manure out of my mouth and resisted the urge to gag. The poop actually didn't taste bad, but the though of it in my mouth was gross. I had to get out of here. Anxiety rose and I began to hyperventilate as a memory rolled in of a horrible time in my childhood, a time after my mom passed away from breast cancer. I was nine and my father left me alone in our Chicago slum to go to a bar to drink.

During the day it wasn't so bad, but at night rats came and scurried over me. Ever since then I became panicked in the dark and to this day I slept with a nightlight. Agnes once told me that

Thomas Edison, inventor of the light bulb, was afraid of the dark, too. If that was true, then I was in good company.

I hated emergencies, especially dark ones. And, I knew if I didn't do something soon I would faint. I counted to ten slowly so I could clear my mind, and by the time I got to five I had begun to breathe in and out as I counted. Better.

Once I could think, I rolled closer to the wall and ended up on all fours. Then I leaned my left hip and shoulder against the wall and slid upward. That, too, was better, even though I was up to my thighs in wet shavings and horse apples.

Next up: a way out. I began to explore my environment. Truth be told, the clogs I'd worn to the party were not the ideal shoes for this. Runny manure leaked in and made the soles of my feet slippery. I lost my left clog twice and twisted each ankle before I kicked them off. They were already ruined. No need to try to keep track of them.

I inched my way around what I now knew was a cargo container with an open top. I knew that on one end of the outside there was a ladder, and I was hoping for the same inside. But no, not that I could find, and I was pretty sure I had inched my way along all four sides. In the process, I realized that the pile of poop was deeper on one end than it was at the other. I slid down a wall to a sitting position at the cleaner, dryer end.

Time for more thought. Why had I ended up on the deeper end, which must have cushioned my fall? Was it by chance, or was it intentional? That thought led to another. How had I gotten here? The last thing I remembered was settling the horses in for the night. I assumed that I did not get here by myself. If that was true then someone—or possibly several someones—had climbed up the ladder on the far end and tipped me over the edge. Surely I did not climb up and topple in all by myself.

I thought about that for a while. If one person dumped me here it had to be a man. The ladder was narrow. There was not enough room for two people. No woman I knew, with the possible exception of Sloan Peters, could hoist me over a shoulder, climb the ladder and let me fall inside. Sloan was tall and fit. But was she strong enough? I was five-foot-six and weigh in at about a hundred thirty pounds. I lose weight during competitions, so subtract five pounds. Could Sloan have done it? Maybe.

I next considered any woman who might have partnered with a man to cause me to be inside this gigantic horse potty. Judy Lansing I eliminated, because as far as I knew, Mike was still in the hospital. And if his injuries were as severe as everyone said, then his assistance would have been impossible. Annie? Not remotely possible, even with Tony. Especially with Tony. Debra Dudley, however, required consideration because of Zach. Could they have teamed up? I didn't know.

Nothing good came of additional speculation, so I moved on. Which of the many turd wagons was I in? There was no way to know. Even in the deep end I could not reach the top of the wall, no matter how high I reached. I was hip deep in doodie there and could see nothing but up.

I stood, raised my eyes and began to move around the edges of the container. I even cut into the center, still looking upward. I hoped to see the edge of a building, a change in lighting—something that might indicate where I was. All my cut into the center did was bring about a fall and give me another view of the same starry sky.

As the Irish would say, I was in "deep shite." I was covered with wet shavings and watery manure from my hair to my toes. Maybe I could try out for a job as Swamp Thing. Probably, if I ever got out of here, I would smell for days.

Last February, Hank urinated into the floor grate of my furnace. My house immediately filled with mutant urine vapor and I could tell from the reaction of people around me that I, too, smelled. That went on for most of a week, so I had no doubt that this smell would linger, too.

Then a horrible possibility struck me. What if I was off the show grounds? What if the bin had been moved to a dump or an abandoned yard? No. Whoever was involved would need special equipment to move the container. There was only one person I knew who could do that, or cause it to be done. Noah.

I wanted to cry but would not let myself. Instead, I put on my practical thinking cap, just as Mrs. Sidnam, my kindergarten teacher, had taught me. Sooner or later morning would come. In the meantime, if I banged on the metal container it might make a loud noise. I rolled from the center, where I had fallen, to the side and tapped my fist on the wall. Nothing. I banged harder. There was a little noise, but not nearly what I had hoped for. The thickness of the metal combined with the heavy, wet shavings and horse poo muffled the sound.

No one had ever called me quiet, though. I had a good voice so I tried it out.

"Help! *Help*!"

There was an echo, and maybe a little amplification from the metal walls. I tried again.

"Help!"

Nothing. But, I looked up and realized the sky was starting to lighten. Eventually morning would come and with it the business of show ground activity. With luck, I could attract someone's attention.

There was nothing else to do, so I sat down in a corner and tried not to think about poop.

I must have dozed off. When I next opened my eyes the sky was gray with dawn and I could see the tan outline of my poop coop. I closed my eyes again, hoping I'd just had a bad dream. But no, I was still trapped inside. In frustration, I banged my fist on the wall and, *ouch*, regretted it almost instantly. Maybe I was a little too frustrated.

I held my now throbbing hand to my chest and two tears fell. I sniffed back the rest but the worst thing about that was there was nothing to wipe my snotty nose on. My clothes were gooey with manure and there wasn't a handy box of Kleenex anywhere in sight.

Sight. I could actually see! The sky was getting lighter by the minute and I hoped it would not be long before I was rescued. I could do with a shower.

Now that I could see the tall sides of my prison another thought came. Maybe I could rock the container to tip it over. I tried, but my best efforts couldn't generate the smallest wiggle, even when I sloshed as fast as I could from one side of the container and banged as hard as I could into the other. All I received for that attempt was a very sore shoulder and the knowledge that running through knee-deep poop was akin to running underwater.

Then I perked up. I heard something. Maybe. Yes! It was the distant sound of a shod horse clip clopping on pavement. At least I now knew I was still on the grounds. I listened more closely. A horse person can tell a lot from the sound of a horse's foot falls, especially when the stride is magnified by the combination of horse shoes and blacktop or cement. I could tell that this horse was at the walk, had no signs of lameness in his or her gait, and best of all, was coming toward me.

I began to yell.

"Help! Please! Help!"

I stopped to listen. The horse's clopping had stopped. Oh, no. I hoped the leader or rider had not turned off onto a grassy area and were now moving away. I tried again.

"Help! I'm in the manure bin!"

I banged on the wall with both of my fists as I yelled. It hurt my sore hand but I kept on, even though the noise from my banging wasn't much. Maybe it would help.

"Hello?" called woman's voice. Not mine.

"Help," I cried again. "Please, help me get out of here."

The rhythmic sound of clopping started again, then became jumbled.

"Stop banging, you're scaring my horse," called the voice.

I stopped and the clopping started again, much nearer now. Then the sound stopped again.

"What on earth?"

I looked up to see Sloan Peters peeking over the top of my prison. She must be sitting on a gigantic horse, but then again, many Dressage horses were quite tall.

"Sloan! Thank God," I cried. "Please, help me out of here."

"Cat Enright? Is that you?"

"Yes! Please find Noah Gregory, or go to my stalls and get Jon, my assistant. I have to get out of here."

She disappeared for a second and I thought I'd lost her. Then I heard footsteps on the ladder outside.

"How did you get in there?" she asked.

I could see her almost from her waist up. She was peering at me from above the deeper end of the poop pile.

"I don't know," I said. "I woke up and here I was."

"Wow, were you drinking?

"No. We can talk later, Sloan. I need to get out of here."

"I can see that," she said. "Hang on."

Sloan pulled out a cell phone, dialed it, then spoke in Spanish to whoever was on the other end. The only thing I understood was, "*Pronto*."

"I'll be right back," she said to me. "Don't go away."

I didn't know whether to laugh or cry at her words.

"Sloan!" I called. What if she left me here? What if she was the one who had dumped me in?

"No worries," called Sloan. "My groom, Miguel, is on his way."

And sure enough, I soon heard the slap of human footsteps on the pavement. By the sound and frequency of the footsteps, Miguel must be running.

Sloan climbed back up the ladder, higher this time, then leaned over. "Grab my wrists," she said.

I looked at her, unsure.

"Grab my wrists, Cat, like in a fireman's hold. I'll grasp your wrists and pull, then you can walk your feet up the wall."

I was untrusting of her, but had no other option. I was also dubious that her plan would work. But, I grabbed anyway and she pulled. Our first attempt did not go well. My hands and wrists were so slimy that neither of us could maintain the grasp and I plopped back into the pit.

"Cat?" Sloan called after a minute. "Miguel has a towel. I've wiped my hands and now I'm going to throw it down to you."

She was smart to wipe first. After I got through with it, it would be of no use to either of us. I wiped, then wrapped the towel around my waist. Least I could do was return it to her.

Our second try was better. Supported by Sloan and the security of our interlocked hands, I inched my way up the wall. The only hiccup came when Sloan needed to take a step down to a lower rung. Our balance shifted and for a moment I was sure I'd plunge head first to the pavement below, but I didn't. Sloan kept pulling, and before I knew it, I was teetering on the top edge. It must have been all of three inches across.

"Hold up," said Sloan. "Let me go down one more rung, then you can swing your leg over."

I waited, then swung, and Sloan guided my feet onto the ladder. When I was finally on the ground all I wanted to do was hug her.

"Ah, not now, Cat," she said eying me. "I was happy to help, though. Do you need Miguel to take you back to your stalls?"

I looked around in an effort to orient myself. I was on the far rear side of the show facility, next to a series of tall bins on a paved track that was rarely used by anyone other than show management. My initial instinct was to refuse Sloan's offer of Miguel, then I considered my state of sliminess and thought it might be a good idea to have a very human-looking escort.

"Good, then," she said as Miguel gave her a leg up onto her horse, a huge bay Warmblood gelding.

"Uh, Sloan?" I said as she prepared to ride off.

She gave me a questioning look.

"Thanks," I said. "Just . . . thanks."

She smiled, turned her gelding, and rode away.

29

MIGUEL AND I ARRIVED AT the barn to find Jon up and filling water buckets. I can only imagine what Jon thought when he realized it was me underneath all the wet horse dung. Unlike Sloan, however, Jon didn't shy away from a poop-covered hug. He wrapped his arms around me while I heard him thank Miguel in his own language. I didn't even know that Jon spoke Spanish.

Jon, of course, had many questions. I filled him in on the basics, then asked him to defer the rest until after I got a shower.

"No. Cat, I know how badly you must want to get clean," he said. "But you have to report this to the police first."

"But—"

"No buts. This sounds like another attempt on your life and you might be carrying evidence under all that . . . ah, slime.

"Don't forget the urine soaked shavings," I said, pulling some out of my hair.

"Never," said Jon, then we both broke into laughter.

I went into the tack room while Jon first called Noah, then the police. It was good timing, as Noah had been smack in the middle of a meeting with two detectives in the show office. Like Miguel, Noah arrived *pronto*, and had a female plain clothed detective and her younger male partner in tow. It was the first time I'd seen either of them. I explained what had happened, including the fact that Sloan Peters assumed I was drunk.

The two detectives looked at each other. "You don't still have one of the cups you were drinking from last night, do you?" the female detective asked. I squinted through the manure that was stuck to my eyelashes. DETECTIVE P. REY.

I looked around. "I don't know. I don't think so." I really could not remember.

The detective looked at her partner, who had been talking on a cell phone. He nodded. The upshot was that they wanted to transport me to the local medical center to get blood and urine samples, and to get a once over from a doctor. They would also take samples of the poop and shavings.

"You think I was drugged, don't you?" I asked.

"It's one possibility," Detective Rey said.

"There are others?"

She looked at her partner again, then at Jon, Noah, and me. "We're aware of what happened to your truck. Is it possible," she asked, "that you were the one who damaged your brakes?"

I stared at her openmouthed before Jon and Noah both began to protest at once.

"Stop," I said to them both. "I'll go with you," I said to the detective, "just to prove you are wrong. But I have classes today. It is my job, my livelihood, to compete, so I hope you can speed things along so I can get back here and not disappoint the owners of my horses.

"Jon," I continued, "can you and Darcy get Sally, Reddi, and Petey prepped? Ask Darcy to get my saddle seat suits, my habits, from my hotel room. I gave her my extra key. There are two habits in the closet in a green clothes bag marked Thursday."

I had never been more aware how important organization was during a show. I was so glad that I had sorted each show outfit into a hanging bag before I left home. That way nothing was left to chance, and if I ran short of time, as might be the case today, I had everything I needed in one place.

Then I turned to Detective Rey. "Do you want to put a tarp down in your car before I get in? I might stain your seats if you don't."

The younger detective pulled a tarp from the trunk of their unmarked car and I left with them. All of a sudden I felt exhausted. So much so that I almost fell asleep on the ten-minute ride to the medical center. I tried to calculate how much sleep I'd had the night before and gave up. I just couldn't remember.

The detectives hustled me in and I was scraped for samples, then gave blood and urine. I first saw an ER doc who asked all the questions a doctor asks if he suspects a patient has a concussion. Then I saw a psych doctor who was the first medical person to seem concerned that I had no memory of last night. After all of that I was finally cleared for a shower. It all happened quite quickly. I'd like to think the detectives fast tracked me because of my classes that day, but it is more likely that the hospital staff did it so I wouldn't continue to smell up their nice facility.

After my shower I donned a cotton hospital gown and a pair of ugly blue paper slippers, and shuffled to a clean trauma cubicle in the emergency suite. Then I waited. The waiting confirmed my suspicion that the smell of horse dooky sped things along. I was not ready, however, to find my clothes and put them back on in an effort to speed things up. I did think about it, though.

Eventually the ER doc returned and sat down on a rolling chair.

"The good news is: no concussion," he said. He was a young cheerful type.

"And the bad?" I asked.

"Well it looks as if you somehow ingested some gamma-hydroxybutyric acid, better known as GHB."

He must have noticed the blank stare on my face.

"GHB is a hypnotic depressant, also known as liquid ecstasy. It's a date-rape drug. I've spoken to the police and we think it was added to something you drank last night."

My mind whirred into gear and I thought of all the people I had seen and talked to at the party. I came up with at least a dozen names. There were probably more, but my memory of the event came in bits and pieces. The doctor was speaking again and I zoned back in on him.

". . . some of the effects are drowsiness, forgetfulness, slowed heartbeat and breathing, loss of muscle tone, and even coma," he said. "The coma lasts one to two hours, with full recovery in about eight hours, so the timing is spot on for you. What also might be of interest is that the drug's effects usually begin fifteen to sixty minutes after ingestion and lasts up to six hours."

I tilted my head in hopes that the new position would allow me to better process this information. Unfortunately, I was still just as flabbergasted as I had been when my head sat evenly between my shoulders.

"As your test results pertain to a crime, and I hear they might be relevant to a murder investigation, I'd like to share the specifics with the police."

I nodded my assent.

"You can refuse," he added, "but they'll just send out a subpoena. Your refusal would just slow the investigation down."

"Okay." What else could I say?

"Good, I'll get the paperwork started. In the meantime, here's some information on date-rape drugs."

I read the pamphlet he gave me and realized how good it was that Jon and the detectives insisted that I come to the medical center, because GHB can only be detected in urine up to twelve hours after ingestion. It was also good that I was not given more than I was, because GHB can cause breathing to slow down enough that a person has to be put on a ventilator, or even life support, until the effects of the drug wears off.

Bottom line: I could have died.

I was just signing my statement for the police when Annie peeked around the corner of the cubicle with a plastic grocery sack filled with clothes. She handed the sack to Detective Rey. I couldn't remember when I was so happy to see someone.

Annie looked at the nurse and the two detectives. They filled the cubicle, so Annie said she'd meet me in the waiting room. I couldn't wait. As soon as all the paperwork had been signed and everyone had left, I turned to the bag and pulled out the clothes. I recognized them instantly as Jon's. His must have been the only spare set around. There was a pair of shorts, a polo shirt, some flop flops and, yes, a pair of his boxers. Jon was about five nine and slim, but Annie knew the clothes would probably be too big, so she had added a length of bailing twine to tie around the waistband of the shorts. The only item of clothing that was not Jon's was a bikini swimsuit top. I didn't know who it was borrowed from, but I was grateful for it.

Ten minutes later I fell into Annie's arms. I was so glad that she was the one who came to pick me up. All of my emotions came bubbling to the surface and I bawled huge tears of anger and relief as my dearest friend held me tight.

By the time we stopped for breakfast at the nearest drive-though and got back to the Miller Coliseum, I had pulled myself together. I had to. I had two classes today and had to support Darcy in her event. I also could not let the horses see how upset I was, so after Annie and I got to the grounds, I went to the spa area before I went to the stalls. I was hoping that either Richard Valdez or the keeper of the vibration plates could work me in. As it turned out, Richard was booked but another trainer had not shown up for a vibration appointment. I vibrated for ten minutes and stepped off feeling much more like myself.

Due to the schedule change after they had canceled classes last Friday afternoon and Saturday morning, all of the saddle seat classes were being held today. As a trainer, I liked to have classes spread out. With the way the schedule was today, Sally's class was first, followed by Reddi's, then Darcy and Petey. All three classes were one after the other.

That meant I'd have a clothing change at the gate, which involved stripping down to change from one outfit to the next right there in front of everyone. I'd have to be sure to wear a tank top and thin leggings underneath my show outfit. Show rules gave a trainer three minutes for tack and clothing changes, but I could do it in about ninety seconds—if I had help.

Usually my helper was Darcy. On occasion it was Annie, and once it was Agnes. That was a disaster I do not care to remember. Suffice it to say that neither the horse nor I made it into our second class. But, Annie and Tony were headed out to

Tennessee Equine Hospital to see Star today and due to Darcy's class, she would not have time.

The other option was to wear the same outfit for both classes. Both Sally and Reddi were chestnut in color, although Sally's coat had a lot of white mixed in, while Reddi was a solid bright chestnut with snowy white hair over her rump. I guessed that my gray saddle seat habit would work for both. I had planned to wear a showier black outfit for Reddi's class, which better set off her fancy style and matched her tack. But Agnes owned both horses and I did not think she'd mind if I wore the one suit. And given the option, I'd rather spend the extra ninety seconds connecting with Reddi before the class.

Jon could ride, but rarely did so. On occasion, however, I had to press him into service and today was one of those days. If he could just keep Reddi at a strong working walk while I was in the class with Sally, do some flexing of her head and neck, maybe move her hips off the rail each direction, she should be loose enough to compete well.

I got to the barn bathroom with enough time to not have to hurry as I changed out of Jon's clothes and into my gray saddle seat habit for the classes. I did my makeup and my hair—which was extra curly as I had not had the luxury of my smoothing hair products, or even a hair dryer, at the medical center. I topped the resulting bun with a gray snap-brim hat, adjusted my traditional man's tie, and pulled a pair of soft gray riding gloves out of my Thursday bag.

Before I went back to the stalls I took a moment to mentally focus on the classes ahead. I did a deep breathing exercise to clear my mind and visualized how I would ride each of the classes in a bluish purple haze. When I walked out of the bathroom, I felt ready.

What I wasn't ready for was bumping into Cam and Hill. Fortunately, the encounter did not last long, because Agnes and Lars also appeared and swooped me away. I will spare you Agnes's comments about my ordeal, but the quaver in her voice let me know how much she cared.

Saddle seat is not Sally's best class. The best horses for the event are slimmer and have longer legs than Sally does. Because we would be competing with elegant Arabian horses, leggy Saddlebreds and Morgans, and gaited Tennessee Walking Horses, I did not hold out much hope that Sally could hold her own.

I finished loosening Sally up in the warm-up arena and saw Cam and Hill near the out-gate. Was Cam the person Hill had met with? Was he the person Hill did not want to tell us about when Bubba had wandered over to our stalls? Did either of them dump me into the dumpster? Or, was it both of them? Zach Avery rode by and I wondered about him, too. Did Zach look surprised that I was here? Or, was it my imagination? Debra was standing near the rail and called something out to Zach. He nodded absently, absorbed in his horse. Was Debra in on it?

Zach was riding a flashy coal black Arabian whose tail was so long that several feet of it dragged on the ground. They would be in our class and I hoped Sally and I wouldn't step on the tail by accident. That would be a disaster, especially if the tail was enhanced by hair extensions. Could be an embarrassing moment for all. I'd make it a point to steer clear of them.

I saw Sloan approach Cam and Hill. She had rescued me, but was it a coincidence that she rode by that morning? Or, was she checking to see if I was still alive? Other than my inner circle,

I realized that I could not trust anyone. It was a terrible thought that left me feeling cold.

I had wanted to be last into the ring, but riders of two Saddlebreds and a Morgan snuck up on our rear and I had to go in ahead of them. I collected Sally and pushed her into a perky working trot. We trotted down the runway that lead to the in-gate, but ten feet from the ring Sally came to a screeching halt and almost caused a wreck as the other three horses piled up behind us.

The riders made their displeasure known through the use of some very creative foul language. I wished their mothers were there to hear them. I am sure several mouths would have been washed out with soap.

I pushed Sally forward with my seat, legs, and voice, and as soon as she entered the arena her balkiness disappeared. Instead of a hunched back and clamped tail, she had forward ears and a swinging gait. Sometimes I could not figure this mare out.

Right away I noticed that many of the horses had long tails. These horses had not been in the warm-up arena so I had not seen them before. A flat shod Tennessee Walker whizzed past us at a running walk. Some breeds do not trot, and instead have an alternative gait. The Walker's tail was extra long, too. Whew, there were a lot of tails to dodge in a busy ring.

There were so many breeds and variations in breed standards that this was going to be a difficult class to judge. Sally remained energetic throughout, but ultimately could not compete with the more graceful breeds in this very elegant style of riding. We did not make the final cut, and thus, did not place.

I did not have time to process this turn of events, as I had to jump off Sally and onto Reddi. Unlike Sally's stocker build, Reddi had more of a saddle seat body—well, as much of one as an Appaloosa can have. Because of that I had hopes that she might do better than Sally. I handed Sally to Jon and he gave me a leg up.

"I'll meet you just past the out-gate, so you can stay to watch Darcy's class," he said over his shoulder as he led Sally away. He was already assuming that Reddi and I would not need to head to the photographer's area for a win photo. I badly wanted to prove him wrong, and we almost did.

Reddi always got a little excited in her classes and today it worked for her. She had a lot of knee action and brightness in her expression, yet executed each gait transition perfectly. We were held for the placings and were awarded a sixth place ribbon. An Arabian, a Morgan, two Saddlebreds, and a Tennessee Walker placed ahead of us, but I was thrilled that we were in there at all. Our sixth place was a big win in my book.

As promised, Jon was right where he was supposed to be and I hopped off Reddi and trotted up into the stands to sit with Lars and Agnes for Darcy's class.

"Basketball," said Agnes patting my knee.

"What?" I couldn't imagine what she was talking about.

"Your story about basketball players when we were watching the Dressage. Dear, dear Cat, I get it now, and I'm as proud of you and my horses as pea soup."

I was pretty sure that whatever she said was meant as a compliment.

Darcy's class was an equitation class, so Petey not being a classic saddle seat breed should not make as much a difference as it had in the pleasure classes I had just ridden in. That didn't make it any easier for Darcy, though. Saddle seat was ideal for people with long legs, and Darcy didn't have nearly the length she needed. That meant her form had to be perfect. In an ideal world, she needed to keep her elbows in at the waist and her forearms parallel to the ground. That should provide a straight line from the bit, through the reins, to Darcy's elbow. But because Darcy was short and Petey was tall, and because Petey carried his head lower than an Arabian or Saddlebred, that straight line could not happen.

Agnes's scream of delight at Darcy's third place was deafening. I was thrilled, too, but had just realized how exhausted I was. I was sore from my head to my toes, and despite the shower at the medical center, I still did not feel clean. I just wanted go back to my hotel room, soak in a hot tub, and call Honeycakes. Yes, I was somewhat surprised at how much I missed Brent.

My hotel would have to do until I could go home, which is where I really wanted to be. But that left another set of problems. The show was scheduled to end Saturday evening. What would happen if the police did not find the person who was causing all the mayhem? I didn't know what others thought, but I still operated on the assumption that one person was behind everything.

It was Thursday night. That left just forty-eight hours for the police to solve these crimes. I was terrified that would not happen, and that I would return home having to constantly look over my shoulder.

Cat's Horse Tip #20

"Fluorescent lights, such as those often found in the barns of show facilities, can quickly tire a horse's eyes and brain."

30

I AWOKE FRIDAY MORNING MORE refreshed than I ever thought possible, and was in a cheery mood when I got to the barn. My good spirits were dashed, however, when I found Jon and Tony in a brawl in the middle of my aisle. Both were yelling, circling each other, and throwing out punches whenever they thought they could land one.

"All right," I yelled. "Enough."

Neither man responded, although it is quite possible that I could not be heard over the insults they shouted at each other. I grabbed the top off of a plastic tote in the tack room and threw it between the two. Then I repeated my words. Both Jon and Tony stopped, and had the decency to look embarrassed.

"Whatever it is between you two. It *will* stop right now," I said. "I will not have two grown men upset my horses by getting into a fist fight in the middle of my aisle. That is beyond unacceptable."

I could almost see the testosterone wafting off the pair. I took a deep breath and blew it out. Then did the same with another. With the third breath Tony joined me. Ah ha! It worked on people as well as horses.

If I'd had a way to put them into time-out I would have, but as I didn't, I told them I did not want to see hide nor hair of either them for at least an hour.

"But," Jon said, "I was going to feed—"

"I'll do it." I was already getting the buckets.

"I'll leave," said Tony, "but not unless Jon stays. I don't want you alone here on the grounds."

"I'm a big girl," I said, as I poured grain into Reddi's bucket.

"A big girl who has had three attempts on her life in the past few days," said Tony. "Be reasonable."

"I am." I held up my phone to show Tony a text that had come in less than a minute ago. "Darcy just got here. She'll stay with me."

Tony looked uneasily at me, and then at Jon. But both of them left when Darcy walked around the corner seconds later.

Darcy and I continued to feed, then we locked up the tack room and she walked with me to the coliseum. The show was finishing up a few classes during the day, then tonight the championship classes would start. Gigi's was the only class we had this evening, and we had none throughout the day.

I had wanted to see some of the jumping, specifically because Reed was riding. It wasn't every day that I got to see an Olympic rider compete. Darcy and I found seats to the left of the announcer's booth, several rows behind the judge's stand. For this early class there must have been all of a hundred people in an arena that sat several thousand. I didn't mind. I was not in the mood to make conversation.

Just after Reed went around with his second horse (in some jumping classes a rider can compete on more than one horse), Tony plopped down on my left. I sighed.

"Darcy, would you excuse us?" Tony asked.

Darcy looked at me and I nodded. I might as well hear what the man had to say.

Tony dangled his hands between his knees.

I waited.

"I don't have a lot of time this morning," Tony finally said. "I'm leading Master Attack, Mike Lansing's colt, in the yearling class and I have to get ready. But I wanted you to know that the reason Jon and I were fighting this morning was because of you."

I opened my mouth to reply, but Tony held up a hand and I closed my mouth back up.

"There's something he and I, together, should have told you a while back. At first, we decided you did not need to know and we were both comfortable with that. But more recently I felt you needed the information. Jon disagreed. That's what our fight was about and I apologize for upsetting you or your horses. You were right. It was unacceptable."

I considered Tony's words as a thousand possibilities skipped through my head. None of them stuck, however, so I had no idea what he was talking about.

"Are you here just to apologize," I asked, "or are you going to fill me in?"

I watched Tony's face as he worked through the pros and cons, and I don't think he knew the answer to my question until the last second.

"Jon," he said. Then the words stuck in his throat. He was quiet for a time before he tried again. "Jon is my son."

"What?"

I was so surprised by the news that I didn't realize that I shouted the words or remember how I had come to be standing.

"What?" I repeated just as loudly. "You knew all this time and never told me?"

"You're going to scare a horse, Cat," Tony, who was now also standing, said. "Let's go outside. I'll tell you more there."

He took my arm, but I shrugged it off and hurried up the stairs. A thought flashed through my brain. What if Tony was the killer? What if he just told me that to get me outside, alone? I moved farther away from him, then called Darcy.

"You busy?" I asked, keeping my voice low.

"No. I'm on the other side of the arena watching you and Tony. Like what's up with you two?"

I explained that Tony and I were going to go outside, out the doors on her side of the coliseum, then sit on the grassy slope and talk.

"Can you watch us through the doors?" I asked. "If we get up to go anywhere but straight back to you, I want you to call the police."

"Yes Cat, but—"

"Tony's coming; I have to go. Just keep your eye on us."

Once more, I hated that I suspected my friend.

Tony and I walked around the mezzanine, through the doors on the opposite side, and sat on the grass. He didn't seem to want to start the conversation so I did that for him.

"Maybe you should start from the beginning," I said.

So he did. Seems when Tony was a kid his best friend was a Native American boy named Dusty. They went to school together, played ball together, the only thing they didn't do was go to church together, as their families were of different faiths. The spring of their junior year in high school, Dusty's church went on a mission trip to help an underprivileged Native community in eastern Oklahoma, and Tony went along.

"Annie and I were dating then and she almost came along, too," he said. "At the last minute her mama took sick and Annie stayed home to help."

According to Tony, the mission group stayed in the destitute town for about a week. They, along with members of the community, fixed houses and cars, cleaned up streets, and helped people along the path to finding Jesus. One person in particular that Tony "helped" was a pretty young thing named Yanita.

"She was sixteen and was a total mess. Drinking, parties, that was her life," said Tony. "I am not proud that I succumbed to her charms."

Tony did not find out that he had a son until Jon was thirteen. By that time Jon was an angry young man and Yanita, in a moment of sobriety, tracked down Dusty's pastor.

"I had only gone on the mission trip the one year, but Dusty's church went every few years," Tony said. "Yanita realized that if she didn't get help for Jon, and quite soon, that he would end up to be just like her. I think it's the only responsible decision she ever made."

Tony went to meet Jon, then weeks later brought him home for a visit.

"He and Annie got along right from the start, even though Annie and I had a long rough patch in there. You know Annie always wanted kids, but that never happened for us. Then I bring home a boy who is mine, but not hers. It was hard for Annie, but she never let Jon know."

I started to ask a question but Tony again held up his hand.

"Let me finish. If I don't get all this out now, I probably never will."

Through Dusty's pastor, Tony found a good high school in a town about thirty miles away from Jon's Native community, and a series of families to host Jon during the week. On weekends Jon went home.

"That was all Yanita would agree to. She wanted better for her son, but she didn't want to lose him in the process. We saw him in the summer between shows, and sometimes during his Christmas break, but I wrote to him every week. This was back before everyone had cell phones and the Internet."

Jon dropped out of school at the end of his junior year, got his GED a few years later, attended community college, and worked a series of jobs, none of which lasted more than a month.

"He was floundering, Cat. He was lost. Three, well, about four years ago now, Jon came to me. He'd always loved the horses, and seemed to understand them instinctively. He asked if I could find him a job. Of course I offered him one but he wouldn't take it. Jon wanted to stand on his own two feet, to make something of himself, by himself.

"I knew you had your hands full and had just finished building that apartment over your barn, so I gave Jon money to go to Tennessee. He called you and, well, you know the rest of the story. I thought if Jon was with you, then I'd get to see him at shows and keep up with him, be sure he was doing all right."

I hugged my knees to my chest. Tony had the good sense to remain silent while I worked through all he had told me. It was a lot.

"Why didn't Jon want me to know?" I asked.

"He thought you'd think less of him if you knew he was my son," said Tony. "Guess that shows what he thinks of me. We've never seen life from the same viewpoint."

I looked at Tony for the first time since he began to talk, and smiled.

"You're a good dad, Tony Zinner, certainly far better than mine ever was." My dad was another story. I rarely saw him and that was just fine with me.

"It's not been easy," he said. "I have a very stubborn Cherokee, Norwegian, German son."

"That is quite a combination," I agreed. "So, your thoughts. Should I tell Jon that I know?"

Tony considered that, then said, "If you want. That's for you to share if and when you want. Jon will not hear from me that I told you, but I don't mind if he hears it from you."

"And Annie?"

"I'll tell Annie," he said. "That night with Yanita was the only time I didn't tell Annie something and look how that worked out. Since then, I have shared everything with her . . . and she with me."

Maybe that explained their closeness, and I wondered again if Brent and I would ever have anything like Tony and Annie had.

Tony and I walked back into the coliseum, and Darcy and I headed back to the stalls. She, of course, wanted to know what our conversation had been about.

"Tony told me a secret and I have to think about it before I can tell anyone," I said. Then I saw her face. "It's not about anything that is going on here. No worries, okay?"

"Okay," she agreed. "Hey Cat? Why can't you tell corn a secret?"

"I don't know Darce, why can't you tell corn a secret?

"Because corn has ears!"

"Pretty lame, kiddo."

"I know, but it made you smile."

That it did.

Noah and Jon were both at the stalls when we arrived and Jon broke away from Noah as soon as he saw me.

"About this morning—"

"It's fine, Jon. Let me get a few things done, then maybe you and I can grab a bite to eat."

I hadn't had breakfast yet and my stomach was long past the growling stage. I turned to Noah.

"I just stopped by to let you know that, as of a few minutes ago, the police had not gotten anything back from either the veterinarians or the state lab on the tox screens for Star or Temptation," he said. "Thought you might ask Annie if she's heard anything from the hospital."

Darn. I'd hoped that information would open up a lead that would help close the case before the competition ended. Some trainers were already loading up and heading out—those who did not have classes today and did not have horses in the championships tonight or tomorrow. One of them might even be the person we'd been looking for, or some of the people who were leaving could have information. It was all so frustrating. There had to be something we all had overlooked.

After Noah left I checked that my show outfit for tonight was not wrinkled, and that Jon had polished Gigi's halter. He had. I looked at the show schedule once more and confirmed that the evening's performance began at seven P.M. Gigi's class was the second in, so we needed to be in the holding area a few minutes after seven. She needed to head to the wash stall at four, and I made a note on our dry erase board about that, as well as a reminder not to feed her any hay this afternoon. Hay can extend a horse's underbelly enough that it can ruin the tight, straight profile needed for a halter class. Gigi could eat all the hay she wanted after her class.

Bubba and Hunter stopped by, but when it became clear they were just hanging around, I sent them over to Cam's stalls to see if he needed his aisle swept. Then Jon and I went to the coliseum, bought several dozen freshly made miniature doughnuts, coffee for him and orange juice for me, and sat in a deserted section of seats.

Some of the jumping was still going on, but these fences were smaller, so I assumed it was a different class than what Reed had competed in earlier. From the impeccable turnout of the horses and riders, it was probably a hunter over fences class. Jumpers are judged solely on whether or not they get over the fence, hunters are judged on how well they get over the fence. Here, form counted.

Jon opened the box of doughnuts and I ate several before I said a word.

"If I tell you something, promise not to get mad?" I asked when my mouth had cleared itself of all traces of my third doughnut.

"Did Tony tell you?" he asked.

"Yeah." I picked up another doughnut. "Why did you feel I would think less of you if I knew?"

"I don't know. Pride, maybe. Ego. Stupidity."

"Well, I'm glad I know," I said. "Makes our little horse show family closer somehow."

I stuffed another doughnut into my mouth.

"That's it?" asked Jon.

I nodded. I'd been taught that it was rude to speak with my mouth full.

"I thought maybe you were going to fire me."

I swallowed. "Fire you? No way! We're a team, Jon. I could not get along without you. I know I don't often say that, but I mean it. You are my rock here at the shows, and at home."

It was his turn to nod, not because his mouth was stuffed with doughnuts, but because he looked like he might cry if he said anything.

Jon and I finished every last one of those doughnuts, then went back to our stalls. He took Gigi for a walk, while I sat in one of our director's chairs. Darcy had Petey in the aisle, and was grooming him.

I turned the events of the show over in my mind, pieces clicking together here, and falling out there. Sally began to kick her stall wall again and I got up to see what her problem was. Maybe she wanted to go for a walk, too. She looked purposefully at me, then lifted her right rear leg and slammed it into the stall wall. Then she made a quarter turn, so I could see the long side of her body. Then she turned her head to look at me and again picked up her right leg and kicked the wall. Just one loud staccato kick.

"What is she doing?" Darcy asked, joining me at Sally's stall.

"I don't know. She did this a few days ago, too. Maybe she just wants to go home. I know I do."

Sally then pinned her ears and shook her head.

"She's, like, saying your answer is wrong," giggled Darcy.

"Well I wish she'd be clearer about the right answer."

Sally kicked her stall wall again, then sighed and began to eat the rest of her morning hay.

I went back to the director's chair and thought some more. I smiled at Ambrose and patted Hank. Then all of a sudden, things in my brain clicked together and I knew not only who it was, but why.

Cat's Horse Tip #21

"If a horse does not follow the societal rules of the herd, the herd leader will banish the horse from any interaction with the other horses."

31

I KNEW. I KNEW WHY the horses and people had been hurt. I knew why my life had been in danger. But even worse, I knew what was about to happen.

What I didn't know was how far the show had progressed, and I raced through the barns. I dodged the hindquarters of several dozen young stallions who were having their final grooming before going to be judged.

As I ran, I ignored one groom's angry call to "slow down," and a trainer's warning to "watch it." I was intent only on reaching the coliseum.

What class were they on? The last I'd heard over the public address system, the jumping was over and the weanling colts were going in. How long ago was that? Two minutes? Twenty? I couldn't remember.

As I got closer, I realized with horror that the final call for the yearling colt class was more than several minutes past. Colts, the two year olds, were coming up to the holding area. The yearlings must already be in the arena and in the process of being judged.

"Oh, God," I prayed, "please let him win. Then it won't happen."

I dashed through the exhibitor entrance, up steps to the mezzanine, halfway around the arena, then down more steps to an area close to the horses in the ring, yet void of spectators.

I sat, gasping for breath, in a front row seat. Looking closely at the handlers of the yearling colts, my heart sank. The gun was tucked into the waistband of his slacks, virtually hidden by his jacket. Before I could think what to do, the public address system crackled and the announcer called out the numbers of the top six finalists.

"Please let him make the cut," I prayed. "Please let him make the cut." He did and I breathed a shaky sigh of relief.

The top six now moved in random order, single file, head-to-tail, down the center of the ring. I moved quickly, so that I was again directly in line with the exhibitors, and as close to him as I could get.

The placings were being announced. As usual, sixth place was read first, working up the line to first. My heart was thumping so loudly I could barely hear the announcer. I could hear the blood pumping through my veins. Oh, God. What was his number? 1207. That's it. 1207. He had to win. Please let his number be called last.

"In sixth place, number 931—"

I couldn't hear which entry 931 was, I was shaking that badly. What if he didn't win? What would I do? Somehow I had to make him stop. Thoughts were tumbling around my brain like clothes in a dryer.

"Fourth place to number 466—"

Fourth? What happened to fifth? Get a grip, Cat, get a grip. I took a few deep breaths. Steady. Think. I looked about, feeling dangerously close to hysteria, and only began to regain control when I saw Tony leading Master Attack, Mike Lansing's yearling, toward the gate, a white fourth place ribbon in hand.

"And in third place—"

I tried to concentrate, but I couldn't focus. Deep breaths, Cat, deep breaths.

"The third place ribbon goes to . . . number 1207—"

"Nooooo," I yelled as I jumped over the arena wall, and dropped into the soft footing. What was I doing? I was acting on instinct and knew I'd have to trust it. Running, yelling, I raced to the center of the arena as he pulled the gun from his waist, waving it wildly in the air.

"No, Cam, please. Don't!"

"Don't come near me, Cat," Cam hissed and I saw the gleam in his eye. What I had always taken as an intense belief in his horses and in himself was far beyond an obsession.

He turned, surveying the crowd of spectators.

"My colt is going to win this class," he shouted to them. "I've got the best colt here. Don't you agree?"

There was a low rumbling from the spectators and a frantic scurry away from some of the closer seats.

"Hey," he screamed. "What's the matter with all of you? I've got the best colt here. Agreed?"

I edged closer to Cam. The remaining two horses and their handlers had scattered when the gun was first pulled, and now they were warily making their way toward the out-gate. Each had one eye on Cam, the other on Noah, who was making frantic hurrying motions with his arms.

"Please, Cam. Let's talk about this," I said when I was within arm's length. "Come. We can go to the show office, they'll let us talk in private and we'll work it out. It will be okay."

For a second there, I thought he believed me. He looked steadily at me and a bit of the wry humor I once loved flickered in his expression. He smiled a gentle, half-smile and slowly put his colt's lead entirely into his right hand, along with the gun. Then he stretched his left hand toward mine. When we made contact, he squeezed my hand briefly, then, with Herculean strength, pulled me to him and pointed the gun to my head.

"Close the gate, Noah," he called. "Close the gate or this will be Cat's last class. Neither of those horses are leaving the arena without everyone agreeing that my colt gets the blue ribbon," he shouted, jerking me a quarter turn so I was facing the gate.

Noah stood there in indecision, waves of anguish flashing across his face. I knew he was weighing his concern for me against the welfare of the other exhibitors and their horses.

"Close it, Noah. Close the gate now," shouted Cam. "You've got until the count of three. One. Two—"

In spite of the fact that this might be my last moment on earth, I was quite calm. I felt as if I was watching a movie in slow motion. Colors sharpened and I could smell the dirt on the arena floor. This wasn't real. Couldn't be. If I reached out now, I knew I'd find a bag of popcorn on the seat next to me, and with it, the comfort and safety of a darkened movie theater. Wouldn't I?

"Okay, Cam," called Noah, interrupting my fantasy. "I'm closing the gate. Leave Cat be. Let her go."

Cam leaned over so I could see his face. "You know I can't do that, don't you?" he asked softly. I looked at his face and stifled a gasp. The concern in his eyes was so real. "I can't let you go until my colt wins this class. Everything depends on it. My farm, it's mortgaged to the hilt. The trust fund, it's gone," he laughed quietly. "I never was any good with money. You know that, Cat. I need the stud fees this win will bring. I can't fail now. I . . . I just can't."

Like quicksilver the concern faded from his eyes and he whirled us another quarter turn to face the judges' stand. There were no judges there, of course, show management having spirited them away at the first sign of trouble, but Cam didn't seem to realize they were gone.

"I want you to come back out here and take another look at these three colts," he yelled to the empty judges' stand. "Come out here you scum bags. Come out here *now*!"

Cam had moved the gun into his left hand. His right arm was now wound tightly across my shoulders, bending at the elbow to bring his fist into my throat. He pushed into my neck just tightly enough to allow some passage of air, as long as I did not move. He also had the colt's leather lead looped around his right hand, and that dug uncomfortably into my neck. My vision was, for the most part, blocked by the gun he held to my forehead with his left hand. All in all, it was a most uncomfortable situation.

Maybe I could get the colt to move, to pull Cam off balance. But then the gun might go off, too. I didn't know what to do. Out of the corner of my right eye I could see the two remaining colts and their handlers standing about thirty feet from the out-gate, as close together as one can with yearling colts. The stands above them, and, I assumed, throughout the arena, had emptied, save for a few morbid spectators perched cautiously in the far top seats. Vision to my left was entirely blocked by Cam's massive chest. I could smell his sweat, and my fear.

"Cam," I pleaded.

"Don't say a word, or you'll die right here and now."

I started to gag as he pushed harder into my throat. There was sweat now too, his warm, mine cold, and the muscles of his body were as tight as piano wires. I knew before this was over that he would kill me.

Finally realizing that the judges were missing his big show, he jerked us a quarter turn back to the right, again facing the gate. Peripheral vision came into use as I caught Noah approaching us diagonally from the rear. I knew better than to let Cam know he was coming, but my relief at help so close at hand made me relax enough that he couldn't help but notice. Cam turned his head toward me, and spotted Noah.

Before any of us had time to think, Noah hit the arena floor, grabbed handfuls of the footing, and threw them at the colt. Noah had the fortitude to do what I couldn't. Already nervous, the unexpected sting of the dirt clods hitting his body made the colt jump forward, knocking loose Cam's grip on my throat. I, too, made a beeline for the ground, and rolled under the colt knowing that his sharp, dancing hooves posed much less danger to me than the gun in Cam's hand. There was a series of pops, however, and the heated sting of something grazing my left shoulder. I heard Noah cry out behind me and sensed his movements had stilled.

Fury welled inside me and my Irish temper raised its ugly head. How dare Cam shoot Noah! Glancing through the colt's prancing legs, I saw Cam turning wildly this way and that, pointing the gun at the stands only to whirl around and aim yet again in another direction. Rising quickly on the colt's right side, I willed my trembling fingers to obey, and somehow unsnapped the chain end of the colt's lead where it fastened to the halter. Using the halter to position the colt, I pushed him between Cam and myself. Cam was so concerned about his colt winning, that I felt the chances of Cam hurting the colt were slim to none. Besides, if my plan worked, the colt wouldn't be between us for long.

There was blood. Mine, I guessed as I saw a few drops splatter on the colt's right front stocking.

To my left I caught the movement of one of Noah's legs, and relief flooded through me. Noah was alive! Just then one of the colts near the gate, a stunning Andalusian, backed away from his handler and reared. Cam's frightened colt took that opportunity to run toward the gate, and as the snap from the lead to the halter had been released, there was nothing to stop him.

As I watched the colt bolt toward the other horses, I glimpsed movement in the stands and saw several armed men take positions.

"How did you know it was me," Cam said finally, pointing the gun at my head.

"I didn't. Not until a few minutes ago." My words were surprisingly steady, considering I was about to be blown to bits. "Then I figured out how you knew Mike Lansing's cinch had been cut long before anyone else did. According to Melanie and Judy, everyone was so concerned about Mike and Rabbit that they just pulled the saddle off and put it in the tack room. No one looked at it until later in the day. You couldn't have known it was cut that early in the game unless you were the one who did it. You also knew Mike would rather scratch his entries than let someone else show them.

"In fact, I think it was you who told me that, once upon a time. By the morning of Mike's accident everyone had security near their stalls. You couldn't have gotten to another colt if your life depended on it. So to keep Mike's yearling out of competition you simply removed Mike. How am I doing?"

"Pretty good, Cat. But then you always were."

I ignored his words. "But you couldn't have known that Judy would take the decision out of Mike's hands and let Tony show the colt."

I had run out of words and there was nothing left between us. No love, no conversation, no colt to physically block the way. I looked down the barrel of the gun and began to shake. This was it. This was all there was. I felt I should be praying, but could only think of all the things I'd wanted to do, and never got around to. Brent and I had talked about spending a week in New England, except we hadn't found the time. Now we never would.

"I didn't want it to end like this, Cat. Really, I didn't." Cam was sobbing now, and so was I. "And I want you to know that you are, by far, the best horsewoman I ever had the privilege to know."

That said, Cam slowly turned the gun from me. He brought his hand up and pressed the gun to his temple. And with tears running down his face, he pulled the trigger.

Epilogue

THE FOLLOWING MONDAY I SAT on my front porch early in the morning nursing a large glass of Sprite, orange juice, and ice as I tried to make sense of all that had happened.

After Cam . . . fired the gun (those are the only words I can use) the arena was filled with silence. No one breathed. No one moved. I stood there, silent and frozen along with what seemed like the entire world.

I tried to move my feet, to start walking to the gate, to run, but there was a disconnection between my brain and my muscles, and all I could do was stand there. Then it seemed as if the universe jump-started itself and everyone nearby poured onto the floor of the arena.

There must have been at least two-dozen police, security, and show staff directing the movement of people and trying to secure the area. Then Jon was there, wrapping his arms around me.

"Breathe, Cat," he said. "Try to breathe."

And little by little, I did.

The arena, of course, was declared a crime scene. I don't think anyone wanted to compete in there anyway, so the classes for the rest of the show were split between the outdoor and warm-up arenas.

Yes, the show did go on. Noah called another meeting and everyone felt that to shut down the competition would be to let Cam win. For it was Cam all along. In his mind, everything he had been given in life, all the money and privilege, had been taken away. His business was not doing well and the only way he could see to revive it was for his yearling colt to win at this prestigious all-breed event. A win like that could set him up with stud fees for the next two decades.

For Cam, competition was not about improving his performance, or the performance of his horse. For Cam, it was all about the win.

Cam did everything he could to ensure that his colt would be named champion. First, he scoped out the toughest contenders. Then he mixed a dried concentrate of persimmon, which is exceedingly caustic to a horse's stomach, with sugar and water and dumped the mix into buckets that he placed in the stalls of Starmaker and Temptation in the middle of the night. By morning, he had retrieved the buckets.

He also slipped the colts lots of fresh persimmon the first two nights they were on the grounds. The colts ate the sweet fruit, seeds and all, which mashed together in their intestines tight enough to cause blockages.

Persimmon contains a lot of tannic acid. Tannic acid lowers blood pressure, and it was enough to cause Temptation to die and for Dr. Carruthers to think, momentarily, that Starmaker was dead.

Cam also added a smaller amount of persimmon powder and sugar to Annie's tea after she began to question him the morning that she fainted. Her questions were innocent. She was only concerned about Star and the other colts, but Cam could not take any chances. As we had all attended the same regional, national, and world championship Appaloosa shows for years, he knew that Annie took medication for high blood pressure. Enough tannic acid combined with her meds could have killed her. Fortunately, Annie only drank a little of the tea.

I don't think murder was on his mind when Cam frayed Mike Lansing's cinch. But, Cam knew that Mike was a threat in any halter class. He was the best at presentation, set up, and in showing a horse perfectly to a judge. Cam felt he had to get Mike out of the way—and he did.

I'll never know if Cam sliced partway through the billets on my Steuben at the same time, or if it was later, or why he felt he had to do that. Was it because I had rejected his offer of dinner? Or, did he think I had seen or heard something that might point to him? Speculation was pointless, but my mind kept turning it around anyway.

There were a lot of things we'd never know. How Cam got to my truck brakes, for instance. The holes in my brake system had been small. Did he do it there in Murfreesboro and it took until the return trip for the brakes to fail? Or, did he follow us to Ashland City and wait until we were asleep?

Cam took a huge risk the night of the exhibitor party when he drugged my drink. What if he did not have the opportunity to get me alone? What if someone saw us together? Maybe he hoped I'd just go into a coma and my breathing would stop.

No one will also ever know if Cam planned to shoot himself if his colt did not win, or if it was a spur of the moment decision. Noah said the police thought Cam planned to shoot all of the colts that placed ahead of his, making his colt the winner by gruesome default. It all came down to the balance between how badly Cam wanted to win and what he would do to make sure that happened. It was the ultimate magnum equation.

Fortunately, the bullet that grazed my shoulder was just that, a graze. The area was still covered by a little cotton and tape, but it was healing nicely. Noah had not fared as well, however. The bullet that struck him broke a rib, but the rib also deflected the bullet, which exited Noah's side without hitting any major organs or arteries. He was patched up and hospitalized overnight, and will soon be fine.

I sighed, and took a swig of my juice mix wishing that I had an apple doughnut to go with it. Out in the field in front of me, Sally and Gigi trotted to the gate as Jon came to bring them up to their stalls for the day. It was going to be a scorcher and they would handle the heat much better inside the barn with fans blowing in front of their stalls, than outside in the sun.

Gigi jigged as Jon led her toward the barn. I was glad that Mason and I had decided to pull the filly out of competition for the rest of the year so she could learn to be a horse. The mare halter championships had been rescheduled for Saturday, and Gigi, as champion yearling, looked beautiful. It is tough for younger horses to compete in championship classes against older horses, and a six-year-old Arabian mare of Debra Dudley's won. I was thrilled for her and for Zach, yet still heartbroken for them over the loss of Temptation. Mason and I both felt that Gigi had done enough winning for a while. She was like a giggly eleven-year-old girl. Now she needed to grow up.

Sally was also getting a little break. Agnes and I had not yet decided if we would enter her at the world championships this fall. Agnes wanted Sally to "tell" us whether or not she was supposed to go. So far the mare had stayed mum on the topic.

Agnes was anything but mum, however, about the many "clues" Sally had given us all week. Agnes bragged to anyone who listened that Sally balked every time she entered the arena because she knew something bad was going to happen there. Then there was the time Sally stood in halter pose in her stall. Agnes claimed the mare was telling us that something would happen in a halter class. The sharp kicks to the stall, in Agnes's mind, were warnings from Sally about gunshots. And the round balls of dirt that Sally spit out? Bullets.

I still was not convinced of Sally Blue's psychic abilities, but I was thrilled, however, that she had been named reserve champion junior performance horse at the all-breed event. It was a huge honor. The grand championship and the bonus money that went with it had been earned by Reed Northbrook's Bavarian Warmblood gelding, Kaspar. While I had been dodging bullets, both figuratively and metaphorically, Reed and Kaspar had quietly cleaned up on all of the competition's big jumping and Dressage events. Reed had also scarfed up the top trainer award.

I was, oddly enough, heartbroken over Cam's death. I no longer cared for him in "that way," but he was someone I had once loved. It had only been three days so the shock was still very new, but I had a feeling I would be processing his death for a long time.

I was also still processing my relationship with Brent. I really cared about Honeycakes. He was comfortable, warm, kind, handsome, and fun. But did I love him? Maybe. I realized I had trust issues, but Brent's jealousy was unsettling. I was glad that Brent was one thing I did not have to deal with right now.

Instead, I got to spend the day with my dear friends. Tony and Annie were staying a few days with me—and with Jon. Starmaker was improving rapidly and the two men were going to pick him up this afternoon, then bring him here for a few days of R&R before Tony and Annie headed home to Oklahoma.

The screen door slammed and Darcy wandered onto the porch in shorts and a tank top. During her Youth Watch search for clues at the show, Darcy had spoken several times to kids who did student security at MTSU, and had even talked with one of the horse science professors.

The good news was that Darcy had decided that, after graduation from her exclusive private high school, she wanted to study horses at our local state school.

She hadn't approached her decision with Mason yet, but it would be a battle when she did. I knew he hoped for Yale or Vassar, or another ivy-league college for her, but the reality was her that grades weren't good enough. Darcy was a bright but uninterested student. What interested her was the subject of horses.

I looked at my young friend and knew I'd go to bat for her, whatever she chose. If I could convince her to tell her dad that she'd reach for a graduate degree, it might make the choice easier on them both.

The most exciting thing on my horizon, though, was that my hot, hunky neighbor Keith Carson had just hired me to teach him to ride. He was doing a duet with a country music starlet and they were going to shoot a video that involved horses for their single this fall. I had a sneaking suspicion that Keith was going to need a lot of lessons. Hot dawg!

THE END

FOOD FOR THOUGHT: BOOK CLUB QUESTIONS

1. Do you agree with Agnes and think that Sally Blue is psychic?

2. How do you think the relationship between Jon and Tony will progress now that their secret is out in the open?

3. Why do you think Cat feels so close to Annie?

4. Is Agnes someone you think you'd like, or do you think she would be an annoying person to know?

5. Will Cat and Brent's relationship stand the test of time? Why or why not?

6. Which horse is your favorite and why?

7. Do you think having Ambrose around deterred any attacks against Cat or her horses?

8. Murder and sabotage aside, would you like to attend an all-breed event such as this? Why or why not?

9. Does Cat have feelings for Keith Carson, or is it just as she says—a schoolgirl crush?

10. What did *The Magnum Equation* teach you about horses that you did not already know? About people?

11. Do you think Cat does well in emergencies, or not?

12. If you could give Cat one piece of advice about life, what would it be?

13. Will Darcy really go to college? If so, to a state school, or to a prestigious university as her father wants?

14. Despite the problems, do you feel this national all-breed show will continue, and be held again in following years?

ABOUT THE AUTHOR

Lisa Wysocky is an award-winning author, clinician, riding instructor, and horsewoman who helps humans grow through horses. She is a PATH International instructor who trains horses for therapeutic riding and other equine assisted activities and therapies. In addition, Lisa is the executive director of the non-profit organization Colby's Army (ColbysArmy.org) formed in memory of her son. Colby's Army helps people, animals, and the environment. Lisa splits her time between Tennessee and Minnesota, and you can find her online at:
Facebook.com/ThePowerofaWhisper
on Twitter @LisaWysocky, or at:
LisaWysocky.com or CatEnrightStables.blogspot.com.

Author photo by Monica Powell, wardrobe by Wrangler/VF Jeanswear, hair by Bill Vandiver at The Edge Salon.

GLOSSARY

At halter: A class where horses are led, and judged on conformation and movement.

Cinch: A broad strap attached to a Western saddle. It goes around the horse's belly to secure the saddle.

Droppings: A polite word for horse poop.

Elimination round: First phase of a class with many entries, where some are eliminated due to low scores.

First call: An announcement that lets exhibitors know to head to the warm-up arena or holding pen for their class.

Flying lead change: At the canter, a horse leads with either the left or the right front leg. In a flying change, the horse changes leads without breaking stride.

Girth: A broad strap attached to an English saddle. It goes around the horse's belly to secure the saddle.

Half-pass: An advanced move where a horse travels sideways and forward at the same time; a lateral movement.

Horn: The knob on the front of a western saddle. It is used to hang things from, or as a place to wrap a rope around. Inexperienced riders use it to hold on, which only serves to give them even less control over their horse.

Hunter: A horse or class that is judged on how well the horse gets over a fence.

Impulsion: The forward movement of a horse; also helps a horse utilize the power in its hindquarters.

In-gate: Term for the side of the gate horses and riders use to enter a competition arena.

Jumper: A horse or class that is judged only on whether the horse gets over the fence.

Junior: A horse four years of age or under; a youth rider at this show aged thirteen or under.

Made the cut: Able to continue on in the competition, versus getting the gate (not being placed)

Open class: A class without age or status restriction for entries. Youths and adults, as well as amateur owners and professional trainers, can enter.

Out-gate: Term for the side of the gate horses and riders use to exit a competition arena.

Own daughter: A next generation descendant; daughter.

Reining: The process of steering the horse; also a western class that focuses on flying lead changes, sliding stops, and spins.

Ring steward: An assistant to the judge who also directs traffic and keeps control of the arena during the class.

Round pen: A sixty-foot "round pen," usually made of pipe panels, used for training horses on the ground and under saddle.

Scratch: Canceling an entry in a class at the last minute.

Senior: For the purposes of this show, any horse over the age of four.

Stock horses: Horse breeds traditionally used for cattle, or stock work. Typically Appaloosas, Quarter Horses and Paints.

The gate: Term meaning a horse and rider did not place in, or was eliminated from, a judged event; a generic term for the entrance and exit to an arena.

Weanling: For horse show purposes, a horse born in the current year.

APPLE BUTTER FROM THE APPLE TREE

Ingredients
3 pounds of apples
1 cup sugar
1 cup brown sugar
1 cup water
1/4 cup apple cider vinegar
Zest and juice of 1 lemon
2 teaspoons ground cinnamon
1/4 teaspoon ground allspice
1/4 teaspoon ground cloves

Use a slow cooker (crock-pot) so you don't have to be concerned with the apples burning. Plus, your house will smell so good with the aroma of the apple butter.

Choose the variety of apple according to your taste. Cat likes a crisp, tart apple, but you may prefer a sweeter apple. You can also use some sweet and some tart.

Instructions:
Wash, peel, core, and slice apples.
Place in slow cooker and stir in all remaining ingredients.
Cover and cook on high until apples are soft.
Mash the mixture into a buttery consistency.
Uncover and continue to cook on warm until the apple butter thickens and is an amber color.
Seal in jars, or keep in refrigerator.

Makes about 2 pints.

Yummy recipe courtesy of Letha Botts.

ACKNOWLEDGEMENTS

After the publication of the first of Cat's adventures, *The Opium Equation*, we were honored with not one, not two, but four prestigious book awards, plus many positive reviews. Cat and I were both blown away with the accolades, and hope you find this adventure just as worthy.

When I began writing about Cat, this book, *The Magnum Equation*, was actually the first book in the series. I had finished about 40 percent of it when I realized that Cat and her crew had a previous story that must be told first. I'm not quite sure how I came to that conclusion, but Cat was very insistent.

Thank you to our publishers, Neville and Cindy Johnson at Cool Titles, for taking another stab at Cat and me. Their commitment to excellence made me strive harder to deliver. Special thanks to Cindy for suggesting the title! Cat and I also very much appreciate Anjuli Harary's eagle eye on the proofing.

Thank you also to Middle Tennessee State University and the Tennessee Miller Coliseum. Both are very real and I have attended many events there. Patrick Kayser and Travis Emore took time out of their busy schedules to give me a comprehensive tour of the venue, and the layout and description are very similar to what you will find when you visit. However, I made a few small adjustments to better adapt the facility to the story.

I also made a sincere attempt not to use real names of horses in any given breed. I could not find any evidence of an Arabian stallion named Jubair, for example. If I erred, and named one of the horses in this book the same name as your horse, my apologies. It was not intentional. On the other hand, my mistake might give your horse something new to talk about at the watering hole.

Thanks to Richard Valdez and Sadler Car Care; and to Jamie, Glenn, and Jenn of the *Horses in the Morning* crew for being such good sports about allowing themselves to be part of this story. Thanks, too, to Danny Haber, DVM, who took time to debate items that might cause Starmaker and Temptation to colic while he gave annual exams to several horses, and who gave me the idea for the specific substance. I also am appreciative of Monty McInturff, DVM and all of the veterinarians and staff at Tennessee Equine Hospital. They treat horses at several therapeutic riding centers that I work with and I know they give those horses the same fabulous care that Starmaker received. I have come to realize that there is a fine line between Cat's world and our real world, and all of these people are important in both.

Special thanks to my cat, Bailey. Without her paws chasing my fingers around on the keyboard, this book would not have been nearly as much fun to write, although I might have been able to complete it much sooner without her "help."

To Wrangler/VF Jeanswear, huge thanks for providing my wardrobe for booksignings and appearances. Otherwise, I might arrive in my 1995-era barn jeans and a horse-slobbered shirt. Many thanks also to Procellera.

Special kudos to Letha Botts (for her apple butter recipe), and to Mary Isenman for all they both do for me.

To you, the reader, I have to say that Cat and I so appreciate you picking up *The Magnum Equation*. I hope you enjoy Cat's story. If you do, please tell others about it, and her. Many adventures lie ahead for Cat, but she has told me that public demand is the only reason she will agree to share them with you. So, let us know what you think. In the meantime, please visit Cat at CatEnrightStables.blogspot.com, and me at LisaWysocky.com.

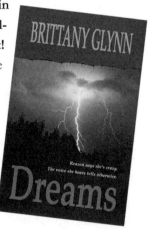

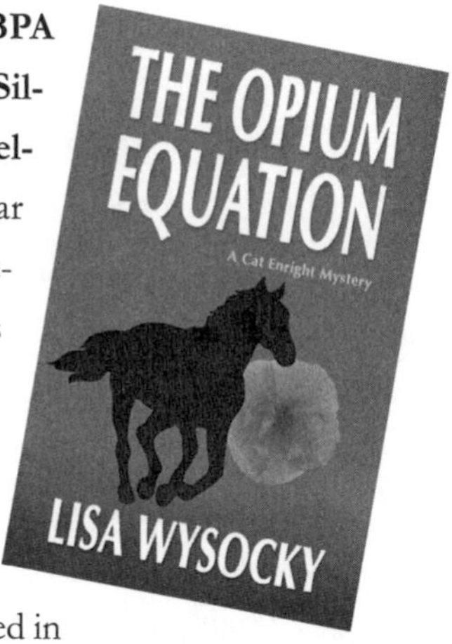

An American Horse Publications, IBPA Book of the Year, and Mom's Choice Silver Medalist; and National Indie Excellence Finalist! When retired movie star Glenda Dupree was murdered in her antebellum mansion in Tennessee, there was much speculation. Prior to leaving life on earth, Glenda had offended everyone, including her neighbor, a (mostly) law-abiding horse trainer named Cat Enright. Cat finds Glenda's body, is implicated in the murder, and also in the disappearance of a ten-year-old neighbor, Bubba Henley. An unpopular sheriff and upcoming election mean the pressure to close the case is on. With the help of her riding students, a (possibly) psychic horse, a local cop, a kid named Frog, and an eccentric client of a certain age with electric blue hair, Cat takes time from her horse training business to try to solve the case and keep herself out of prison.

John Wooden was arguably the greatest coach and the greatest leader of all time. These Woodenisms, a collection of his wisdom and sayings, inspire, motivate, and prepare you for any challenge. Woodensims provide common sense, assist you in being a leader and a team player, and also give you strength. Many of these Woodenisms have been distributed individually. They have also been used in print, and in presentations by Coach and other speakers. Now they are collected here, yours to cherish and enjoy as you strive for success.

Coming Soon:

The Fame Equation

Join Cat and her crew for their third adventure! Back home in Ashland City, Tennessee, Cat preps hunky Keith Carson and his duet partner, an innocent, up-and-coming female country music star, for a music video by giving them riding lessons.

When the sweet young thang is found floating face down in the river soon after, it is discovered that Cat was the last person to see her alive. Well, the last person except for the person who murdered her . . . or did she just fall?

Raves for the Cat Enright Equestrian Mystery Series:

"From the first page to the last *The Opium Equation* will keep you engaged and wanting more, horse lover or not."
—Glenn the Geek, founder, Horse Radio Network

"A murder, a mystery, and a psychic horse. What's not to love?"
—*Horsemen's Yankee Pedlar*

"Wysocky puts out an excellent product. Readers will be waiting to lap up more Cat Enright adventures. And there is that hunky country singer."
—*Midwest Book Review*

"This quick and entertaining read will amuse fans of Carolyn Banks's equine mysteries."
—*Library Journal*

Special Offers for Friends of Cat Enright